Fairytale of the Other New York

By

Joseph Kiel

Copyright and Legal Notice

www.josephkiel.com

Get a Free Joseph Kiel Novella

Visit the link at the end of this book or visit my website at **www.josephkiel.com** to join my Readers' Club.

Signing up to my list won't result in endless spammy emails, so don't worry. You'll receive a free eBook (a novella from *The Dark Harbour Tales*) and you'll be the first to know of any news I have or announcements about forthcoming releases. You can unsubscribe at any time.

Acknowledgments

I would like to give special thanks to all the people who helped me on my *Fairytale* journey...

To my parents, aunts, uncles, brothers and cousins who helped me research our family histories.

To my good friend Daniel Sumpton, who did some all-nighters to create some awesome artwork for the front cover and who also put in many good words about this project.

To Colin McFarlane, who assisted me in my research of the Second World War.

To all my good friends who may have inspired little parts of this story.

To all those family members no longer of this world, who inspired the characters and ideas I wrote about.

And to my dear wife, who allows me to indulge in my strange fascination with a certain Lincolnshire village, and who is a constant source of support and inspiration.

Foreword

The novel you are about to read is set in that same world we've all been muddling through these last two years, the one with covid in it. Although it may seem foolish to try to predict how this pandemic will play out, and how our world might operate this Christmas, even just a couple of months before that period in time, I hope that the reasons for including the pandemic in this fictional status quo are self-evident.

Running parallel to this novel, I also conducted research into the lives of my grandparents and what they did during another traumatic era, the Second World War. This process really came alive when I discovered forgotten photo albums of that period among the family heirlooms. As you'll see in my afterword, these photographs paint stories that fascinate and intrigue. I would hope that, in many years to come, I've also left a document that gives an interesting insight into the challenging times we are going through at the moment.

I am no soothsayer. If this world turns upside down immediately after I put the book on the shelf, and its depiction of reality turns inaccurate, then I'm just going to call dramatic licence.

It is a fairytale, after all...

~ Joseph Kiel, October 2021

Chapter 1

BUT IT'S STILL NOVEMBER!

You knew Christmas fast approached when those familiar festive tunes crept onto the radio playlists. Yesterday was Advent Sunday so I shouldn't have been surprised. Traditionally it was the day my home borough would switch on its Christmas lights and last night I'd popped out to admire them. One final look before it was no longer my home.

I wondered what song they might play, what was actually the first Christmas record of the season, the DJ from the local BBC radio station informed his listeners. Perhaps a bit of *Last Christmas* and I would be Whamageddoned before December had even started? Some Slade? Mariah? Songs I'd had no reason to think about for the past eleven months, but ones I would no doubt be hearing regularly in the coming weeks.

That pointless mental exercise distracted my mind momentarily.

"What do you reckon, kids?" I asked the two in the back.

The other seats of my Renault Clio, or 'Clarence' as I called my car, were stacked up with storage boxes crammed with tat and bin bags filled with clothes, and sitting upon all that junk were my two 'passengers', my tatty childhood teddy bear who sat alongside a giant orange stuffed bear. That one was something I'd won at a fair. Well, my boyfriend at the time had won him, expertly throwing some winning darts. He'd fluked it really. Last week I chucked that big old fella out, stuffing him inside the wheelie bin, but then I felt so bad for him, like I'd genuinely murdered someone, so I fished him back out and loaded him in the washing machine, one at the launderette down the road as he was too big for my own washer.

It was a pretty sad state of affairs when you realised you could fit *all* your belongings inside a mid-sized car. And some of the crap I was lugging, like that giant bear, was stuff I shouldn't have kept, a relic of an old relationship I really didn't need any reminders of. I supposed it made moving that much easier when you were light on possessions, no need to hire a removal van. Silver linings and all that.

That covid virus sure had a lot to answer for. One tiny rogue sequence of genetic code had the power to unstitch my entire life and force me to retreat to my childhood home. I had nowhere else to go. At first I'd fought against the dreary winds of fate, hunting around for another job as everyone else whom the virus had kicked in the teeth was doing.

Nope. Going back home was the only option I had.

I was on the other side of Peterborough when I'd tuned the radio into the Lincolnshire BBC station. The presenter of the breakfast show had changed, yet I still recognised his silky tones. He'd probably been moved from a different time slot, or maybe I'd heard him on another frequency. Plenty more changes surely awaited the more I acclimatised myself within my old stomping ground.

I'd risen early that morning, a lot of my belongings already packed inside the car the night before. Nothing in view constituted stuff that might tempt a passing thief to smash the window and grab. In reality, I doubted anything I owned was worth the bother. Living in London had been so ruthless on my purse, and it wasn't as though I had some crummy, living-wage job, but an actual career job in publishing. Even with the salary it paid, I found I could barely tread water. How did people do it?

They get a rich partner, Hazel, that's what they do!

That was something else I was leaving behind in London. Well, it was officially over two months ago, but you know how these things go. You split up, you get lonely, and you realise another lonely person is your ex, so you hook up for the convenience of it, because it's preferable to going on Tinder or hanging around in bars.

Not that those options were always on the table in these covid times. That virus had left all the poor singletons abandoned in the desert. A romantic date was more likely to take place over Skype than in a restaurant. How tragic was that? Fortunately, I had flatmates to lean on and provide companionship. And let's just say my *'it's-only-a-bit-of-flu'* ex wasn't a keen observer of the rules. Heck, even the people who *set* the rules couldn't keep to them. Social distancing went against our humanity, it seemed. The ex was too easy a fallback. If only he'd been an anxious germophobe, barricading himself in his flat with his hand gel supplies and antiviral wipes, and I could have made it a cleaner break between us. As alert as I had been, my ex with benefits was a virus I could not control.

But by moving back to Lincolnshire I was properly getting him out of my system, especially with where I was headed. There was nothing even remotely conducive to romance there.

But before then, I had a stop to make. I was taking the scenic route to my new home, finally leaving the never ending A1 (the Lincolnshire bypass, my ex called that road) at Newark as I drove to the county capital. From miles back I took in the majestic sight of Lincoln Cathedral sitting commandingly on the hill. If anything could be considered the yellowbelly's Mecca, then it's surely that building, 'Cathy' as some folk call it. But that wasn't the hill I gravitated towards.

Driving out of the city centre, Clarence chugged his way up Canwick Hill to the International Bomber Command Centre. Along with the new road layout in central Lincoln, this was another recent change, at least since I was last there. Reaching tall into the cool November morning air was the memorial spire. My nan had told me about it a few years ago when things were much more lucid for her, but I hadn't got round to visiting, hadn't carved out any time to do so. I had no excuse now.

She'd mentioned that the names of Grandad's friends were on display there. Grandad had been part of Bomber Command in the war, flying in the Lancasters and dropping bombs on Nazi Germany, but he was one of the lucky ones who had returned. I can't tell you what role he had within his Lancaster crew, or even what squadron he belonged to. Such details aren't things that a pre-teen girl might think to ask, her whole life ahead of her, but failing to appreciate that her grandfather didn't have a great many days left ahead of him. And when you got to a dryer-eared age, and such matters interest you, that's when he's no longer around to answer your questions.

And asking my nan, the grandparent that was still kicking around, wasn't a brilliant option anymore, sadly.

I felt stiff after the non-stop journey from London, my legs appreciating a stretch as I escaped from the confines of Clarence. Well, there had been one stop actually, somewhere along the A1. My bladder isn't *that* strong. In fact, it was complaining once more, but I was supposed to be acting solemn right now, not searching for the bogs.

I checked my mask was still in my pocket before walking over to the car park ticket machine. It was covered up, however, a covid thing, the sign telling me to get a ticket from the building, so I headed there next. As I reached the glass doors, I cursed myself as I realised the place was closed. Damn. Perhaps I should have looked it up online before turning up. But how come there were other cars here?

Just as I turned round, I spotted an old guy with a walking stick heading in my direction, a black baseball cap on his head.

"It's not open," I told him once he was in earshot.

"Oh, I know," he replied, making sure not to get too close to me; a hangover of a pandemic. "That's why I came. Place is best when it's quiet."

I followed him as he carried on along the perimeter path, passing by the 'International Peace Garden' before the path opened out to the memorial garden, the thirty-one metre monument reaching up into the sky before us. That was one fact I had conducted prior research on. It was the tallest spire in the whole of the UK, its height the same as the width of a Lancaster bomber's wing.

The old chap toddled off ahead, disappearing behind one of the many walls that circled the spire. I wandered in the other direction to give him some space. Name after name had been etched into these obelisks. There must have been tens of thousands of them, a few with my surname. Unknown distant relatives, perhaps?

Beyond us, the valley cut into the land before the city of Lincoln, the cathedral atop the opposite hill. I read on an information panel how the building was a welcome sight for the crews returning home. So many hadn't made it back.

In the corner of my eye, I noticed the old guy sitting down, peering up at the obelisk nearby him. Was one of the particular names on it significant to him? I glanced at the one closest to me, a collection of painted rocks at its base, a long list of surnames beginning with the letter G, poppies pinned here and there.

I didn't know the names of any of my grandfather's friends, the information now lost in time. Perhaps it *might* be worth asking Nan.

It had been a much different ordeal for our generation. These guys had travelled to all corners of the globe in the battle against fascist armies. For us, all we'd had to do was sit on our backsides at home watching Phil and Holly on

This Morning, staying away from where this malicious virus might be lurking. The death toll had still been catastrophic. Perhaps twice as many as the names that were on display here?

Were we coming through it now? Would we ever? That virus was still out there, and plenty were still coming down with it.

Christmas would be different to last year though, surely, something that was more resembling normal. Across the city, up Steep Hill, they'd hopefully be holding the Christmas Market soon, an event that had been cancelled in 2020. It was something to look forward to.

I felt cold, a breeze sweeping through the valley, so I made my way back to the car. The old chap caught my eye as I was leaving, so I waved goodbye. There was something a little Captain Tom about him.

Back inside Clarence I entered Nan's house into the sat nav. My knowledge of the Lincolnshire roads had become somewhat rusty in recent years. That's what living in London did to you; You forgot about the rest of the country.

One thing I was soon reminded about, two miles down the road, was the many tractors you found on these roads, getting stuck behind a bright green John Deere dragging a plough. I hung back, unable to overtake him. At least I was in no hurry.

If I talked about my childhood home, my discordant accent might confuse you. The mention of New York makes one think of Central Park, Times Square, hot dog stands, and yellow cabs, miracles and disasters, Lady Liberty holding her torch up high, Trump Tower, Ross and Rachel and Joey and the gang in Central Perk, John Lennon getting shot, Kevin McCallister lost alone setting booby traps for Joe Pesci and his fellow thief, Robert De Niro driving a taxi, King Kong climbing the Empire State Building, Frank Sinatra singing how he wanted to be a part of it. Culture, character, drama, and romance, as rich as you will find anywhere on the globe.

If you could conceive of some other settlement on our planet that was the complete opposite of all that, you would end up somewhere with the same name: New York, found in deepest, darkest Lincolnshire. So good they named it once. That was where I grew up.

Christopher Cross once sang poetically about getting caught between the earth's satellite and New York City in a Dudley Moore film. With *that* New York, yes, you might indeed think of that as a romantic experience. Get caught between the moon and New York *village*? There's no falling in love with that. Oh no, missy. Know what would happen? You'd asphyxiate and die. Or burn up in the solar rays. I'm not too sure, actually. I'm no scientist, so all I've got to go on are films. Maybe check out *Event Horizon* if you really want to know. Or *The Last Jedi*, possibly, if you have any force tendencies.

It seemed apt that as I first saw the hamlet mentioned on a road sign, the DJ started playing a song about New York. Not the Christopher Cross one, but his second Christmas tune of the season, The Pogues and Kirsty MacColl. I would not find a local police force ahead singing *Galway Bay*, no bells ringing out, no dreams of a better time. It most certainly *was* a place for the old, my nan being testament to that.

There was nothing in New York. Nothing. You could whizz past the small scattering of houses and not realise you had just driven through this little apple. There was no pub there, but it did have a school down the road, a primary school. It no longer had a church, at least one that wasn't now privately owned. There was the village hall, but the events held there didn't typically grab me. Set within the level Lincolnshire Fens, the landscape as desolate as a desert, the only thing that pertained to a grand scale was the sky.

I had not come back here with much of a plan. New York was simply a place to exist, but I would find some sort of meaning in doing that, providing care for Nan. She sure wasn't getting any younger. We were all on the slide and there was only one way it went.

I needn't have worried about being at a loose end there. If my very first acts were anything to go by, my presence would prove to be much needed.

I would get going on her care the second I stepped out of the car.

The Snowman (1982)
Directed by Dianne Jackson
Film Review by Hazel Nightingale

It's a rare thing in these polarising
times to find a film that is so universally
loved, but the 1982 TV movie based on Raymond
Briggs' wordless book achieves that. The film
has become a staple of the festive season, as
important as turkey and trees, baubles and
fairy lights. Christmas is simply not
complete without a viewing of *The Snowman*.

Aside from the three different
introductions the filmmakers have created
over the years (my personal favourite has
always been the *less-is-more* original
featuring Raymond Briggs that had me, as a
little girl, wondering if all this *really*
happened??), no words are needed to tell its
story of the young James who builds an effigy
in his front garden one snowy day only for
that figure to come to life by magic later
that night. Viewers could almost believe some
real magic was woven into this film.

Each frame was hand drawn by a team of
animators and, knowing that, the result is
breathtaking, the enthralled youngster in
flight with the snowman as they soar over the
English countryside. The film always takes me
back to my own childhood, growing up in rural
Lincolnshire (I was delighted to learn that
Lincoln's very own university, my alma mater,
provided animators for *The Snowdog* sequel,
and it may have just been me, but I thought

one or two of those flying shots were reminiscent of certain angles of Lincolnshire). Rural England is a place sometimes haunting, sometimes desolate, always enticing. Accompanying the visuals is Howard Blake's beautiful soundtrack which, too, captures the dissonance of the festive period, its darkness, and its light.

Passion and pure artistry are present in every single frame. You can forgive it if occasionally it's a little rough around the edges, or if the style of one sequence is marginally different from another. There is a perfection within the imperfections. These qualities only make the film more human, and subsequently more appealing than the sterile computer generated fare that studios prefer to manufacture these days. The latter is plastic, the former is blood, sweat, and tears... and so it has a soul.

In these days of infinite content being spewed onto our screens, this is a story that viewers return to again and again, despite the heartbreak in its conclusion. The life of the Snowman may be fleeting, his magic even more ephemeral, but this film will live forever.

Verdict: 10 / 10

Chapter 2

"HERE'S WHERE IT BEGINS," I muttered to myself as I pulled into Nan's drive. I could have arrived there at any point today, after lunch, just before bedtime. In fact, it could have been a different day entirely, as I still had a couple of days left on my contract, but the very second I switched off Clarence's engine, fate gave me this snapshot of the life of my grandmother Dora Nightingale.

It was half eleven in the morning and there she was in her full Kesteven Morris gear, black leggings, a multicoloured skirt, bell pads around her shins, wooden rods in her hands. Flowing from her tattercoat was a slew of ribbons, their colours coordinated with her gown: yellow, red, black, making her look like a giant pom-pom. Crazy to some, normal for Lincolnshire.

She stood on her neighbour's doorstep and Kitty was trying her best to restore some order to her confusion.

"It was yesterday, Dora. Don't you remember? At the Christmas market?" I saw the relief on her face as she clocked me. Here came the granddaughter to save the day.

"Good morning, Kitty," I said. "Hello Nan. What's going on here then?"

She turned round to me, her eyebrows raising, a twinkle of recognition in her eyes. "Martin, you're here. Will you take me?"

Martin was my brother. She'd muddled us up all my life. At best I would be called Mar-Philli-Hazel as the names of all three siblings span through her mind till she got the right one. The fact that I was a granddaughter and not a grandson didn't mean a thing to her. My nan never did have a firm grasp on gender identity. It's a marvel she and Grandad ever reproduced. When I was a child, she kept a big tomcat that

16

would prowl the fens like a panther catching rabbits and pheasants and most probably impregnating every lady cat in a five-mile radius. What was his name? Lilly.

"Where am I taking you?" I asked her. "To the circus?"

"We're dancing in the market place in Sleaford."

"That was yesterday, Dora," Kitty told her for what was likely the tenth time.

So that Christmas market had gone ahead then? Boded well for the Lincoln one.

"Was there a good turnout?" I asked.

"No," Kitty replied, her face scrunched up as she shook her head. "It was just a *virtual* thing, so they described it. The public could watch the lights switch-on ceremony from home through their computers or mobile telephones, or however it works. The town crier did explain it to me. But no, there was no real market on, as such."

For the older community members here, *wireless* technologies still meant anything to do with the radio. Anything involving the internet was regarded as space-aged wizardry.

I turned to Nan and said, "Why don't we go home and put the kettle on?" Often the best tactic was to distract her. "I've come all the way from London today to see you."

"Cor," she scoffed, as though I'd just told her I'd been rolling around in manure. "What did you want to go to London for?"

I ushered her towards her bungalow, mouthing, "Sorry," to poor Kitty. I was aware that my nan was increasingly finding herself in a confused state and bothering her neighbours, but catching her in the act like this gave me the impression it was happening all the time.

"It's all right, Hazel," Kitty said as Nan sauntered off home, her ribbons rustling in the breeze like she was some human pinata. "It was me who got her onto the team in the first place. I asked for it. Nice to see you back, anyway. I didn't realise you were due here today."

"You know, I just woke up this morning and had a feeling Nan was going to terrorise the neighbourhood."

I gave her the spiel as to the actual reason I'd returned to the Shire and I also wrote my number for her in case I might ever be out somewhere and Nan was being, well, Nan again.

Following the dementia patient into her bungalow, I collapsed on the sofa as she jingled off to her bedroom. She was prattling on to me about something, as though her voice could magically carry through rooms with no muffling.

"What are you yakking about?" I called out to her. "Do you need a hand getting your costume off?" The only sound that followed was her wheezing and panting as I pictured her wrestling herself to remove the outfit.

She'd been waving her hankies with the Morris dancers for about fifteen years now. How in the heck she remembered the sets, I had no idea. Perhaps their routines had imprinted on her brain just in time before the dementia had properly kicked in.

I'd seen photos of some of her performances. Some of the older snaps involved the same sort of costume she dressed in this morning but with the dancers' faces painted black. It wasn't even worth bothering to explain to her the modern day queasiness with that particular custom.

I found *the Morris* utterly bonkers. It was no wonder my nan had taken to it so well. Although her noodle was conking out, we could not say the same for her physical condition. I often wondered if her body hadn't seemed to age simply because it had *forgotten* to do so. If I were to ask her how old she was, I suspected she wouldn't answer that she was ninety-two years of age. The concept of time was something else she struggled with. Whenever she reeled off the date, she would typically go back in time to the early nineteen-hundreds. Most of her life she'd been saying *nineteen* sixty-four, *nineteen* eighty-three, *nineteen* ninety-one... and with *nineteen* tidily stored in her hippocampus, when we hit the turn of the century, instead of going on to *twenty*, Dora Nightingale had reverted to 1900. Her very own mental millennium bug.

Back when Grandad was around, her dancing hobby was much different. Those were the tea dance days where some guy would play old Glenn Miller vinyls in a village hall as they danced the jitterbug. Whenever we'd tagged along as kids, child-minded on school holidays, they'd give us each a strip of raffle tickets for the interval tombola. The top prizes were usually a bottle of wine or a box of chocolates. When my luck was in, I'd be picking from the dregs, a tin of peaches or some corned beef.

After about ten minutes of fannying around in her bedroom, Nan joined me in the lounge. I sighed. She was still wearing all her Morris gear.

"What the heck were you...?" I began, my fingers clenching into my palms.

"Huh?" she replied before I'd even got the whole of my question out.

I shook my head. "No matter." I'd been there ten minutes and already I was exhausted.

"Have you come for lunch then?" she asked me.

"No. I mean, yes, I will have something to eat later. I've come forever, Nan."

"Ooh," she replied in that way old folk react to something controversial or saucy on television. It implied she understood I was here permanently. "What about Maddox?"

For the love of God.

She got my name wrong *every* time, but as for my ex? His sticks like dog dirt to your shoe, doesn't it? It's not like he even had an easy, regular name to remember. Maddox? That's not a proper name to my nan. It's just a random

19

sound. A word you might see on a bottle of manly bubble bath, if indeed such an oxymoronic concept was possible.

"I'm not with him anymore, Nan."

"Well, why ever not?" she asked as though it was all *my* fault I hadn't been able to keep a man. *Why can't you be like your siblings, Hazel, and settle down with someone?*

"I don't want to talk about him. What are we having for lunch?"

I'd save her from the truth about that Maddox rogue. Evidently he was a charming gentleman to my nan, not a sly little cheat who didn't know how to get by on an honest living. Explaining that he was part of a team that scammed victims over the telephone, getting them to part with their money, really didn't show me in a great light either. *You sure can pick 'em, Hazel!* In my defence, he'd duped me, too. I thought he just worked at a call centre. Which, I supposed he did, but I had the impression he was trying to persuade people to change their mobile phone plan, not suckering them to pay in advance for their covid jab or telling them there was something fraudulent going on with their national insurance number.

"Have a look and see what I've got in," she said as I got up to investigate the food situation.

In the kitchen I found half a mouldy loaf of white bread in the bread bin, next to which was a punnet of grapes that was a day away from being a punnet of raisins. At least she had some butter for the bread, looking lonely on the top shelf of the fridge. Plenty of UHT milk in there. I didn't know why she never drank regular milk. The cupboards held a substantial supply of tuna and rice pudding and porridge sachets, but not much else.

Beside a collection of dusty cordial bottles, congealed formations floating within them, I spotted a half empty bottle of whisky. Had Nan taken to quaffing this stuff? It was always Grandad's favourite tipple, so I wondered if this bottle had just been kicking around the bungalow since his passing. The label looked new though, and on closer inspection there was some promo competition with a closing date of 2020. Right. Nan was knocking back liquor then. Dementia and drink. A winning combination.

"Is *Sherman's* still there in Coningsby?" I asked as she rustled into the room like a giant tumbleweed. I should have checked this on the drive in.

"Oh yes, it's still there."

Not that I would take her word for it. It remained a fifty-fifty matter, but asking her such questions would help me gauge how many marbles she still owned. If that mini supermarket was no longer in existence, I could carry on to Tattershall which had a grocer.

"Do you want to come for a ride out with me, then?"

"Let me get my coat."

"How about you put some proper clothes on first? Can't take you into the village like that, can I?" She was jingling and rustling with every step.

While she found a less outrageous outfit to wear, I checked out one of the spare bedrooms, what had evolved into a storage room for her many dancing shoes and dresses. This room had been my quarters, growing up. When Phillipa and I came to live here as kids, I should have been entitled to the bigger room next door, but somehow my little sister had staked her claim over it. I could have inherited it when she moved out, but I'd become attached to this room. The lavender grew just outside, and on summer days the scent would carry through the window.

I suddenly thought about all my boxed-up belongings in Clarence, so I made a start on lugging them inside. Hopefully, by the time I'd done that, Nan would be ready to go.

"So how long are you staying for, did you say?" Nan asked me as we drove down the fen road to civilisation. I was certain there weren't as many potholes as the last time I was here. It was like driving over the surface of the moon.

"At least for the rest of the year," I said.

"So you'll be here for Christmas?"

"Most definitely." Maddox would attempt to lure me back to London by then. Of that I had no doubt. But I'd promised myself I would not let him suck me in.

"That'll be nice."

"Yes, it will," I agreed, wondering what decorations were up in the attic. When we were kids, my favourite one was this pair of light-up bells that chirped Christmas carols, something she'd brought back from a trip to America. Were they still in existence? Or had she stored them away in a place she'd now forgotten about? Thanks to that virus, I hadn't visited her at all last Christmas. I doubted she'd even put her tree up. It wasn't like there was a great deal to celebrate last year. Covid had stolen everyone's fun.

Although I'd stayed over plenty in the summer, in-between waves when things looked to be settling, her bubble in the winter months had comprised Martin and his family, seeing as he lived locally to her, just down the road in Sleaford. But my brother had little time on his hands, working at the council and raising two kids. He'd done his best.

"You'll have to see Robin," she said. "See if he needs any help at *The Mall*."

She raised an important point, something I hadn't dwelt on. What would I do for work now? Would I indeed need a job? There had been a slightly selfish aspect to coming to live with Nan, that I could make use of the solitude of the

Lincolnshire fens to focus on my book, the one I'd been meaning to start writing for the past four years.

Although her care could well turn into a full-time position, I feared my sanity would suffer somewhat if I didn't take time to get out of the bungalow. And I couldn't ignore the goal of the long game, that I needed to get back on my feet somehow. As much as I didn't like to think about it, Nan could drop dead the next day and what would I do then? That's the end of my role as carer, the end of my residence in New York.

Years ago, I used to work at a pub-restaurant in Woodhall Spa. It had started as a weekend job when I was doing my A-Levels, then later on my employment was confined to the holidays as I studied English at Lincoln University. The landlord Robin and landlady Sunny lived above the pub with their children. I suspected his kids were old enough now to help their father run the place, but it was worth popping in there to have a chat.

"I may go see him tomorrow," I said. "Maybe we should have lunch there."

"That's a good idea."

I hadn't actually done much of that sort of thing, going out for a meal or hitting the pub for a drink after work. It was another hangover from the pandemic. The outside world just seemed dirty now. Public venues were giant petri dishes teeming with infections. Although I'd long had both my vaccination jabs, the ghost of that virus lingered. With all the sanitisation procedures in place, pubs and restaurants were possibly the cleanest they'd ever been.

Last summer I'd come down with covid. I was still in my twenties, admittedly only just, but with age on my side, its residence in my body was manifest. I wasn't one of those lucky asymptomatic ones. The weirdest aspect was losing my taste. It really did steal that from you, and it was weeks before I was properly right again.

But as for my passenger? The one who didn't have the mental capacity to retain the threat of a killer virus in her brain? It was impossible to impress on her, despite all the government messages, the need to wash one's hands regularly. Dora Nightingale was a lifelong country bumpkin with only a casual sense of cleanliness at the best of times. Germs and viruses? Ah, they're an old wives' tale!

It truly was the miracle of this whole pandemic that she never came down with it. My body's reaction may have indicated how the Nightingale genes coped with the virus, so I doubted Dora would have been a silent carrier. No, my inkling was she'd ridden the luck of that outbreak like a surfer bum riding a giant wave, performing cartwheels on her board as the breaker crashed. That covid wave would not get the better of my nan and wipe her out, oh no.

Still, when there's a nasty viral outbreak brewing out there, the last place you want to be is in the capital. The isolation of New York, Lincolnshire was the place to be. Sometimes the idea of putting her in a care home was mooted, but Martin had been absolutely right as the pestilence had spread. Nan was better off in her own home.

Her biggest risk was contracting the virus from the various visitors that came to her house, namely the carers. Martin had arranged for them to come each morning to make sure she was up and had taken her medication. With me now living with her, we'd cancelled those visits. As her primary caregiver, it was my way of singing for my supper.

We soon arrived in Coningsby and it looked as I remembered it, a lot of the old shops still trading, the church with the massive clock face towering over everything. Had they designed it for the benefit of the local RAF pilots who could check the time by peering down from their cockpits?

"Oh look," I said, pointing up to the sky. "The Lancaster is out. They must have known Hazel Nightingale was back in town today." The Battle of Britain Memorial Flight Visitor Centre was based in this village from which they maintained working relics of certain wartime aircraft: the Lancaster, the Spitfire, the Dakota and various others that I could never remember the name of.

"Your father used to fly in those," Nan said.

"Yes. My grandfather, you mean."

"Yes," she replied, shaking her head in frustration with herself. She made that mistake often.

As I turned into Silver Street, I saw *Sherman's* was indeed still trading. Nice one, Nan. Much like her, the geriatric fen-dweller, these remote Lincolnshire village shops knew how to endure.

I parked up in the adjacent car park. Nan raced on ahead and for a moment I wished she *was* still wearing those damned bells. Perhaps I would get her to wear them when we went out again. Sure would make keeping track of her much easier.

Chapter 3

THIS COUNTY ISN'T CALLED THE land of the big sky for nothing. Yes, it has some flat areas but then it often contradicts its reputation. Steep Hill, anyone? The Wolds? That's part of the magic of Lincolnshire. Once you go exploring, among the prosaic villages and bland fenland, you'll occasionally come upon a gem.

The village of Woodhall Spa was one such Lincolnshire gem, a place that to me always seemed bizarrely un-Lincolnshirey. This is a resort with distinct character and, dare I say it, some class. Lining the high street are fancy cafes, bookshops, sweetshops, shoe shops. Further within the village you'll find a golf course, an outdoor swimming pool, and the coolest cinema in the whole of Britain, the Kinema.

One weekend in the summer, the entire community is sucked into a time warp and sent back to the war for the 1940s festival, a great big fancy dress party. Roads are closed as people wander around in their floral shirtwaist dresses, men in army uniform as they explore the vintage vehicles lining the street, wave their flags, and listen to Vera Lynn singing *We'll Meet* Again. Throughout the day, the villagers gaze skywards to catch sight of the Lancaster or the Dakota. Even 'Winston Churchill' makes an appearance. More exhibits are found in the woods and Jubilee Park, not to mention at the Petwood Hotel where the actual Dambusters stayed and one of the last remaining Barnes Wallace bouncing bombs sits on display in the car park.

I knew the festival fell victim to the virus in 2020 as I'd been up visiting nan on the weekend it should have taken place, but as I sat there in *The Mall*, I couldn't remember if I'd heard of its resurrection this year.

"Did the 1940s event happen this summer?" I asked Nan. I realised asking her to recall something that had transpired over four months ago was a big ask.

After a few seconds, her eyes lit up with a memory. "Oh yes. Very hot weekend. I bumped into Ron selling little Union Jacks. I'll show it to you when we get back."

I seemed to recall seeing her buy this flag a few years back, so I sensed there was some blurring going on with her memories. They'd definitely cancelled the Lincolnshire Show, so it was most likely the forties weekend had come a bit too early for the nation's recovery and had to be put off too.

That virus had robbed us of so much, but if there's one thing we're good at, it's that we can adapt. I remembered the VE Day celebrations in London last year on its seventy-fifth anniversary, all the people in my old neighbourhood throwing little tea parties in their front yards, red, white and blue bunting festooning the street. The revellers may have pushed the boundaries that day, neglecting that mandate of two metres' distance after a few beers as they encroached on their neighbours' parties. As the nation observed this anniversary from a traumatic era, in 2020 we were going through our own trauma, tormented by an invisible nemesis.

Romanticising wartime always struck me as rather odd, although there was probably something about that time that appealed, an innocence perhaps, a black and whiteness as we were so sure of the fight, so sure the Nazis were utterly evil and needed stopping. They made everyone else look good.

It wasn't until the end of that conflict, when those two bombs dropped on Japan, that we directly looked our mortality in the eye. Humanity had not been so self-aware till then, not in terms of what destruction we could wreak. Nothing would be the same again for us once we'd opened that Pandora's box. No wonder we yearned to go back.

Such retrospectives meant returning to a time of fewer vehicles, no budget airlines taking you to exotic climes, no virtual worlds. Back then technology didn't nag you to get in your daily amount of steps, food labels didn't remind you about consuming your five-a-day, the climate behaved as it should because there weren't so many vehicles on the roads or planes in the sky, you knew who your enemies were because bullies did their work to your face rather than via their computers. Life was simpler, or at least it was in the villages. Did the nostalgia for this era appeal because we knew the result? We knew that, ultimately, the allies succeeded. When they halted the professional football leagues last year, the broadcasters tended to replay the matches England won, not those that ended up in penalty-shoot-out elimination.

Or perhaps these nostalgic celebrations of wartime were a way of dealing with the trauma of it all. Would we be doing the same with the coronavirus experience considering the suffering it had brought us? In years to come, might our descendants celebrate with a weekend of Zoom conference calls, baking cakes, juggling loo rolls, wearing face masks, decorating our front windows with rainbows and messages to the NHS, banging our pots and pans at six o'clock?

"What do you want to eat then?" I asked her. The menu was in her hands, but she'd been distracted, watching the world go by through the window. Parked along the road I noticed two very large lorries. They were most probably either delivering farming machinery or were lost.

She wrinkled her nose. "I'll just have a shandy, I suppose."

"You're not hungry? The whole point of coming here was to get some lunch."

I grabbed the menu and looked for a lighter bite for her. Undoubtedly, when my steak came out, she would wonder where her meal was. Second guessing my nan didn't always work, but it was a sensible policy.

Melissa came to our table to take our order. She was one of Robin's kids, a twin.

"Oh hi Hazel," she said. "Lovely to see you back in the Shire."

"Hi Melissa. Come up for Christmas, yes." I preferred saying that instead of having to explain how I was back in Lincolnshire because I'd lost my job and my whole life had subsequently unravelled because I was a total failure. "Your dad keeping you busy at work, then?"

"Yes, doing a few shifts in-between my studies."

"Oh right, what are you studying now?"

"Media at Lincoln College."

"Last I saw you I think you were just about to start your GCSEs." I made a quick survey of the room. "Things picking up after lockdown?"

"Seem to be getting there, yes. A lot of people just want to get back to how we were before."

"Is your dad around today? I'd love to catch up with him."

"Yeah, he's upstairs having a nap. Let me take your order then I'll go rouse him."

I changed my mind at the last moment, going for some simple crispy chicken strips instead. Perhaps I wasn't so hungry either. It made sense to watch the pennies too, until I sorted the job situation. I ordered a jacket potato topped with tuna for Nan.

Once the food was in front of her, she swiftly got stuck in, and once she'd demolished that, she picked up the other menu.

"Fancy a dessert?" she asked.

"I'd better not."

"Don't fuss about the cost; I'll get it."

I knew for a fact she didn't need to worry about money

with Martin obtaining power of attorney early last year and keeping me apprised of her finances. With her state pension and Grandad's pension, free bus passes, no television licence fee, no council tax, Nan had more moolah in her bank account than she knew how to spend. But I'd told myself before coming back to Lincolnshire that I wouldn't lean on her. It was a slippery slope.

"They've got *portifilios*," I said. That was her way of pronouncing the cream-filled choux pastry dessert known to the rest of the English-speaking world as 'profiteroles'. But for us grandchildren, the Dora Nightingale version was so amusing that we'd adopted it ever since she'd coined it.

"Ooh and apple crumble and custard," she read from the menu. "I've never known you to turn down a crumble."

It was true. The ones she made when I was a child were epic.

"Go on then. You twisted my arm."

By the time we'd both polished off those, Robin had still not appeared. Maybe he was under the weather today and needed rest. However, just as we were getting up to leave, I heard a voice.

"Is that Hazel Nightingale I see? Revered London film critic?"

I turned to find a grinning Robin in one of his yellow t-shirts, The Black Grass Bandits emblazoned on the front. It was a three-piece folk band, and he was the lead singer. Kind of like The Pogues, but with a Lincolnshire bent rather than Irish. They'd produced a couple of albums, every track themed around particular facets of rural life round here, whether it was the need to puff on your inhaler as you scaled Lincoln's Steep Hill or about falling in love with a girl because she ate chine. I was certain they were the only band in the world that had written a song about sugar beet.

I'm not sure how the heck it had happened, but they'd even performed over in America, in none other than New

York, of course.

"Hi Robin." I pointed to his t-shirt and said, "The Bandits still going strong then? They survived the Rona?"

"Absolutely. Come down in a few weeks as we've got a little Christmas gig on right here."

"I'm there."

"So what brings you back home, then?"

I gave a subtle flick of my eyes to indicate the old dear behind me. "Keeping an eye on this one."

He nodded understandingly. "Won't that magazine miss you?"

"Sadly, it is no more," I confessed. "Tomorrow the final edition is out."

"Oh no. I'm sorry to hear that."

"So if you have any shifts going, don't hesitate to call me."

"Yeah, sure. Absolutely." He sounded too enthusiastic about that, unconsciously peering behind himself. There stood his daughter Melissa at the coffee machine pouring drinks. He may as well have said, *'Soz, duck, after you went on to better things I built up the family workforce. All covered, thanks!'*

That's what my life had come to, trying to wrestle some hours off a youngster as they earned some pocket money. Talk about a fall from grace.

We'd just said our goodbyes, and I was putting on my coat when Melissa came back over.

"Hey Hazel. Before you go, let me show you something."

"Sure." I turned to Nan and said, "Wait here."

Melissa beckoned me over to the fireplace.

"Sorry, I couldn't help overhearing. If you're looking for some work, this might interest you. Especially as you're a cinefile."

She pointed to the community notice board, upon which was a poster. *Would you like to be in a feature film?*

"They're shooting a movie here in Woodhall Spa next week," she explained.

"Oh, that sounds intriguing. What's it about?"

"Some sort of war film, of course. I don't know if it's a Netflix production or what, but it's got a cool cast. I looked it up."

Maybe that accounted for those big lorries down the road, Hollywood getting set up before the cameras rolled.

"I'm not so sure, but thanks for thinking of me. I've never done anything like this before. I don't know how to act."

"They tell you what to do. Easy stuff. It's not like you have to recite Shakespeare or anything. You often just mooch around in the background or something."

"Have you signed up for this, then?"

"Definitely. I had my fitting and covid test yesterday. I've done a few productions now. Bet you hadn't realised I was in *The Crown*?"

"Oh wow. Well, I guess if you're on this I'd at least know someone to show me the ropes."

"Yeah, go for it. You've nothing to lose, Hazel. Be quick though. Do it when you get home."

I'd written about films no end, but I'd had no firsthand experience of the production process. Was I the right material to step in front of the camera? Was I what they were looking for?

A clattering of porcelain resounded behind me, Nan knocking her dessert bowl and spoon onto the floor. I cursed. How the hell had she managed to do that?

"Don't worry, I'll tidy it up," Melissa said. She prodded her forefinger on the flyer. "You get enlisted for this. It's been there weeks so there isn't much time."

"Sure," I replied, nodding. To humour her, I took a photograph of the poster so I would have all the details. Not that I could see myself going for it. If they were filming next week, then surely they'd have already sorted all their extras by now.

"Ready?" I asked Nan as I returned to her.

"Yes."

"Let's get out of here before you wreck the place. Be seeing you, Melissa," I said as she got up from clearing up the debris.

"Later Hazel. Yes, see you on set!"

Nan and I stepped outside. We'd only just had lunch, but it was that time of year when, by that point in the day, it already felt very old.

"Well, what do you fancy doing this afternoon?" she asked me.

"How about a film?"

As I drove us back to New York, it occurred to me we hadn't watched any Christmas films yet. December awaited its grand entrance in a little under ten hours. The music had started yesterday, so what festive flick could we watch to kick off the season?

Love Actually (2003)
Written and Directed by
Richard Curtis
Film Review by Hazel Nightingale

Appearing just two years after the darkest
day in recent history, the terror attacks of
9/11 which Hugh Grant mentions in the opening
scene, one can't help but wonder if Curtis
wrote this as a direct reaction to that event
much like Bernie Taupin had scribbled down in
a few minutes a new version of *Candle in the
Wind* in the immediate aftermath of Princess
Diana's death.

Love Actually is a celebration of the
varied facets of love, and it is unashamedly
a feel-good film, sometimes gooey, sometimes
poignant, thoroughly witty. When I first
watched it back in the early noughties, I did
have the sneaking suspicion that Dickie may
have written it on the toilet, perhaps on
September twelfth 2001, but even a Curtis
story from the bog can pack a serious smack
on the lips.

You've likely seen it all before, and
heard it all before too, like the song *Love
Is All Around* that he *did* in one of his other
films. This time it has a festive twist. This
time it's all a Curtis Christmas special. His
characters share that same drive, hold to
that same meaning of life: fall in love, get
married, live happily ever after.

And what a world it was back then, when we

were allowed to meet new people, where it was possible to conduct a romance *in person*. The opening footage of strangers greeting their loved ones in the airport seems a long time ago. Yes, we used to go on planes and fly to other countries. We used to hug each other.

Despite this festival of affection, it doesn't necessarily always work out for the characters. Sometimes they take a kamikaze shot (Andrew Lincoln and those cue cards). Sometimes they twist when they should have stuck (looking at you now, Alan Rickman). Sometimes the love for their family is greater than the love they can afford to a suitor (Laura Linney and her doomed workplace crush). It's all there. The all-star cast certainly goes a long way to draw you in to their interweaving romances, but a lot must be said for the themes that hold the narrative together.

'5 weeks to Christmas' a caption reads over a shot of a mall, the hustle and bustle of shoppers as they swarm through the decked out hall, on a mission to do their Christmas shopping. A man carries a tree, skaters skate on an outdoor ice rink, buskers play festive tunes. The film captures that feeling we all get in late November / early December, that sense of light and happiness on the horizon, that sense of heading somewhere. A sense of purpose.

Filled with that warm sweetness, we're soon sucked in, so high on love that we'd even put politics aside to root for the prime minister (a most un-British thing). What would normally merit a parliamentary investigation, headlines in the tabloids, a vote of no confidence as PM Hugh Grant abuses his powers to chase after some foul-mouthed girl who used to work for him, instead provides the heartwarming conclusion. He even has a smooch with her in a primary school of all places and we laugh at the sight of lipstick smudged over his lips.

Love Actually has the audacity to switch from 'political scandal' to comedy sketch show in a blink, as the exuberant Kris Marshall fulfils a horny teenager's fantasy, heading to America and instantly pulling a bed-full of hotties. By then the film *has* you so you go with it. And next year you'll actually go through it all again.

Verdict: 7 / 10

Chapter 4

"ANYTHING FROM MADDOX YET?"

Sometimes I couldn't believe her. It was barely a few minutes past seven in the morning, and she comes out with that. I often wondered if, instead of going to sleep like most normal people did, she lay awake in bed all night trying to cook up dumb questions.

"No," I replied. "And I'm not sitting here waiting for the telephone to ring."

You still have that stupid teddy bear he won for you at the fete, don't you, Hazel? Is that possibly a sign you're unable to let go of him completely?

"Ah," she replied, going silent for a few moments. "Do you suppose it's over between you two, then?"

"That's what I'm trying to get across to you, yes. Me and Maddox are done. I laid a whisper on his pillow, I've deadheaded all the flowers he planted in my backyard, and the winner took it all. In other words, we broke up."

I realised all my pop music references would go straight over her head, but, despite that, it still felt good to say it all. She sat in a stunned silence, but it didn't last long.

"What were you growing?"

"Huh?"

"In your back garden. What were you growing? Carnations?"

You really think I had time to do any gardening in London? I just shook my head, my attempt to abort that conversation as I lowered my gaze to my mug on the coffee table.

Beside it was a pile of magazines, on top of which was the December issue, the final magazine we'd published. I grabbed it and flicked through the pages, wondering if Nan had read it. I sent her them every month (although this particular issue I'd been able to hand deliver, of course). With her dementia, perhaps she picked it up each morning and re-read all the articles, any memory of perusing them the day before escaping her head. Or maybe she'd forgotten it was even there three seconds after placing it on her coffee table.

"What about that chap at the magazine?" she said. "You had your eye on him for a while, didn't you?"

Was she making it her mission to sort out my love life or something? Dora Nightingale, the fenland Love Doctor? I could practically hear her thoughts, the conundrum that eternally troubled her brain. *Why can't Hazel find someone to settle down with like her siblings have?*

"Are you talking about Dan?"

He was our head distributor, shipping tens of thousands of our community magazines each month to our bank of youngsters who would deliver them door to door. I'd mentioned him to Nan just the once, but it was one of those weird details that stuck in her mind. *Ooh, a potential suitor for Hazel! Let's keep going on about him until the end of time!*

"Yeah. Dan. You said he was a nice man."

"Well, first off I don't work at the magazine anymore because it's gone under, and secondly I no longer live in London either, so I'm not really rating our chances."

"Don't think so negatively…"

"And besides all that, I'm afraid there was one other killer blow. He shaved off his lovely beard."

"Oh, how could he do such a thing?" she replied, chuckling. That's what I liked about my nan most of all. My strange sense of humour would tickle her. We had the same genes, after all. If I wanted a vision of how I would turn out in sixty years' time, I only had to look across the room. "Well, you'll have to keep your eye out. Sometimes romance comes calling when you're least expecting it."

"I expect the most eligible bachelor here is Barry at number thirty-seven, and he's an octogenarian widower. It's not beyond the realm of possibility that I'm literally the only living girl in New York." I babbled these words into the pages of my defunct publication. Ironic how they called New York one of the most romantic places in the world. This place couldn't be any further from such a reputation.

"Montgomery's still around, you know."

I rolled my eyes. Why was she so intent on pairing me off? Montgomery was whom I would describe as the local eccentric. He wasn't the village idiot, but possibly the closest thing we had to one. He'd never married, and well into his fifties he still lived with his mother, spending his days lolling in the surrounding fields painting his watercolours. I'd never been aware of him ever having a job, although I was aware he sold a lot of his paintings. In fact, we had one of them hanging in this very bungalow, a portrait sitting of me and my siblings when we were young.

I hadn't actually seen Montgomery in a few years. That's the thing with this village. You were more likely to pass them in the car, a little wave as you raised your hand from the steering wheel. That was about the limits of New Yorkers' social needs.

"He must be getting on now," I said.

"Well, I'll keep thinking."

"Please don't," I muttered under my breath.

"Anyway, what would you like for breakfast?"

"I'm not hungry."

"What about a pancake and maple syrup?"

She did amuse me sometimes. Morning pancakes were a staple of our summers when we were shipped over to hers for the holiday. She still saw the young girl in me.

"Okay then. For old times' sake," I replied. "Although, the rate you're fattening me up, I think even Barry Harrison would pass on me."

"You could do with a bit more meat on you," she remarked as she got up, heading for the kitchen.

While she did that, I returned to my bedroom to throw on some clothes whilst they still fit me. So often last year, when I was furloughed, I'd stopped bothering to get dressed in the morning. Staying in your pyjamas all day saved those few minutes when you went to bed at night and got changed again.

With my return to work looming earlier this year, I'd forced myself into the habit of making an effort. But not that much of an effort. Jeans and a hoodie were quite acceptable, especially here.

After my highly nutritious breakfast I felt inclined to get outside, burn off those calories, so I set off for a little walk. I left Nan with a task to keep her occupied, replenishing the bird feeders that hung from a cherry blossom tree in her back garden. Hopefully that would keep her out of mischief.

I'd never done this as a girl, go for walks from the bungalow, and I was soon reminded why. There weren't many decent strolls you could make, only follow the road out, which wasn't much fun with all the vehicles tearing past. As I trailed down Sandy Bank Road, a long straight passage before me, I felt like I was miles from anywhere.

New York really was a desert, nestling within a featureless landscape. There were no focal points here, no park to walk the dog, no pond to sit by writing poetry, no village green to play cricket. In fact, it wasn't even a village but a hamlet.

As I plodded along I realised the only thing it had in common with the New York of America was its long, linear roads. Here those roads took you into the settlement and then they took you straight out again.

And yet there was something about its blankness that appealed to me, that sense of being disconnected from the rest of the world. I loved that feeling, even as a child, the isolation.

It was a way of life that had been widespread in our country the past two years, even in the capital, as we all followed that mantra: stay home, protect the NHS, save lives. I sure wouldn't pass another soul on this little walk, wouldn't get within two metres of anyone. Such distancing was second nature to these New Yorkers.

Elegant trees lined the route, making the view vaguely reminiscent of the giant elms on either side of the mall of Central Park. Perhaps that was another similarity these namesakes shared, but I realised I was at the bottom of the commonalities barrel.

"Talk of the devil," I muttered as I spotted someone sitting on a wooden chair by an easel in the field across the road. Montgomery. He was painting whatever, a tweed flat cap on his head, a paintbrush clamped in his jaws, another in his hand. After all these years, was there actually anything left of this area to paint, an angle he hadn't yet tapped? The guy looked older with more lines on his face, and so my brain updated the 'library image' I had of him. This was a distinct phenomenon I'd noticed this year. So many people were looking old all of a sudden, like the pandemic had prematurely aged us. Where once a famous actress might have always played the love interest, now she was suddenly playing the maternal mentor figure.

My fellow villager saw me, raising his paintbrush into the air as he waved.

"Hazel," he mumbled to acknowledge me, the other paintbrush still protruding from his jaw. He'd said it as though it had only been a couple of days since we'd last seen each other and there was absolutely nothing to catch up on. The reality was that years had separated the last words that had passed between us, certainly many changes going on in my life in that time, but most likely none in his world. With the pace of life round here, he probably hadn't even realised I'd been living away.

"Hi, Montgomery," I replied. "Nice to see you still painting."

He said nothing else, just attempted a distorted smile with the brush in his mouth like a bit. His focus soon returned to the skies to the west, from where I heard the thundering roar in the distance. Of course, he was composing a scene that involved the Coningsby jets. I left him to it, plodding on out of the village.

The dynamics of the New York community had always been a wonder to me. With limitations on where the villagers could mingle, somehow everyone seemed to know everyone else's business. Perhaps they might meet in the aisle of *Sherman's*, or see each other on a Sunday morning in the pews of Saint Peter's down the road in Wildmore. Somehow, this was enough for information to spread. Were they all conditioned to avoid the chitchat, blurting nothing but essential matters while they had the chance in those fleeting moments? Or perhaps out here there just wasn't much to talk about.

In more recent years, the New York Facebook group had come along, not that it was a useful resource for a significant contingent of the population, those, like my nan, who didn't have the internet. I'd remained a member of the group, even during my years away down south. It was so tight-knit, so *'we don't care for outsiders, mate'*, but it seemed the admins had considered me an honorary New Yorker rather than one of them *frim folk* from out of the county. A middle-aged couple called the Bakers ran it and their ship was tight. I often had the impression they thought of themselves as the Taylor Dooses of our village. The rumour mill made suggestions that they weren't thoroughbred yellowbellies, but were actually from the faraway land of Leicestershire, yet no one had ever had the guts to put this slur to them.

The road trailed on and on, offering me nothing but more and more fields. I was just turning round to head back to the bungalow when something caught my eye. Prowling across the field was a cat with a ginger coat and white socks. I wondered what the chances were that it was related to Nan's Lilly, one of his descendants. As I crouched down, the feline saw me and put off his hunting to come and investigate me. I removed my phone and took a few snaps.

"Hey puddy tat. You're a big fellow. I may have known your great-great-great-grandfather. Although, his fur was a different colour to yours."

He was soon done posing for photographs, rubbing the side of his mouth over my hand to scent me, so close now the camera wouldn't even focus. He certainly seemed affectionate like Nan's cat. Perhaps it wasn't such a crazy idea.

"I'm heading off now, fella. See you again."

"Enjoy your walk?" Nan asked when I returned home and plonked myself down on the sofa.

"Yeah, look what I saw," I replied, fishing out my phone and bringing up the photographs of the cat.

"Ooh, where was she?"

"On Sandy Bank. And I'm certain she was a he. Reminded me of your Lilly."

Her face lit up with the mention of her old pet. Perhaps she might benefit from some more animal company.

"Have you thought about getting another cat?" I asked.

"Pah," she said. "I don't want a ginger tom."

"Well, I don't necessarily mean the same colour as this one. And what do you have against gingers, anyway? You could get another black one like Lilly."

What was I saying? She could barely look after herself at times. How would she cope with a pet in her charge? Certainly with me around it would work, but was I really going to be here forever? What would happen to it when I got my life together again and moved on?

That poor moggie will be long dead by then, Hazel!

Perhaps I was just trying to recapture the past. Sometimes it hit you how it was long gone.

My thumb continued to scroll through the images, and we gazed on them in silence. That was, until I came to the photo I'd taken yesterday.

Nan squinted and leant forward in her seat. "Do you want to be in a film?" she read. "What's that about?"

"Oh, that was just some poster I saw in *The Mall* yesterday."

"Is it a Hollywood film being made round here?"

"So it seems, yes."

"Are you going to do it?"

"I hadn't thought anymore about it, to be honest."

"You like films. You'd enjoy that."

"Oh, I don't know. I'm sure they'd be long days, and who will look after you then?"

"Ah, you don't need to worry about me," she said, wafting her hand. She got to her feet. "You give it a go, my beauty. We could see you on the big screen in the Kinema. Wouldn't that be something?"

As she left the room, I gazed through the patio door to the back garden. The bird feeders hanging from the tree looked to be still empty.

"Definitely a better idea than getting a cat," I spoke to myself, my eyes returning to my phone.

Her reaction kind of felt like a nudge from the universe. Maybe I'd do it for Nan, something for her to look forward to, seeing her granddaughter on the silver screen. Even though she would most likely forget she'd suggested it within five minutes.

And that's if they were actually still looking for extras. That's if, even after doing it, my scene wouldn't end up on the cutting room floor. And if I didn't talk myself out of it. That was something I was an expert at.

An hour later I was still attempting to come up with reasons I should pass on that film extra thing when my phone lit up with a text. It was an unknown number, but the first line explained it was from Robin's daughter Melissa. She was asking if I'd signed up yet. I gave her a quick call.

"Hi Hazel."

"Hi Melissa," I replied, putting her on speaker. "I was literally just going over the entry form for that agency when you messaged me." It was a bit of a lie, but as I spoke, my fingers worked hard to bring up the link on my phone. Cool Cat Casting, they were called. *Cat*; was that another little sign from the universe there?

"Great," she replied. "So you're up for it?"

I paused for a moment, but no excuses came to mind.

"No harm in giving it a shot, I suppose."

I angled my ear away as she gave a girlie cheer. "That's so cool. Nice one, Hazel. The reason I got in touch was because the agency emailed me this morning to ask if I have any friends or relatives who would be interested, so it sounds like they're struggling to get the numbers."

Interesting. So it kind of meant that I'd be doing them a favour, not that I was doing it because I was desperate and it was the only work I could get my hands on. I preferred looking at it that way.

"I thought loads of people would have gone for it."

"People like the idea of being in a film, but get intimidated when it comes down to it, I think."

"Oh, not me," I lied once more.

"So when you fill in your measurements, make sure they're accurate. I know some like to be lenient..."

"Whatever are you trying to say?"

"It's just the fitters can get uptight if you're half an inch off, like it's a massive deal and you've ruined their entire day."

"I swear to tell the whole truth and nothing but the truth about my expanding waistline."

"And if you know of anyone else who'd do this, then point them the way of Cool Cat Casting too."

"I know you and my nan, so that will be no."

"Ooh, they'll want some selfies of you as well. I can give you a hand if you want, or will your nan be able to help you?"

I chuckled. "She can barely work the television remote. Asking her to take a photo would be like asking me to perform brain surgery."

"Well, I'm around all day."

"Thanks Melissa," I said. I was actually really grateful she'd persisted with me on this.

"No worries. Give me a shout if you get stuck on anything."

After hanging up, I sat there in the lounge, staring at my phone. There we had it. I could put this off no longer. Couldn't be letting Melissa down now by backing out. Glancing to my right, I noticed nan outside. She'd re-discovered the packets of seeds I'd left out for her and was replenishing the feeders. Only three hours late.

I got up and slid the door open.

"Do you have a tape measure?" I asked her.

Chapter 5

UPSTAIRS IN *THE MALL*, MELISSA demonstrated how well the living room doubled as a makeshift photo studio. In fact, all she'd had to do was shift a sofa ninety degrees. With the midday sun streaming through the bay window, I stood against the white emulsion of the wall as she took a few snaps on my phone, capturing me from the front, side, and rear of my head.

"Should I have smiled?" I asked as I swiped through the collection.

"No, neutral expression, like a passport photo."

"But..."

"They're fine. Just get them sent off."

"Okay."

"They're not going to *not* pick you. Submitting your details is just a formality, really."

"Let's do it now," I said as I sat down on the skew-whiff sofa. It was best I did it right away in case I tried to talk myself out of it back home. Melissa perched herself on the armrest. "So, are you working tonight?"

"Nope. First night of the Lincoln Christmas Market so I'm heading there with Randal."

"Nice one."

"Last year just wasn't the same without it."

The series of photographs finished uploading to my profile. My fingertip evinced my last dreg of hesitancy before I prodded it down on the screen to hit submit.

"There," I announced. "All done."

As I got up to leave, Melissa said, "Hey, are you doing anything tonight? Do you want to come with us?"

"Yeah, sure. I'd like that."

"Would your nan like to come as well?"

"I doubt it, but I'll ask her."

We made our arrangements for getting together again later, and I returned to Clarence and made my way home. Driving out of the village, I passed by the old RAF base, a facility that had been repurposed during the first wave. Transformed into a temporary mortuary, it was where the covid dead were stored. With so many excess deaths it had resulted in a bottleneck as corpses awaited their funerals. I heard the villagers found it a grim prospect, but they had to be taken somewhere, and I don't think there was much, if anything, going on at this base beforehand.

Eighty-two years since the start of the conflict, there remained many of these relics dotting the Lincolnshire landscape, leftovers from the war machine the country had converted into. Our shire was given the moniker of 'Bomber County' as most RAF bombers took off from there. There may have been over a hundred military airfields, but only a handful of them were still in use.

The fragments of runways and control towers and POW camps that remained, ghosts of the war, gave the impression of how immense the entire operation must have been. For my generation, we'd mobilised against a much different threat, but I wondered how long the ghosts of covid would last.

In years to come, would we appreciate the collective efforts we'd undertaken to fight the virus? Would covid-era remnants linger? The posters in shop windows, battery-drained temperature guns stored away in drawers (or perhaps an item on *Antiques Roadshow 2101*), forgotten road signs that directed drivers to testing centres lying in ditches, discarded face masks littering the streets.

How long before we forgot how facilities had been recast? Social venues like the Lincolnshire Showground had become vaccination centres, mothballed gymnasiums had become testing centres. And what about the laboratories where covid tests were processed? What sciencey stuff would be going on in those after the covid storm?

When humanity properly focussed on something, when everyone got together for the same cause, we can achieve great things. That's something I would take away from this time.

It's one reason I always had faith that a vaccine would come along before too long. If humans could endeavour to put men on the moon when it was still the 1960s, then I knew we would succeed with this challenge.

I gazed up at the giant fir tree standing tall in Minster Yard, rivers of bright lights flowing around its branches, a star upon its apex. Behind it the cathedral was lit up blue. For the first time, I had that Christmassy feeling.

Unsurprisingly, Nan had opted to stay in the warmth of her bungalow this evening. Although we'd visited the market many times when I was younger, she probably no longer found the hike around the trail of stalls to be that appealing, certainly with the merciless breeze that was slicing past us tonight. I'd left her in front of the television watching the soaps.

It was refreshing to mix with people closer to my own age, although there was still a hefty nine years' difference between me and the twins. *I* was the old one with these two, but nowhere near as high maintenance as my nan. I hoped. Along with the twins was Randal's buddy Brian, a lanky lad who sipped from an energy drink. I'd never met him before.

Immersing ourselves in the stream of visitors through Exchequer Gate, we began investigating the stalls. With the goal of finding something I could bring back for Nan, I hit upon the perfect solution with the first vendor, Christmas puddings. I bought a trio of those, all infused with different flavours.

I always found the market to have such a cool atmosphere, festive tunes piped through speakers along the cobblestoned route, stallholders dressed up in top hats and tailcoats like they were out of *A Christmas Carol*, the fairy lights, the smell of mulled wine. Starting outside the cathedral, the trail worked its way into the castle grounds, then on to The Lawns, then back along the outer castle wall where you'd find the big wheel and other fairground rides nestled beside the Cobb Hall medieval tower. It was absolutely best to visit at night. With hundreds of thousands of people flocking there each year, it was sometimes tricky to even get to the stalls. The sight of such an event last year would have made me wince.

"Who's hungry?" Randal asked as we exited down the ramp of the castle's west gate. Ahead of us a vendor cooked German sausages on a giant spinning skillet, and they smelled delicious. The twins were well in tune with each other, sharing an almost psychic bond, so I assumed the question was for my benefit. And Brian, who continued to slurp his sustenance from his drink.

"I might get a hot chocolate," I replied, spotting a stall on the opposite side.

"We're going to grab some hot dogs," Randal announced, as though they'd decided on that telepathically. "We'll see you over there."

My fingers welcomed the steaming cup of cocoa as I wrapped them around it. I'd forgotten to bring my gloves tonight and my digits were turning red raw. I found a quiet spot to stand in, away from the flurry of the human river. As I sipped my drink, the haunting tune of *Coventry Carol* gently hovered over the hubbub, echoing along the castle walls. A little later, the other three joined me there as the twins munched on their bratwursts.

It was Melissa who spotted him first. I noticed her squinting at something behind me, so turned to follow her gaze.

Initially, I saw a group of youngsters beside a roasted chestnut stall, their eyes wide as they practically danced on their heels. What were they so worked up about? It took me a few seconds to clock the object of their excitement. One of them approached a nearby man and asked him for a selfie. He acquiesced to her wish, and that caused even more of the rosy-faced teenagers to pluck up the courage and approach him.

"That's Eddy Partridge," Melissa said. "He was in that film with Will Smith."

I knew exactly whom she meant, and suddenly even I felt the twinge, that star-struck sensation that might turn me into a giddy teenager again.

Get a hold of yourself, Hazel! He's only human, like the rest of us. Just a very good-looking human, that's all. And talented.

I'd seen him in a number of films. Come to think of it, I'd probably seen all his films. Last year he'd been on the news with the protest marches following the George Floyd incident. Partridge, as an African American himself, had leant on his A-list status to voice his support.

"Ooh, do you think he's over here for our movie?" Melissa asked.

"Has to be," I replied. It wasn't wishful thinking. Surely it was the only reason. As cool as the Lincoln Christmas Market was, despite dragging in the crowds from far-flung corners of Britain, I doubted its pull extended quite as far as Hollywood.

"We've had an illustrious flow of cinematic dignitaries visiting our shire when you think about it," Melissa remarked. "Tom Hanks and Ian McKellen filming *The Da Vinci Code* in the cathedral, Rob Lowe over in Boston. Keira

Knightley and Jamie Dornan in Stamford."

"And don't forget," Randal butted in, "trumping those lot are the guys from *Top Gear*."

"One of my favourite directors too," I added, recalling how Castle Square, which we'd recently walked through, had been transformed into a film set for a period piece. "Mike Leigh when he did *Peterloo*."

"Never heard of it," Brian offered to the conversation. Randal pulled a face suggesting his ignorance on that matter too.

"You know the one she means," his sister retorted, slapping her brother's shoulder. "I told you about it. I was in it!"

"That would have been an awesome film to work on," I said, but Melissa's focus had returned to the here and now of Eddy Partridge. She handed me her phone.

"Take a picture, Hazel."

She popped her head into frame as I activated the camera function, Partridge plenty of yards behind her, oblivious to yet another photographer getting a snap of him. I took a couple of shots before the superstar called time on posing with yellowbelly teenagers, two members of his entourage wearing suits and black ties appearing next to him to extricate him from the throng. And just like that, his posse melted into the crowds and was gone.

"Let me see, let me see," Melissa gushed as she grabbed her phone back to view what I'd captured. With her so close to the camera, everything behind her was blurry, the drama occurring there a tad ambiguous. "Oh look, me and Eddy Partridge."

"That could be anyone," Randal chipped in as he stuffed the last of his hot dog into his mouth. He had a point.

Melissa clutched her phone to her chest. "Well, you just wait till you see the film we're going to make with him. We'll be hanging out with him in the coming days. His new besties."

Randal rolled his eyes, angling his body back towards the route of the market trail.

"Probably wasn't even him," Brian said, before belching. "Could have been some impersonator having a thrill."

"He looked pretty real to me," Melissa replied.

"Besides, I thought they were making a war film," he went on, draining the last drop from his can and scrunching it up.

"Yeah, they are."

"And there were... black guys in the war, were there? Is this another Bridgerton thing?" He mumbled a little so it was difficult to make out all his words.

"Of course there were."

"Bet... bet there weren't any American ones."

"God's sake, Brian. What did you get in GCSE History? An F?"

Whatever retort he was going to give next appeared to get caught in his throat. Seemed the lad had a bit of a stammer.

"Come on, we've still got plenty of stalls to see," I said, changing the subject.

"Who's up for a go on the big wheel?" Melissa asked.

It was nearing nine o'clock by the time I arrived back home, bags hanging from my arms. I'd bought some lovely Christmas decorations to put on the tree whenever I got round to digging the thing out of the attic.

The blaring sound of the television greeted me as I stepped inside. Nan was asleep on the sofa, her head arched back as she snored, Ant and Dec bantering on the box. I turned the volume down to a gentler level before settling into the seat.

Just at that moment I noticed something odd, my eyes resting on the dining table by the patio door. It was all set out, her best tablecloth, a plate and a knife and fork, even a glass of drink. We'd both eaten before I'd gone out, a lasagna that we'd devoured at the kitchen table. So what was going on here?

I shook her arm to wake her. "Were you expecting company this evening?"

"Eh?" she asked, probably not hearing me, or perhaps she was still half asleep.

I pointed to the opposite end of the room. "Who did you get all that out for?"

Her eyes squinted in confusion for a moment before she looked at where I was pointing. "Oh, Warren was here." It was all so matter-of-fact as though this happened every week and there was nothing for me to be surprised about, as ordinary as the starlings that visited the feeder each morning.

"Warren as in...?"

"Your father."

And by *father* she actually meant *grandfather*.

"Grandad was here?"

"Yes. I don't think he was hungry, though," she said as she got up to clear the table.

Had I unknowingly fallen down a rabbit hole? I felt like I'd stumbled directly into the mouth of madness. My grandfather had died a long time ago, three years after the turn of the millennium.

"Does he visit you a lot?" I asked as I picked up the drink. It was alcoholic. Whisky. So that explained that little mystery.

"Most nights, yes," she replied, collecting up the cutlery to put back in the drawer. I followed her into the kitchen.

"And... how is he doing?" I wasn't quite sure what

54

questions to ask, but I found this whole thing so fascinating. Martin had never mentioned anything like this going on with her, her daily rendezvousing with the dead.

"Not sure, really. He never says a word."

"So he just rises from his grave to hang out with you watching *I'm a Celeb*?"

"Yes, and then he goes off to bed. In fact, he might even be in there now."

The hairs on the back of my neck prickled.

"Well, should we have a look?" I suggested.

"Go on then."

I led her into her bedroom. The bed was unmade and I couldn't remember if she'd neatened it up this morning after rising.

"There's no one here, Nan."

"You can't see him because he's not here." Perhaps that statement made more sense in her own mind, but the way she'd said it carried no suggestion that she realised she was contradicting herself.

"Yeah, exactly. There's no one else here. Are you sure he visited you?"

"Oh yes. You'll see him tomorrow night, I should think." She pottered off back to the living room to finish clearing the table.

Although I kept an open mind with supernatural matters like this, at the same time I really didn't expect the ghost of my grandfather to visit tomorrow or indeed any day this month. It was easy to dismiss this as a part of her dementia, her way of coping with the loss of her husband, even though almost two decades had passed since then.

But... what if she did have *the gift*? What if the alterations of her mental faculties had somehow unveiled this ability? It all seemed like madness to anyone else of sound mind, but what if all us full-shilling folk were wrong?

A distant memory drifted into my mind. It was

something that had taken place right here in Nan's bungalow, except we were out in the garden watering the tomato plants in the greenhouse. Earlier I'd been watching a film, *Casper*, and with its subject matter on my mind I asked her if she believed in ghosts, and she told me of an incident when she was younger, when Great-Nanny had died. Nan had been laying awake in bed one night, the day after her mother's passing, and she'd seen a ball of light hovering over the bed. It was her mother, she said, checking over her, still with her.

She'd never spoken of any other incidents like this, so I didn't know if this was a random anomaly or whether it happened regularly, but my flesh continued to crawl as I pondered on this memory.

"Who ya gonna call?" I muttered to myself. "We're in the wrong New York for this kind of stuff, Nan."

The Man Who Invented Christmas (2017)
Directed by Bharat Nalluri
Film Review by Hazel Nightingale

It seems that every few years there's a
new version of Charles Dickens's *A Christmas
Carol* coming out (there's well over a hundred
of them now!) but this film offers a unique
take on the greatest Christmas tale ever
told. This time we go behind the scenes,
exploring the writer's journey, witnessing
Dickens drawing inspiration from the
different characters he meets in London,
random little details that trigger ideas. A
cold-hearted curmudgeon stands in a graveyard
muttering 'humbug', a wealthy snob talks of
his disgust of 'the surplus population', a
young maid tells a story of ghosts appearing
on Christmas Eve. All of these moments echo
in Dickens's mind as he rushes to complete
his new book in time. Indeed, the characters
are alive as he strives to transfer them to
the page.

The masterful Christopher Plummer as
Ebenezer Scrooge sits there in Dickens's
study while his creator swiftly jots down all
his miserly sentiments, telling him that the
two of them will do wonderful things. Dickens
is much in need of a hit after a succession
of flops. With this book he struck his
audience hard, a direct hit with his
'sledgehammer' story. Its effect would change
Christmas forever.

Not only did the author 'invent' Christmas

('reinvigorate' may be a more accurate description but a little hyperbole never hurt anyone), it seems he may have invented self publishing too, overseeing its printing and even commissioning some illustrations for his novella. The background to how Dickens released his book might explain a curious minor discrepancy that always puzzled me. The ghost of Jacob Marley warned his former partner that the three ghosts would appear on consecutive nights, yet as the narrative unfolds, they all appear on the same night. Come Christmas morning, the transformed Scrooge casually shrugs off this feat, "The spirits have done it all in one night. They can do anything they like. Of course they can." It's a shame you never got to use word processors, Charles. You can easily go back and change your manuscript then.

And then there's his Ghost of Christmas Present, a character that looks like an early prototype for Father Christmas. He embodies the Christmas spirit, a warm and bountiful figure spreading his incense on those most in need. Dickens certainly was on a roll with this project.

Is there also an argument for Dickens creating (or, again, 'reinvigorating') a sub-genre as he marries together ghostly visitations with Christmastime? Indeed, in Victorian times this was a tradition, recounting spooky tales by the fireplace. In more recent times, one thinks of the ghost stories of MR James, the telling of which would become a staple of Christmas television on the BBC. As a young girl I remember being spooked out by Christopher Lee's narration of these tales. Andy Williams mentions ghost stories as an important festive component in

It's the Most Wonderful Time of the Year. In the world of cinema, horror is commonly blended with a festive backdrop in such classics as *Gremlins* and *The Nightmare Before Christmas.*

But as far as ghosts go, perhaps the festive period is the time spirits come to the fore as we reflect on those who are no longer with us, the lost ones we shared Christmas with in the past.

Dickens would have further stabs at the Christmas ghost story himself, starting with *The Chimes.* Nothing would ever be as good as *A Christmas Carol,* however.

You feel Dickens's struggle in *TMWIC,* his frustrations in the creative journey as he is continually disturbed by people intruding upon him working, most particularly by his father. Old memories of Dickens's childhood resurface, but he only pours them into the pages of *A Christmas Carol,* raising awareness for the poor souls of that era that society forced to work like slaves in the workhouses.

This film may surprise you with how good, how *inspired,* it is. It's beautifully shot, with expert performances all round. I'm not sure it earned all the love it deserves, but, as with what happened with the forgotten masterpiece *It's a Wonderful Life,* audiences may grow to appreciate it even more as they return to it in Christmases yet-to-come.

Verdict: 9 / 10

Chapter 6

I WOKE THE FOLLOWING MORNING to find a strange new notification on my phone. It was Cool Cat Casting with an enquiry through their app. They'd processed my application and were asking me about my availability for the coming week. There were various filming days listed, and they also wanted to know whether I could attend a fitting either today or tomorrow. Still lying there in bed, I responded to it, ticking every available date.

Yep, I have all the time in the world for you guys!

It said I had to keep free any day that I committed to, that I would be on a *pencil* for those dates. I couldn't exactly see much else coming up to make any demands on my schedule, other than Nan, of course.

The title of the film was *Flying Colours*, but Melissa had mentioned last night that they often go by code names, especially if it's a high-profile flick with a pre-existing fanbase that might lurk around the sets to get a glimpse of filming. Back when they were making the original *Star Wars* sequels, she told me, they'd once gone by the fake name of *Blue Harvest*, something dull with no intrigue. Although this production apparently had some A-listers on it, I didn't think they had much to gain through any subterfuge, not while they were filming in these backwaters. Perhaps *Flying Colours* was merely a working title in this case.

Once that was done, I got up. Nan was already awake, watching *Good Morning Britain* in the living room, her pink dressing gown wrapped around her. As usual, I grabbed the remote to turn down the volume. It was far too early for such a din. Surely I was going to wear out that button before too long.

"Fancy another pancake?" she asked me as I sat next to her.

"Nope. Looks like I may get to work on that film, so I definitely need to watch the calories now."

"Ooh, that sounds exciting. What film is this?"

"You know, that one I told you about, that they're making round here." As I showed her the photo of the poster, I sensed we were about to repeat our conversation from the other day.

"Do you want to be in a film?" she read as though it was for the first time. "Is it going to be on at the Kinema?"

"Let's hope so. We'll go and see it if you like."

"Wonderful." She stood up and left the room.

After dabbing the volume down button a few more times, I got to my feet too. I thought I might find her in the kitchen, but it was empty. Perhaps she was getting dressed. The kettle was still warm, so I re-boiled the water before making some brews.

With a mug in each hand, her drink loaded with sweetener, I returned to the empty lounge and sat down. I'd almost finished drinking my tea by the time Nan reappeared.

She plonked herself on the single-seater sofa, her cheeks flushed. She was puffing and panting, her lips fixed in an O as the wind blew from her mouth.

"Everything okay there?" I asked.

She nodded. "Oh yes. I don't know about kids... I think I just dropped the entire school off at the pool."

It was early. I hadn't even made it to second gear, the caffeine still soaking into my bloodstream. The sound of the toilet cistern filling registered in my brain, and then I realised exactly what she was talking about. I put my head in my hands, as though that would take me away from this conversation of which I did not want to be a participant.

"Nan!" I shouted into my palms. "Too much

information!"

"Cor," she wheezed. "Think I need to go back for round two."

My head was still buried, so I didn't see her toddling off to the loo once more. It was a good few seconds before I could face reality again, until I felt safe enough to remove my hands.

It could have been worse, I supposed. I just had to be grateful that she could still toilet herself.

So with that wonderful start to the day, I had a bowl of cereal and some grapefruit before stepping outside for my morning walk. This was an activity I would think twice about doing in London, the simple act of heading out of the flat on my own. So often when I'd ventured outside for my one hour 'Boris Walk', too many guys would feel they were entitled to throw creepy comments my way. *Give me a smile, sugar. Slow down, hon; why are you in a hurry?* The wolf whistles, the winks, the air kisses. I didn't get any of that sleaze here, didn't have to cross the street to avoid anyone, didn't have to pretend I was on my phone. I could stroll the length of the road and back again and not pass another soul. No one besides Montgomery, that was, who was about as threatening as Tinky-Winky the Teletubbie. The crime I was most likely to witness was probably hare coursing rather than harassment.

It was frosty outside, the front lawn glistening in the strained sunlight like it was fairy dust. Today I walked up the main road, pausing by the village sign. You'd often drive by that sign and see randomers taking selfies by it, amusement on their faces that they were in New York! There was at least one clown on YouTube who'd shot some silly video of himself by it before jump-cutting to him walking into Times Square in the *other* New York.

It's just a name, people! And what's in a name? A Lincolnshire village by any other name would still smell like manure.

I found no one there on this occasion as I paused by the Catchwater Drain, a long, straight ditch that ran beside the fen. It was frozen this morning. In true Lincolnshire style, whoever had come up with that name had employed absolutely zero poetry. *Well, it's a drain that catches runoff, so how about the 'Catchwater Drain'?* To be fair, the river was as functional as its name, not a romantic stretch of water that caused your soul to soar or inspired an art movement. A far cry from the Hudson.

It certainly wasn't what I would call a peaceful place to relax, with all the cars tearing past on their morning commute to Boston. The jets from Coningsby were roaring overhead too. I peered up into the icy skies to see the triangular shape of a typhoon.

There was a vibration against my hip, so I removed my phone. My brother was calling me.

"Hey Martin."

"Aha! Caught you," he replied. "Are you in the middle of doing a runner?"

"Don't put ideas in my head."

No doubt he was checking in on me to see how I was getting on caring for Nan. My big bro was a responsible chap like that. Heaven knows how he juggled his job, raising two kids and looking after an elderly lady twenty miles away, but as he always said, *if you want something doing, ask a busy person.* Even with the coronavirus pandemic thrown into the mix, he'd taken it all in his stride.

His life invariably seemed to contrast with mine, definitely the successful one of the family. While he'd continued his job at the council during lockdown, I'd been furloughed, reduced to watching daytime television each day and going out for that hour of exercise Boris had permitted us. Before the boredom had got too much (or perhaps it was the guilt), I signed up as a GoodSAM volunteer for the NHS. I just felt I had to do my bit, and almost every day I would receive tasks, phoning up the vulnerable, fetching their shopping or prescriptions.

Later on I got involved with the vaccine program, volunteering my time one week as a marshal in a snazzy high vis jacket, beckoning pale-faced drivers towards the car park. Once or twice, a paramedic would pass me. I hadn't been privy to the reason they were summoned to the centre, but I suspected someone had either had a bad reaction to their jab or simply fainted at the sight of the needle.

These activities made good use of my idle thumbs, but, knowing Martin, he'd probably done all this kind of stuff *as well* as everything else.

"Nan told me you'd popped out for a walk," he said. "I just spoke to her on her landline. Almost fell out my chair that she managed to answer it."

"She has her moments, although I do think she's declined from when I last saw her."

"I suppose it's more noticeable with you having not been around her so frequently."

"Martin, did Nan ever mention to you about having nightly visits from Grandad?"

"What?" he replied with a chuckle.

"Last night she'd set the table for him and everything."

"She's never told me anything like that. You're probably going to get more of an insight living with her, seeing her at all times of the day."

"Lucky me. I wonder what other ghosts she'll invite round."

"Are you still coming over with her for Christmas?"

"Definitely. Although I can't guarantee I won't go mad myself in the meantime."

"We're Nightingales, Hazel. We all have a little madness in us."

My phone pinged with another notification.

"Sounds like someone is trying to get through," I said. "I've applied for some work so it might be that."

"Righto, I won't keep you. Good luck with everything, snowblower, and we'll see you at Christmas if not before."

"Take care, laser lips. Nice to speak to you."

"Cheers."

Hanging up, I saw my phone had collected a new notification. It was Cool Cat again.

Congratulations! You have been booked.

"That was quick," I muttered.

So that was it. I was officially now working in the film industry. All these years writing reviews of films, and now I would actively work on one. I would be *in* it.

My fitting was scheduled for half three this afternoon at the Petwood Hotel.

There wasn't a great deal of information on offer as to the nature of my scenes, just that I was a 'villager' and we'd be filming somewhere in Woodhall Spa. Were they not going to give me any basic direction, so I'd at least know what the mood of these scenes would be? I figured it would unravel in time. They'd confirmed that they'd need me for two days next week, with the possibility of one or two more. Production would let me know in due course.

They fed me the usual spiel about safety and coronavirus, to stay away from sick people and not to attend if I had any of those certain symptoms everyone knew was the sign of the disease. I remembered seeing that video of Tom Cruise berating some crew members who weren't wearing their masks on set. With such a simple requirement to wear a covering over one's mouth, I understood where he was coming from. I really didn't want to go viral with a ticking off from a Hollywood superstar, so I would have to make sure I read all their guidelines thoroughly.

That leaked video had been reminiscent of another time an actor lost his rag, some audio of the moment appearing online. Christian Bale had given a crew member an earful and wouldn't let it rest. They got awfully highly strung these film people. I hoped my experience wouldn't involve such incidents.

My ears were numb from the cold, so I headed back to the bungalow, wondering if Nan had remembered to take her meds this morning. If I had any silly o'clock starts on this job, then I had to remember to leave her pills out before I left, now that I was the primary caregiver. Melissa had warned me that productions typically got going really early, but at least we didn't have a long journey before our six or seven o'clock call time.

Arriving home, I found Nan still in the living room. She'd fallen asleep, and also restored the television to a ridiculously high volume. Lorraine was now on, talking to some young pop star I didn't recognise. How the heck did she sleep through that? I woke her up and laid out her tablets on the coffee table beside a glass of water.

"Now then, I've had some good news," I told her, projecting my voice over the sound of the television. I reached for the remote and turned it down. "They've picked me to work on that film next week."

"Ooh lovely. I knew you'd soon find something. What film is it?"

Here we go again.

I went over it all once more with her, hoping it would stick in her brain eventually. The casting agency had also sent me through a PDF document, a guideline on how supporting artists should conduct themselves on a film shoot. As I'd done nothing like this before, I considered it best to digest it all thoroughly.

It was all common sense. Don't go chatting up the actors, asking for their autograph or trying to get a selfie with them or any such nonsense. Don't take photographs on set. Don't go broadcasting any details of the production over social media. There was a lot to take in, and it was making me feel nervous. I would surely mess up one way or the other. It was something I, Hazel Nightingale, excelled at.

Chapter 7

MY COSTUME FITTING THAT AFTERNOON was my first introduction to their world. Before entering the hotel, I'd been instructed to visit the Lab Team. They were operating from a trailer in the car park, a gazebo erected beside it. Covid test time. Awesome. I'd taken a test last year when I'd exhibited symptoms, but on that occasion I was in control of the swab that I had to ram down my throat.

This time round I had a nurse doing the swab, but fortunately she was careful and didn't trigger my gag reflex. After that lovely experience, I then had to wait in my car for half an hour for the lateral flow test to come up good.

With the all clear, I then checked in with the assistant director at the desk in the Woodland Suite. She ticked me off, and I sat down with a group of four other people all doing the same thing as me. Although I'd arrived there early, it seemed production were a little behind in getting the supporting artists fitted. Melissa had warned me that half the job was just waiting around. I'd come prepared though, loading a couple of e-books onto my phone, not that I got round to reading anything.

Instead, I took the opportunity to chat with the people I would presumably be working with, chaps such as Leonard who talked of this production and that production, how he'd mixed with this Oscar winner and that national treasure. He definitely sounded like the seasoned professional in the field of background work. Only last week he'd performed in a period drama at some stately home in Yorkshire. He'd grown his hair and sideburns especially for it.

Next to me was Craig, a vaguely familiar face. It took me a while to recall where I'd seen him before, but when he mentioned about being involved with amateur dramatics, I finally placed him. He'd performed on stage years ago at the Blackfriars in Boston doing *Accrington Pals*. After they called him through to get fitted, I heard him bellowing some show tune from beyond the dividers. I really hoped they weren't expecting any kind of performance skills from me!

In the next seat was another older chap of Leonard's ilk whose name I didn't catch, but the way he was going on, it sounded like he went from background role to background role too. He almost seemed jaded by the prospect of working on this film. I had the impression he knew Leonard well. I supposed there would be these little networks of friends amongst the supporting talent, a bit like that Ricky Gervais comedy. Did any of these people ever have hopes of being the 'bride' on a production one day, delivering lines rather than taking the silent 'bridesmaid' role? Or perhaps they'd come to accept their lowly lot in life as the out-of-focus human set decoration.

There was only one other lady, Sophie. She was about my age and lived in North Lincolnshire. I was instinctively drawn to her and sparked up some conversation. She seemed a little nervy, possibly somewhat overawed like I was.

They all had unique looks. They weren't necessarily *good* lookers, but they certainly had a filmic quality to their features. I supposed the producers wouldn't want anyone that would detract from the main talent. I'd probably seen numerous films that Leonard and his buddy had been in, yet they'd only registered in my subconscious at best. That was the purpose of this job, injecting life into any scene to make it more authentic.

No one ever watched a film and said, *'Oh the background actors in this were so amazing! Took my breath away!'* There was no BAFTA for Best Supporting Artist, right?

Further extras joined us as they came for their

appointments, their presence suggesting this was a rather big production. Safety in numbers, though; I'd blend into the crowd easily with so many people around me. Eventually the assistant director called me through where a fitter ushered me towards the ladies' area.

My costume designer, a middle-aged lady named Evie, had a tape measure round her neck and exuded the air of someone snowed under with work. Her temper seemed so short that I feared she might use that tape measure to hang herself later on if it all got too much. She looked me up and down and darted along the collection of costumes as she took one off the racks, held it up against me, frowned, then fetched another. I couldn't tell what was wrong with any of her rejects, but she was the professional here.

I realised she did this sort of thing all the time, but it was difficult to contain my excitement for having a 1940s makeover, plus I was getting paid for it! She draped another dress against my form, a wine coloured frock with a winged collar and a buttoned front, before wincing and shaking her head. But then she shifted her gaze on me and her eyebrows curled.

"Okay, try this one," she told me. "You're a size six shoe, yes?"

"That's right. What scene are we doing with these glad rags?"

"It's a Christmas party in the village."

"Great. Do you know where we're filming?"

"Nope. Haven't been told yet."

"How will I know where to go on the day?"

She flicked her eyes up at me, her face clearly readable: *We've got ourselves another panicked newbie here.*

"The agency will email you the details, most probably the evening before."

"Right."

I stripped off and slid myself into the dress, standing by

the full-length mirror with Evie.

"Yes," she purred, pulling on the fabric to smooth it. "This works well."

I agreed with her. I'd never dressed up in vintage clothing like this before, despite attending the Woodhall Forties Weekend several times.

"Really loving this. I might have to keep on to it when we've finished filming."

It was a little attempt at some humour, but Evie found no amusement in my exuberance, smiling a smile that was more like a frown. She was already onto the next item, handing me a pair of elegant black heels.

"How do those fit?" she asked as I slid them on.

I took a few paces in them before saying, "I think they're okay."

"It's you who has to wear them all day so speak now if they're no good."

"They'll be fine," I reassured her.

Once my costume was sorted, they then steered me on to the final department, hair and make-up. The ladies there were much less tightly wound than Evie. I sat down by a mirror as a motherly lady called Viola introduced herself.

"Let's see what we can do here then," she said as I removed the bobble from my ponytail, my strands running free as they poured over my shoulders. She began dragging a brush through my locks. I'd been carrying quite a length of hair the past couple of years, the successive lockdowns having a lot to do with that. It swirled from my head in cinnamon curls.

As I glanced aside, I noticed a large mood board the artists were going by, vintage photographs of 1940s hairstyles and fashions, slick short back and sides for the men, glamorous victory rolls and voluminous bobs for the ladies. If they were ever to make a film set during the coronavirus pandemic, then the hairstyle of that time would surely be haystacks or bad DIY efforts.

She opted for the rolls, sweeping my hair from my face in a side parting, and creating the curls with my mane as they rested on my shoulders. I was positively exuding more glamour than I had in a long time, certainly since the virus had come along, but then I had been in the hands of experts here. I suspected they could make anyone look like a million dollars.

"There we are," Viola said once she'd finished. "You'd make a bona fide movie star, my dear."

I noticed in the mirror my cheeks reddening. "Don't know about that," I replied. "All down to your skill, more like."

With my appearance styled, they then handed me a small whiteboard with my name and artist ID number scribbled on it. As I stood on a spot, they took a series of mug shots, presumably for reference when they re-assembled my getup on filming days.

And with that, I'd completed my work for the day.

I emerged from the changing area just as the old chap Leonard was leaving the men's changing room. His hair was now a lot shorter.

"I will see you Monday," I said to him as though I were some longstanding workmate and we had this exchange every week.

After saying our goodbyes, I wandered along the corridor, wondering what the mood would have been like within these same walls during the war. It must have been an incredibly anxious time back then with loved ones separated, so many getting killed. And yet, how come we had such nostalgia for that period? I remembered reading a magazine article that ranked the 1940s as the best decade of the twentieth century. Made no sense to me.

I paused by a dramatic painting of a Lancaster soaring through the clouds, the plane that my grandfather had flown in. I often regarded it as something of a miracle that my generation had never resorted to a world war, that perhaps the collective memory of the second one (not to mention the first) had proved so harrowing that no one, not even that guy in North Korea who liked to parade his missiles around, had the stomach for another worldwide conflict. Or was it that these days, guys satiated their compulsion to fight via their computer games? Were those our opiates?

Farther down, a young runner strode out of a room and carried on past me to the stairs. I caught the words 'Covid Marshal' printed on the rear of his fluorescent jacket. Melissa had mentioned about these. On a shoot she'd worked on earlier in the year, one that had taken place in the centre of Nottingham where the public could cast a scrutinising gaze their way, the marshals were constantly milling around telling the extras to maintain distance, to please put their mask on in-between every take. And it wasn't just the supporting artists they would nag. Even the figures at the top of the filmmaking hierarchy didn't escape their badgering. Whether these marshals were still exacting these orders with such zeal, I would have to wait to find out.

Once the lad had disappeared, I nosily poked my head into the room he'd come from, what was evidently being used for storage.

There were more mood boards on display, with black and white photographs tacked to them. I gazed at them closely, wondering who all these people were, what squadrons they were part of. Maybe they were the Dambusters? Young men dressed in uniform, all slick and dapper, presenting themselves like movie stars, or perhaps that was because I was so used to associating these wartime styles with cinema. Haircuts were neatly cropped, at least fifty percent of them wearing an Errol Flynn moustache. A good percentage of them had a cigarette burning between their fingers too.

So what story from that world war were we about to enact for this film? And what other stars would we be rubbing shoulders with in the coming weeks? We'd already spotted Eddy Partridge. Who else might be on the cast list? Who would play his fellow airmen? Or perhaps a love interest?

Shaking my mind out of this daydreaming, I decided to carry on to my car before I got caught. I couldn't be getting fired before I'd even started. As I strolled out of the hotel, I felt like some hotshot superstar, although there wasn't exactly a limo waiting for me in the car park, no agent or entourage.

"Let's go home then, Clarence," I said as I slipped behind the wheel of my Clio. Back down to earth. "With any luck, I may be able to afford to fill your tank before Christmas."

I'd had my first taste of the world of filmmaking, a dress rehearsal, and I couldn't wait to get started properly.

Chapter 8

THE FOLLOWING MORNING CAME WITH a surprise I had not seen coming.

For a few moments, I believed I'd descended into madness. *Caught the crazy*; Isn't that what they say? I was fast asleep in bed when I felt someone shaking my shoulder. My eyes pulled open to reveal Nan standing by me, a shiny conical hat on her head. She blew on the party blower between her lips and it unfolded before her, brushing my nose as it made that annoying noise.

"Surprise!" she said. "Happy birthday, my beauty."

I was still gathering my faculties as I sat up, endeavouring to put my head space into the now rather than the random dream I'd been in mere seconds ago. It wasn't quite *kissing Valentino* by that Italian watercourse, more like plodding along the muddy bank of the Catchwater Drain in my wellies. Whatever it was now melted from my mind.

"Thanks?" I muttered.

She pulled back my curtains, and I saw the icicles hanging from the guttering over the window. *Right, yes. That's where we were. Winter time. December. Now what's this about a birthday?*

"Open your presents, then," she said, pointing to my bedside cabinet. She'd piled three gifts on it.

I gazed at them wide-eyed, summoning some excitement to demonstrate my appreciation for her efforts. She'd clearly put a lot of planning into this. How on earth she'd managed to plan *anything* was a complete mystery. I had to play along.

"You didn't need to get me any presents."

"Course I do. Go on. They're not going to open

themselves."

First off, I opened the white envelope resting on top of them. Inside, I found a birthday card that would have been more suitable for an old man. There was an image of a green racing car on the front. I didn't actually know a thing about the sport, but I could tell from the style of the vehicle that it was some vintage model from aeons ago. She'd attempted an arthritic signing of her name that was almost impossible to decipher.

"Ah thanks, Nan. That's great. What have we got here then?" I asked as I picked up the first of the presents.

"Now, don't worry if it's the wrong size. We can always get them exchanged."

I tore it open, noticing the wrapping paper looked rather festive, images of snowflakes and holly decorating it. Wrapped up inside were two jumpers, one pink, one white, both cashmere, both the same design. Why two? You'd have to ask my nan that question. It was most likely she wouldn't be able to answer you.

"They're lovely," I enthused. "Thanks Nan." They were perfect. Perfect, that was, if I were sixty years older.

She seemed to forget I still had more presents to open as she said, "Right, I think it's time to make the birthday girl some breakfast."

"Yeah. That would be nice."

I sighed once she'd left the room. She was such a sweetie. I just didn't have the heart to tell her my birthday was in May. I couldn't even come up with an explanation *for* her confusion. It wasn't Martin or Phillipa's birthday, not even her own. How puzzling.

"You are not thirty-one yet, Hazel," I reassured myself as I unwrapped another gift. Inside was a pot of anti-ageing cream.

"What are you trying to tell me here, Nan?" I continued my commentary. "What's in the next one? A walking stick?"

I couldn't contain my laughter once I opened it. She'd bought me a Cliff Richard calendar. How much more surreal could this moment get?

"Yeah, that's me. Biggest Cliff fan in Lincolnshire."

It suddenly hit me. December fourth was Grandad's birthday. If I'd had any concern that Nan would get confused once my actual birthday came along, it may have been worth trying to explain her mistake, but I was certain that come May fifteenth, she would have forgotten about this false celebration.

"Just another crazy day in New York."

After wrapping my dressing gown around me and putting on my bunny slippers, I joined Nan in the kitchen to make sure she wasn't burning down the place. It was on the tip of my tongue to ask her what year Grandad was born, but then she may have realised her mistake. I had an inkling though it would have been his one hundredth birthday today.

"What do you want on it today?" she asked. "Syrup? Lemon juice? Or how about some fruit?"

"What the heck, let's go for the maple syrup. It's only your birthday once a year." She smiled as she rooted through the cupboard, and I muttered, "Or twice if you're the queen or Hazel Nightingale."

Later on in the morning I offered to take her out somewhere. She insisted I chose where. Often on my birthday, which, as I said, traditionally takes place in a warmer month, I would have opted for the coast, but I always welcomed a visit there whatever the time of year. So Skegness was where we headed for.

Not that Nan ever called it Skegness. From Dora Nightingale's lips, it came out as *Skeg's Nest*, as though there was a nature reserve nearby where a migrating bird known as the skeg would come to breed. It was a common quirk of hers, getting names of things wrong, like profiteroles. A couple of years ago I took her to the Kinema to see *Bohemian Rhapsody*, a film about that flamboyant singer named Freddie Murph-cury.

"I'm not going to be around much next week," I said as we passed by the ruins of Revesby Abbey, a scattering of deer in the field before it. I thought it best to warn her, for what it was worth. "So you'll have to look after yourself, okay?"

"Oh, don't you worry about me. I'll be fine."

Although she was an early riser, I would most likely be leaving the house before she got up, and so I wouldn't be around for her breakfast.

"Are you going to take your tablets if I leave them out?"

"Yes," she crooned, as though she could not understand why I would be so concerned about that matter.

I wondered about writing out a big dummy board with basic instructions on it, something she couldn't miss.

"I'll make you a sandwich for your lunch and pop it in the fridge."

"Don't you fuss. You enjoy yourself making your film."

Hurrah! She'd got it in her head at last that I was working on a film. Perhaps I was fretting needlessly.

A little farther down the road we came to East Kirkby, a former RAF station that was now an aviation museum.

"That's where your grandfather was stationed," Nan announced, the same line she spoke every time we drove through this village. After the nutty start to the day with my bogus birthday, she was now on a roll, calling him my grandfather rather than my father.

"Of course, back in the war there were bases everywhere you went round here." This is something else she did, turn into Uncle Albert from *Only Fools and Horses*. "Spilsby, there was a base where Popsy worked. Anderby, where my brother trained. Then further up you'd have Grimsby and Goxhill where the Americans were. Clark Gable served there, you know?"

"You may have mentioned that once or twice before."

"I still feel it to this day. The ghosts of the war. They still linger. Everywhere there are fragments, broken runways, rusty Nissen huts, all those ruins over in the trees at Oscar's plantation, where they found that mustard gas." By that she meant *Ostler's* Plantation, a woodland just outside Woodhall Spa. A few years ago the police arrested a couple after the discovery of some wartime gas canisters there.

"Ooh, think I see the Lancaster," she announced, gazing beyond me to the old airfield. "That's the plane your grandfather flew in, until he got shot down."

He what? I'd never actually heard that one before. Sure, I knew about him being a flight engineer, and obviously he'd come through the war with his life, meeting and marrying Dora around five years later. Was she confusing his story with someone else? Perhaps she'd seen this happen in a film. She was usually very good with distant memories, but I could believe it if she'd forgotten that it was supposed to be a secret.

"You never told me about that," I said. "Where was he shot down?"

"Off the coast of Holland. A U-boat surfaced nearby and rescued them. Blind luck, Warren described it."

"A U-boat? So the Germans got him?"

"He spent the rest of the war in Starling Luff until the Russians set him free," by which she meant he was in one of the Stalag Luft camps.

"I did not know any of that."

And sadly I didn't know if it was true with it coming from my nan's unreliable mind, the organ in her body that was clearly running on fumes. Something about it *felt* true, though, if that counted for anything. Grandad never spoke much about the war, preferring to look to the future. Perhaps his experience as a prisoner of war was a chapter he preferred to put behind him.

There were ice blue skies in Skegness, the sun doing its best to provide what warmth it could. True to its reputation, the town was indeed bracing, but then it was December. After a walk along the promenade, observing the changes that had gone on since my last visit, we headed into the newly revamped Pier Amusements where we got some lunch from the cafe followed by a warm drink each.

It was refreshing to flock to the soothing environment of the seaside once more without journalists and news crews getting shots of the irresponsible daytrippers congregating on the sands as they spread their covid germs. *'That's not two meters' distance!'* all the outraged readers would have shouted at their morning newspapers.

Not that any one individual on those beaches was the problem, of course. It was all everyone else that was forming the crowd. They shouldn't have had the same idea that day to head to the coast.

I'd related with that desire to do so, to flee that virus, like the characters in *On The Beach* fleeing the nuclear fallout. Nan had always talked about sea air having a healing quality, so perhaps those crowds were unconsciously seeking to heal themselves from this infection.

"I bet you're looking forward to your job next week," Nan said as she sprinkled the third sachet of sweetener into her tea. "Having a bit of a break from me."

I waved away her last comment before saying, "Not every day you get to work on a Hollywood film, I suppose."

"And maybe you'll meet someone."

Here we go with that again.

"Well, if the other extras are anything like the chaps I

met yesterday, they're probably nearer your age."

"There'll be lots of young ones surely, if it's a war film. I'll have to show you the photos of your grandfather in his RAF uniform. He was so handsome."

"Yes, I'd like to see those." I'd have to remind her later. She was likely the last remaining custodian of Grandad's wartime stories, and even then they were second hand as she hadn't met him until 1948. And when she was gone, it would fall to me and my siblings. Hopefully Martin had thought to quiz our grandparents, digging into their personal histories. He was smart like that, more methodical than I. He knew the benefits of thinking ahead.

Or perhaps I could ask Grandad himself, on one of his evening visits that Nan talked of. So far, I just had not been lucky enough to catch him.

My eyes rested on a row of nearby fruit machines, their bright lights flashing as they chirped cheerfully, desperately trying to get my attention like an impatient kid. Grandad loved playing on those things. 'Bandits,' he called them.

"What time are we heading on home?" Nan asked.

"Soon," I replied. "Don't worry, I know you won't want to miss *Strictly*. You do remember our man from Woodhall Spa dropped out weeks ago, right? Anyway, how about a little game on the fruit machine and then we'll head off?" Seeing as it was really Grandad's birthday today, it felt a fitting way to honour his memory.

"Good idea, my beauty. Let's see what luck you have."

If my spinning of the reels on that slot machine in *Skeg's Nest* was anything to go by, then it seemed I had a thundering deficiency of good fortune. We put at least five quid into it and made only a pitiful return that went straight back in.

Or perhaps this lack of luck just underlined that I was due some better fortune soon. I wouldn't hold my breath waiting, however.

Chapter 9

THE ALARM SOUNDED AT A quarter to six and I quite likely grumbled more curses than the start of *Four Weddings and a Funeral* as my hand flapped around, seeking to silence my phone. I wasn't sure what was worse, being woken when it was so dark outside, or being woken by someone blowing a party streamer in my face. Back in London I frequently used to rise at this kind of hour. With only a week living with my nan, I had soon become accustomed to starting the day at whatever time my body decided it wanted to wake (barring the fake birthday incident).

I was nervous for the long day ahead, one that would see me venturing way beyond my comfort zone. The first thing I needed was a strong cup of coffee, swiftly followed by another.

My call time was seven o'clock at the Petwood in Woodhall Spa, the same place I'd been for my fitting. It would take me only fifteen minutes to get there. I didn't expect to meet much traffic at that time of day, not that it was ever like downtown Manhattan or anything. I assumed filming would take place nearby or in the hotel itself. That particular matter hadn't been covered in my instructions.

My details about the shoot day had come through around five o'clock yesterday evening, as my costume fitter had said they would. The message offered little information about what we were filming. I wasn't exactly expecting a script, but there wasn't even a general outline as to what the nature of our scene would be. Evidently we were on a *need-to-know* basis, and us supporting artists were right at the bottom of the food chain.

The email also mentioned that there would be breakfast available at the catering van, so I didn't bother eating anything at the bungalow. I wasn't hungry, anyway. After slowly easing myself into the day, my bloodstream sufficiently caffeinated, I threw on some clothes, got inside Clarence and set off for Woodhall Spa.

The dark skies hovered over the landscape like a colossal shroud, offering no clue that we were soon to creep into the light of the sun. Stars continued to coruscate above, and with scant light pollution on these broad fens, those distant beacons were plentiful and luminous. It may as well have been the dead of the night, owls still on the hunt, foxes stalking in the pale glow of the crescent moon, treading over the hard fields upon which Jack Frost had been coating an icy glaze all night. I encountered two or three other cars and wondered if these fellow early birds were also heading to the film set, or were they just going to their shift at the factory?

Minutes later, when I pulled into the hotel car park, there was as much activity as you would expect in the middle of the day. Most of the individuals converged around the waggon giving out full English breakfasts. As I exited Clarence, I still had little appetite, certainly none for fried bacon and eggs at this early hour, but I found less heavy duty foodstuffs on offer as I grabbed a cinnamon pastry.

As I nibbled on that, I spotted Leonard, the older chap.

"Morning," I said. "Ready to party like it's nineteen thirty-nine?"

"Hopefully. The back's aching a bit. Slept on it wrong."

"Oh no. Whereabouts did you stay?"

"Here," he replied, a finger pointing down.

"You had a room at the Petwood?"

"Nah. Slept in my car."

"Well, I suppose that's one way to make sure you're not late."

Come seven o'clock, we got signed in with the assistant directors before making our way to the changing areas. Once they called me through to that room, they directed me towards my costume which had been tagged with my identification number. As I was slipping into my dress, I spotted a familiar face across the hall. I waved over at Melissa, and she smiled back.

Once we were costumed, we then queued for the next stage, hair and makeup. By the time I'd completed that, it had gone nine. No wonder these film people had to get started so early. The extras that were camera-ready were instructed to assemble in the terrace bar that overlooked the lavish gardens. Although a sight to behold in the summer months, the outdoor areas still carried a beauty in December, glistening in the delicate dawn light with an extra hint of mystique.

I was glad to find a refreshments table as I made myself another coffee. The amount I was drinking I feared I might have to bring this whole multi-million dollar production to a halt later on while I popped to the loo.

"Hey, Hazel," Melissa said as she joined me in the room sporting a veal coloured hourglass dress. "You're looking rather glam there."

"Likewise." She looked like a different person. Catching sight of myself in a mirror, I thought I did too. Certainly this wasn't a style I'd ever rocked before. I felt I'd discovered a new aspect of myself. Lost in my narcissistic moment, a young black man in an RAF uniform approached us.

"Excuse me, ladies," he said in an east London accent. "In desperate need of caffeine."

"Sorry," I said, shifting aside so he could get to the cardboard cups. "Have you come up from London this morning?"

"What makes you think I'm from there?" he suddenly asked in an affected British accent like you heard in those old war films. "Chocks away. Flak's heavy over Dresden today, chaps. Do take care."

The guy sounded like a right joker. I could already tell I would get along nicely with him, if we were to be thrown together in the scene. There were more people here than I thought there would be, though, so I possibly wouldn't cross paths with him again this week.

"What is *flak* exactly?" Melissa asked.

"Shells the Germans hurled five miles into the air at the bombers," the guy was swift to reply, as though he really was an air force officer. I sensed he'd likely been reading up on the subject of war recently, maybe as research for his minor role. These days, five minutes of Googling could turn anyone into an expert about anything.

"I'm not sure my nerves could take all those bombing raids," I responded, "knowing you might get shot down any second."

"Totally," Melissa agreed. "I don't have any killer instinct at all. I'd be so useless storming up the Normandy beaches into a shower of bullets. The Germans would shoot me right off the bat."

"Breakfast with ten crewmen, dinner with two," the uniformed man said. "It was all a long game of Russian roulette. And even less fun for us West Indians. We had extra incentive not to get captured by the Jerries." His voice had now switched to a Jamaican accent.

"You're a right man of a million voices, aren't you?" I said. "Yeah, I think I read somewhere the Nazis weren't so progressive when it came to minorities."

He chuckled and said, "I'm Seymour," offering his hand once he'd finished stirring his coffee.

"Hazel," I replied. "And this is my friend Melissa. We're both locals."

"Hi. And yes, I'm from Dagenham, innit."

"I was actually living in Sumpton until recently." I suddenly noticed my voice was sounding posher than usual, my syllables nicely rounded. Perhaps it was from wearing this frock, becoming a character from another period. "Moved back up here last week to look after my nan."

Not to mention the fact I became unemployed!

"Are you an actor then?" Melissa asked him.

"Occasionally," Seymour replied. "Or a film extra. Or a barista. A million voices and a million jobs too."

"They didn't provide you with your own trailer, no?" I asked.

He shook his head. "Criminal, right? I'm a featured extra tomorrow, as well. Doing a scene with Eddy Partridge."

"Oh, we saw him in Lincoln last week," I told him. "So am I right in seeing the pattern here, this film has something to do with BAME in the RAF? A Commonwealth *Red Tails*?"

"Something like that, it seems. Afraid they didn't give me a script. Eddy is the primary love interest though, I can tell you that much. Not mine, I don't mean."

"And you're both playing West Indians?"

"Aye."

"Do you get killed?"

"I don't have a death scene; Put it that way. But I suspect my chances aren't that great. Twenty-five percent was the going rate, I believe."

An AD called us to attention. The lounge was now buzzing with excited background performers primed to step into the forties. She ordered us all to stand in a line around the room in our various categories: female villagers, male villagers, and the uniformed personnel. A final check before we headed to the set, I presumed.

They indeed came round inspecting our costumes, making sure nothing was out of place, no extraneous items had appeared on our bodies, no one with a mobile phone-shaped object in their pockets. One guy had to remove his wedding ring as it was too silver-looking for the period. No detail went by unnoticed, it seemed. I'd opted to leave my phone with my clothes, as I didn't have a pocket big enough for it. Melissa had successfully smuggled hers along, she informed me. I made a mental note to ask her to take a snap of me later. Although a crew member passed down the line taking their own photos, undoubtedly for continuity, I suspected they wouldn't be sending them out to us as souvenirs.

"Okay, we're just waiting for confirmation," the AD said, "and then we'll be ferrying you over to set in mini buses, leaving from the main entrance."

"I need to pee," I muttered to Melissa from the corner of my mouth, before swiftly stepping away for a little comfort break. It made sense to go while I had the chance.

I was relieved to find my fellow extras still present in the lounge once I returned. It would have been just like me to get left behind.

As we waited, I couldn't resist peering into the mirror once more. Yes, I think that lady who fixed my hair the other day was right; I could pass as a movie star.

Another hour had passed before they started transporting us to set. I caught the third minibus, although we would have been quicker walking, as the location was only a few hundred yards down the road.

Situated by the golf course, the Edrow House was an elegant Edwardian lodge now run as a hotel, a popular place for getting married. Not that there would be anything like that going on this week with Hollywood in town taking over. The car park was rammed full with those big white lorries, giant lights set up in the garden pointing towards the windows.

Crew members were milling around as they ushered us through to the set, a function hall dressed up with

Christmas decorations, although I couldn't see a Christmas tree anywhere. Was that custom too inappropriately German for this era? I'd been in this hall only once before, a Burns Night event I took Nan to one January.

Beyond the view of the camera there were cables running, bulky equipment cases cluttering up the floor, monitors on desks. I could barely work out what each person's reason for being there was, what their role in this production was. Who even was the director? I had no clue.

As the third ADs positioned us around the hall, decorating the place with their human props, I couldn't help the feeling that I shouldn't be there, that I'd somehow intruded on this important film set and someone would blow the whistle on me at any second. And yet no one was telling me to clear off or get out of the way. I had front row tickets for this film's production. This was so awesome.

Initially, an AD positioned me at a table with a posse of other ladies near the bar, but for some reason known only to production, I was then transferred to a spot on the other side of the hall. There I stood with two other extras, one a dolled up lady like me, the other a young lad, who I presumed was just under the age to be in the military. Or perhaps he represented the Private Pikes of wartime who had medical conditions.

With the scene filling up with background actors, a man then came round offering us cigarettes, and I figured he was in charge of the non-human props. I found it jarring to have characters puffing away indoors, but, of course, we were in a different era, decades before the attitudes of indoor smoking had changed. Not having ever taken up the habit, I didn't take the props master up on his offer, even though these were only herbal cigarettes.

A third AD returned to our group to give us some direction.

"So you three are having a great time enjoying the

Christmas party. Hazel and Gale, you're maybe discussing if Franklin should be in bed by now..." It seemed to roll off his tongue directly from the top of his head. With all the background actors here today, I was impressed that he'd memorised all our names. I'd only told him my name once back at the Petwood. Despite working on this major production, he was the most laid-back guy I'd ever met. "And then bam! There's going to be a bit of a disturbance at this shindig, so just react how you'd naturally react to that. Turn to look, gasp, raise eyebrows, but nothing too pantomime-y. Less is more."

"Right," I replied, trying to get this all straight in my head. I had the impression that short spiel would be the limits of our direction on this scene. "And what's going to happen over there?"

The crew member was silent for a moment, staring into space, and then I realised he was listening in on an earpiece and most likely hadn't heard my question.

"Okay, so you guys are set," he announced once his mind was back on us. He moved on to the next pocket of characters.

"Well, nice to meet you," I said, turning to face my co-stars. "Gale and Franklin, was it?"

"That's right," she said, offering her hand. Franklin smiled sheepishly. He looked somewhat overawed, grouped with us two glamour pusses.

"So do you guys know what this scene is about, other than it's a Christmas party?"

"Not a clue," Gale replied.

"Oh my," I said. "I think I've just clocked the director." Standing beside the cameraman was Opal Anderson, an Oscar winner from three years ago. It hadn't occurred to me that this production might have a female director at the helm.

"Who?" Gale asked.

"Opal Anderson. She directed *Menagerie of the Mind.*"

"Oh, I saw that film," she replied, her eyes lighting up. "Couldn't tell you who directed it though."

I'd reviewed her film for the magazine, for which I'd read up on her. My role as a reviewer suddenly seemed very handy in this situation. It wasn't every day I could put my film knowledge to such use. For the next few minutes I studied the director closely as she hovered behind the camera, observing how her shot was coming together with its human decorations. She never spoke to any of them, never went up to anyone and said, 'Hey, could you possibly move a few inches to your left?' We were all operating within a hierarchy here, any such instructions passed on via the assistants.

"So have you done this before then?" I asked Gale.

"Been in quite a lot now, yes. A couple of weeks ago I worked on a historical docudrama. Even had some lines on that."

"Wow. So that makes you a genuine actress then."

"That's the plan. Been living the cliched life of waitressing while I climb up the acting ladder."

I wondered how many of my fellow extras were in a similar boat as her, taking these background jobs in-between trying to become the next star. Several times I'd heard of well-known actors having taken these lowly roles at the dawn of their careers, like Jennifer Aniston and Clint Eastwood.

"And how about you, Franklin?"

"I've done... uh, yeah I've done about three films now and one television show."

I nodded, waiting for him to expand on that, but it seemed I'd exhausted his sociability.

"That's great."

It was all so surreal. One moment I'd be having small-talk with strangers, then glance across the room to see a

Hollywood icon as Eddy Partridge stood nearby preparing for the first take. Back when we'd spotted him at the Christmas market, he must have been fifty yards away, but this was less than ten. And I had now become his *co-worker* rather than a randomer in the street. When I was driving back home to Lincolnshire last Monday, I had not imagined I would be in this position the following week.

It was funny how I felt the need to compare my encounters with Eddy in terms of how many yards away I was from him, as though the goal was to reduce that figure as much as possible.

By the time the cameras started rolling and an AD called, *"Background action!"* we remained standing there in our group of three, continuing our desultory chat. There we were making a film, and all we were doing was chatting about what we'd eaten for breakfast this morning.

I didn't pay any attention to the proper actors, the ones that had read the script, anticipating our cue, but I realised when that 'bam' moment came, a fracas erupting across the hall. *Oh my goodness*, I thought. I'd now just spotted star of stage and screen Glen Wood. I was certain he'd now come to that point in his career where he'd be regarded as a national treasure.

The atmosphere in the room suddenly turned, booming voices firing away, racial abuse spouted at Eddy Partridge. We reacted as they'd instructed us to, our eyes fixed on the action, but not one of us was about to step in and tell Glen Wood he was using inappropriate language, call him out. That wasn't the story here.

The director called, "Cut!"

Gale turned to me and muttered, "Who needs Nazis with allies like these?"

Chapter 10

IT WAS A LONG MORNING, repeating that intense scene over and over, the actors summoning the emotion each take as they delivered their lines again and again at that same level. From this fly-on-the-wall perspective I had so much appreciation for their professionalism.

My stomach was rumbling by the time we stopped for lunch. That took place back at the Petwood, and seeing as most people had memorised that simple journey through the woods and past the cinema, they opted to make their own way there instead of waiting their turn for the minibus.

In the car park we found the catering waggon, steam rising from the freshly cooked dishes on offer. Normally I was always a little weary eating grub from food trucks, but this was for a Hollywood production, not some dodgy burger van they'd dragged up from the A1. I figured they'd have high standards. These hotshots would surely sue the pants off them if they gave everyone food poisoning. The pecking order saw them queuing up first, naturally.

We ate inside the hotel, another hall I'd dined in before, on the occasion of my friend's wedding. There I took my chance to catch up with Melissa after becoming separated on set.

"I'd forgotten how hungry I get when I'm on these film shoots," she said as she tucked into her vegan sausages. I'd plumped for the teriyaki stir fry.

"You turned meat free since the Christmas Market?" I asked her.

"No. Only today," she whispered. "Didn't fancy any of the other options, but don't tell catering I'm not actually a vegan."

"Any idea what we're filming this afternoon?"

"Don't know but I think it may involve Janice Daniels."

"Oh my giddy aunt," I gushed once I'd swallowed my mouthful of bean shoots. "She's in this too?"

"Yeah, you probably couldn't see her from where you were, but she popped her head into the hall as we were doing that scene."

"Wow. This day just gets better and better."

Janice Daniels. I was such a big fan. I must have seen all her films, even before her star had risen over this past couple of years. Early on in her career she'd regularly popped up in the films of Killian Hamer, *Blood Stained Windows* and the first two *Electrified* films. Low budget but effective horrors that must have given the budding actor useful showreel material. Her breakthrough role saw her playing a rookie detective on some television series for three seasons, before going on to play a superhero. I just found it so cool that she possessed the range to go from down-to-earth Josephine Schmo to kick-ass warrior, perfectly steeped in each character. And then there was all the charitable work she'd done over lockdown. I mean, it wasn't quite Captain Tom level, but she'd helped raise a lot of money for the NHS. Her achievements seriously put my life to shame, and she was two years younger than me.

But just knowing I was working on a film with her in it made me feel as though I'd found a perch higher up the echelons, albeit a fleeting one. It sure would make an interesting addition to my CV for when I started applying for jobs.

All of a sudden I remembered where I was, how I'd got here. The purpose of my return to Lincolnshire was to look after my grandmother, and I felt a pang of guilt as I realised I had not thought of her once all morning. What a crap carer I was.

The caterers had puddings to dish out, too. This job was the gift that kept giving! With wide eyes I opted for the apple crumble and custard, a worthy effort, although it didn't quite compare to the ones Nan used to make. Once we'd finished eating, I tore off the plastic protector, essentially a giant bib that covered my costume. They looked exactly like the PPE that doctors and nurses would wear in all those news reports from covid wards, but ours were merely to avoid getting gravy stains on our frocks.

The crew asked us to line up again as the costumers came and checked that their background actors were still looking immaculate. One of the stylists adjusted my hair slightly, applying more hairspray.

An AD informed the crowd we would head back to the Edrow House. Although they were ferrying us with the minibuses once more, I walked this time, as did Melissa and a few others. As we trailed up the road that cut through the broadleaf trees, we passed some strangers who stopped to observe the costumed individuals walking past. I read the expressions on their starry-eyed faces: *These must be some of the actors from that movie they're making in the village! Ooh, can I spot anyone famous?*

The filming that afternoon took place in the hall once more, what I assumed was a continuation of what we'd done this morning. I had the feeling there'd be another scene in-between these scenes though, the film perhaps cutting to a Lancaster crew as they flew over the North Sea, or something.

Poor Eddy had to endure even more abuse being hurled at him, but then the tide turned when his co-star Janice Daniels made her entrance. Clearly she was romantically involved with his character. A subplot? Or perhaps their relationship was the main plot. That kind of information was not for some humble background extra.

I actually found it a moving experience, being in the same room as these stars, entitled to stand over their shoulders as I watched them work. How lucky was I to be a part of this production? At one point, Janice and Eddy were between me and the camera, meaning I was in the *same shot* as them. I really hoped that one would make the final cut.

It was late afternoon when the ADs sent some of us back to base. It seemed to be a lottery who they picked, depending on their position in the scene, but both Melissa and I were amongst the extras who weren't needed for the next sequence. Neither were the two stars, Eddy and Janice, as they were escorted in a fancy saloon car. You wouldn't see them cramming into the minibuses with the riffraff, of course.

Darkness had firmly set in as we stepped outside and walked up the street, recently unravelled Christmas lights flickering in the windows of the houses we passed.

"Do you think we're done for the day, then?" I asked. We still technically had a few hours left of our workday, but I wondered if we would have an early finish.

"Possibly," Melissa replied. "They may want us to hang around until they've finished filming, in case they need us."

As we strolled along the drive of the hotel grounds, I realised I needed another comfort break.

"I'll meet you in the bus then, yeah?" Melissa asked.

"The bus?"

"Yeah, the big double-decker in the car park. It's our holding area."

How on earth had I missed that? It was my first day, and there was a lot to take in.

"All right. See you there."

Melissa had not told me what colour this bus was, and I did not think to ask her. I had not imagined there would be any issue when I stepped outside after the trip to the ladies. Familiar with the layout of this hotel, I'd emerged from a different exit to the ones my fellow extras had been using.

And there I found it, the double-decker bus. I had not been through this section of the grounds today, so that explained why I hadn't noticed it earlier. Why had they parked it so out of sight here?

I opened the door and clambered aboard, drifting on like a carefree summer breeze, ready to put my feet up and hang out with my fellow background talent. But none of them were there.

A man sat at a table, his hands rubbing his brow, a baseball cap over his crown that was completely out of place with his attire. On the front of the cap was a familiar-looking emblem, most probably for a sports team, although I could not tell you what particular team it was. He seemed utterly drained, and it was at least five seconds before he raised his head to see who'd entered. But I knew who he was, even before I saw his face. I recognised his costume. He was Eddy Partridge.

"Oh..." I uttered. It was the only word I could bring to my tongue, barely even a word. It was more a grunt. What a Neanderthal I must have seemed.

I heard movement from the other end of the aisle, where Janice Daniels raised her head from her script to deal with the intruder.

"You want the other bus, honey," she told me, her voice full of authority, her manicured hand pointing the way I'd come. She'd spoken to me like I was some five-year-old girl.

"Sorry," I mumbled. "I didn't..."

Eddy just stared at me. Our eyes locked. God, he was handsome, more so in real life than he was in the movies, even in the dim light of this bus.

I didn't know what the look on his face meant to convey, whether he was despising this ignoramus who'd stumbled into the sacred ground where only Hollywood superstars were allowed to tread, not unknown randomers like me, or whether he was just weary from a day of intense filming. Either way, the poor guy surely needed some quiet to unwind. Yet here I was, disturbing him, rooted to the spot instead of leaving. Why was I still there?

Nice one, Hazel. Nice one.

"It's right over there," Janice told me, annoyance mixing with her granite authority. "The red one, not this one." I had the impression she was two seconds away from calling security. Or perhaps she would get out of her seat and use her superhero abilities to dispatch with me, throw me so hard from that bus that I'd hurl through the air, over the hotel and into the Jubilee swimming pool across the road.

Didn't she know I was a massive fan of hers? Didn't she realise she could very well *lose* a fan by talking down to someone like this?

Like she'd really care a damn about that, Hazel!

I threw Eddy an awkward smile, ducking my head into my neck like an idiot, and at last I tore my eyes from that beautiful vision as I delicately retraced my footsteps, edging backwards as though I might effectively press rewind on this little blunder. Once I stepped back outside and closed the door behind me, I sighed. My rosy cheeks were positively humming with embarrassment.

The day had been going so brilliantly, one of those days I would remember for the rest of my life, but then I had to go and do this, wander into the leading actors' VIP area from where I was swiftly booted.

Over yonder stood the red bus, the one designated for the extras, many of whom I could see through the windows. So obvious now. As I glanced back at Eddy and Janice's six-wheeled suite, I noticed how all its windows were tinted. In fact, it wasn't even a bus. It was some sort of camper trailer. How on earth had I been so mistaken? This was the sort of thing my nan would do!

I returned my gaze to the other bus as I schlepped across the tarmac. Climbing aboard with my brethren, a much different atmosphere greeted me. Melissa stood in the aisle and she turned as I cleared my throat.

"So when you said to meet you on the bus," I began, "you didn't mean that one over there, no? The one with Eddy Partridge and Janice Daniels getting some downtime as they go over their lines. Not that one, no?"

"Oh my God," Melissa replied, her eyes lighting up. "You didn't go on their trailer, did you?"

There had been quite a rowdy atmosphere when I'd first entered, but now the others aboard were listening in on the conversation, sensing an amusing story.

"Yeah, I did. For a whole ten seconds before Miss Daniels tells me to clear off."

Standing nearby was Seymour, the tie on his RAF costume loosened. He chuckled, a laugh from deep down in his belly.

"You went in there with them?"

I firmed my upper lip and nodded.

"I can tell you a thing or two about getting booted off the bus," he said. "Come have a drink with me, sister."

He wrapped an arm round my shoulder as he steered me to a refreshments table, something that contrasted greatly with the plush interior of Eddy's trailer. There were no hot drinks here, only bottles of water and pouches with fruit juice, alongside packets of biscuits. The corresponding bar on the other bus, resplendent with Perrier, decanters of sparkling elderflower and otter tears or whatever luxury nonsense these hallowed people drank made this one seem really crummy. Seymour tossed me a pouch and stabbed his little plastic straw in another, and we cheers-ed our drinks, as though I'd just pulled off a dare I hadn't realised I was pulling off. Whatever. I just went along with him.

"Great to have you in the club. Hazel, wasn't it? Now you know our place in this world, us humble extras. Right at the bottom, my friend."

I found myself chuckling too. With my heartbeat returning to its normal rate, I was soon seeing the funny side. Well, it would make an entertaining story to tell the grandchildren.

Chapter 11

I WAS NOT REQUIRED FOR any more filming that day. Although we hung around in our designated holding area for over an hour, eventually a few supporting artists were called back to set while the rest of us were free to go home. As we made our way to the changing areas, an AD reminded us to get signed out on our chit, which merely entailed getting marked off on the spreadsheet on their laptop. Once I was de-frocked, I queued up for that, gazing at my reflection. Back to being Hazel Nightingale again, rather than Unknown Glamorous Villager from the 1940s.

As I shuffled along the queue, I came to a leaflet stand, advertisement for the various attractions and historical landmarks in the area. Among them was a program for the Kinema with a rundown of their bill for the week. I picked it up to peruse.

It was half five when I sat inside Clarence, about the time Nan would normally have her tea. I dialled the bungalow landline on handsfree to check in with her. It was usually hit and miss whether she would successfully answer the phone.

On this occasion, I was in luck.

"Hello?"

"Hey, Nan, it's Hazel. Just..."

"Sorry?" she cut me off. "Speak up a bit."

"I'm just phoning to see how you are. Had a good day?" I delivered my voice in a bellow, and it seemed to do the trick.

"It's been all right, mostly pottering around."

She sounded a little glum, fed up. Perhaps she was feeling under the weather.

"Had any visits today?"

"Well, your grandfather popped round about half an hour ago but I think he's gone now."

It was all so matter-of-fact, like we had this conversation every day. If anyone was listening in, they would not raise their eyebrows at all, unless they happened to know that... *Oh yes, Grandad was dead!*

"Right. And how was he?"

"He never says anything to me. Just sits there."

It was so strange. I didn't understand it at all. Why did her mind never fabricate any words coming from his mouth? Or were spirits physically incapable of producing any sounds from the beyond? My nan would constantly have you scratching your head. The two of them had argued frequently, I recalled from my youth. Perhaps as Grandad had already had a lifetime's worth of bickering with her, he now knew to keep his mouth shut.

"Anyway, I'm all finished for the day, so I'm heading home. Did you eat yet or do you want me to pick up something on my way back? I could grab a Chinese from Tattershall?"

"No, I'm not really hungry. I was just thinking of going to bed, actually. You get yourself one though."

"You're off to bed already?"

"Yeah. Think that's what I'll do."

"All right," I said. "Well, I'll check on you when I get in. Remember to take your pills."

"Righto, duck. Goodnight."

"Night."

She hung up. I started the engine and set off, driving back into the centre of the village. At the roundabout, the strands of multicoloured lights hanging over the street caught my eye, stirring up deep-seated memories of Christmases past. I hadn't properly admired them yet this year, so I made a left onto Station Road instead of heading on home.

Opposite the Dambusters memorial, little Christmas trees protruded above the shop doors, ribbons of twinkling fairy lights in the windows, a view worthy of any Hallmark movie. Many of the houses farther on had their decorations up too, really going to town on it all. I recalled how a lot of the folk down in Sumpton had enthusiastically embraced the festive season last year. What else was there to do for fun when you were in the middle of a global pandemic, but turn Christmas up to 11 in your home? The bigwigs of the music industry had undoubtedly missed a trick. In 2020 they should have made a tweak to that Bing Crosby classic and recorded *I'll Stay Home For Christmas*.

There seemed little point in returning to the bungalow and sitting on my own in the living room watching junk on television, not if Nan had turned in for the night, so I parked up in the village. Down the street I'd passed my favourite pizza place, so I decided to treat myself to a nine inch Margherita, seeing as I'd been so busy today.

I sat in Clarence as I chomped down on that, enjoying the Christmassy view before me, people returning home from work. I later spotted Melissa walking back to *The Mall*. She had been one of the few that had been asked to stay on for more filming, but perhaps it was all done and dusted for the day now, *in the can* as these film folk say.

I soon polished off the pizza. With grease around my chops, I reached into my purse for a napkin, but my fingers first came to that flyer for the Kinema. I unfolded it as I wiped my lips on a tissue.

"What's playing tonight then?"

Monday night's program included some superhero film on the main screen.

"Won't be watching that. Especially if that mardy Janice Daniels is in it."

On the other screen they were showing an oldie, *The Shop Around the Corner*, as part of their festive season, a different Christmas film on all week.

This evening's flick had come out in 1940, the same era I'd stepped into today. It seemed like a little synchronicity as my mind joined those dots, a subtle nudge from the universe that I should go see this film tonight. Or it merely could have been the film critic within me demanding some cinematic stimuli. I'd been doing this for years, going to my local cinema each week before writing my reviews. I missed doing that. Plus, this would be the perfect way to unwind.

"Sure don't have any better offers," I muttered to myself. I'd heard of this old classic, and seemed to remember reading it had been remade in the nineties. James Stewart was the leading man, the same guy from *It's a Wonderful Life*. Boy, he was really on a roll with his Christmas classics that decade.

"Oh, and the wizard from *Wizard of Oz* is in it," I noted as I looked it up on IMDb. "Well, that settles it. *Shop Around the Corner* it is."

The showing wasn't on for another half hour, so I left Clarence where he was and strolled down there, killing some time. Pretty Christmas lights lined the fascias of the Kinema in the Wood's pitched roof. For a Monday night, there appeared to be plenty of cars outside. Folk were keen to flock back to the cinemas after it being denied to us of late because of this virus. I had feared that people may have some reticence in crowding out the pubs and gyms and whatnot, the spectre of covid lingering, but it seemed they were finding it a relief to return to *the old normal* once more. Which was great timing for this particular venue, the Kinema soon approaching its one hundredth birthday. It had grown an extra screen since I'd last visited.

I joined a queue as I stepped inside the porch, putting on my mask.

"I'd like a ticket for *Shop Around the Corner*," I said to the woman as I reached the kiosk.

"Just one, is it?" she asked.

"Yes, just me."

"You've got the very last seat."

Good job I hadn't killed too much time!

I hadn't expected this old black and white number to be so popular. Perhaps people were so keen to get back they'd go see anything. *A remake of* Police Academy? *Great, I'm there! A third* Mamma Mia *film? See me at the midnight showing!*

"Thanks," I replied, as she handed me my ticket.

"You're in Kinema Too on the left."

I enjoyed all the build-up to the main feature, getting ice cream or popcorn to munch on, catching all the preceding adverts. It was all part of the cinematic experience. And the great thing about this place was that they still observed the tradition of an intermission halfway through the picture. For those with weaker bladders, this was a clincher.

I bought a lemonade and a bag of jelly babies before entering the auditorium. The initial trailers had already started, and the seats were filling up, mostly with older couples, but the younger generations were represented too. As I edged up the centre aisle, I checked my ticket to see if I'd been allocated a seat number, what with this being a sell-out. The number indicated I was on the second from last row, which I was pleased about. As a film critic, I usually sat at the back so I could take in the audience's reactions.

"Excuse me," I said to the two pensioners on the inner seats.

They got to their feet, and I carefully squeezed past them. Besides mine, there was one other seat on our row and I just could not believe who was sitting there.

Oh no. This is not good. What kind of weirdo do I look like now?

No one else would have known who he was. That was the thing with wearing these masks all the time, wasn't it?

You'd often pass by someone you knew in the street but be oblivious as to who they were, or you might have an inkling that's your old mate Bobby at the self-service checkout next to you but didn't want to say hello just in case it wasn't him and you ended up looking a tool. Face coverings brought inadvertent anonymity, convenient for some.

And so if Elvis Presley had been sitting in that movie theatre, a mask covering half his face, a hat casting his eyes into shadow within the already dim light, you could easily have missed the discovery of the century.

But I knew the giveaway. I'd seen that very baseball cap before, that emblem.

For a split second the panicked impulse flashed through my mind to one-eighty and scoot away from that whole awkward situation, before I realised that would look even worse. I had no choice but to sit down next to him.

In the corner of my eye I could tell he was turning his head, casting his gaze towards me, an eyebrow cocking with recognition. But perhaps my mask disguised me. Perhaps I was perfectly concealed, perfectly anonymous.

I risked angling my face his way. Eddy Partridge was still looking me over.

"You were at the shoot today, weren't you?" he muttered to me in a hushed voice, so only I would hear.

I sighed. This was so embarrassing, what with that faux pas earlier.

"I'm sorry. I realise how bad this looks, but I just want to assure you I absolutely am not stalking you. I had no idea you were here."

Next door to the cinema were the old spa baths that had sat derelict since before I was born. The story went that they discovered a spring whilst they were drilling for coal. Right now I clung to the anorexic hope that I might be sitting over one of those ancient shafts and a sinkhole would open up at that very moment and swallow me away.

Eddy's eyes smiled at me. Perhaps this situation wasn't so bad.

"You mean to say you did not know I'd be on row H in this quaint little cinema watching an eighty-year-old film? A likely story, miss."

His voice was different, or at least different to the voice I'd heard earlier when he was in character. It was now his natural American accent, soft and lilting.

I felt myself blushing once more. Thank goodness for this mask.

"I'm so sorry about bursting in on you," I said. All of a sudden I found him so easy to talk to. Or perhaps it was because the barriers were down, that I was no longer at the bottom of the hierarchy, not worthy enough to say anything to those lofty film folk high above me. But still, this was Eddy Partridge, a Hollywood superstar. "It's my first day on the job today and I knew I'd mess up somehow."

"I'm over it. I'm glad you're here, actually. Now I don't look like that sad-sack weirdo that goes to the movies on his own."

"Well, I'm delighted to be of service, Mr Partridge."

His face covering had a quirky design on it, a skeletal jaw amid blood-coloured roses. These superstar types just couldn't wear something normal, a standard mask from a pack of a hundred.

The general adverts had finished, and the first of the movie trailers, some kind of gritty thriller, erupted onto the screen with pulsating orchestral stabs. The feature would start in minutes, but I was quite happy to sit there chatting with Eddy. I now understood what Einstein had meant when he talked of the relativity of time, how it could go so quickly when you wanted it to go slowly.

"Have you seen this film before then?" he asked as he produced the same flyer I'd picked up.

"I haven't. I see lots of films, but never this one. How

about you?"

"It's my mother's favourite. Watch it every year. A guy on the crew told me about this cool cinema nearby and when I saw it was on, I couldn't resist. He mentioned there's a wurlitzer that pops up during the intermission too, right?"

"Correct. Except that's next door. We're in the wrong screen for that."

"Damn. Well, next time then. Plenty more to choose from." He continued peering at the leaflet, tilting it into the light. *"The Christmas That Almost Wasn't.* Why have I never heard of that before? Sounds like Christmas 2020."

"Oh, that's on tomorrow, isn't it? That is hands down one of the oddest films in the history of cinema. Definitely walks to the beat of its own drum, and let me tell you that beat is *off.* You just have to see it to believe it."

This was unreal. I was chilling there with Eddy Partridge, discussing movies, and nobody else had a clue.

"With that build-up, maybe I'll have to come back again tomorrow, if I get finished in time."

A silence drifted along. The trailers were still playing, but the words on my tongue had dried up. Perhaps he'd spent enough time shooting the breeze with some random woman, and he would much now prefer me to shut my trap.

"Jelly baby?" I asked as I held up my packet of sweets.

He opened his palm, and I sprinkled a few onto it.

"Thanks," he said, pulling down his mask. "What's your name?"

"Hazel. Hazel Nightingale. Or just Hazel." He raised a fist, and I bumped it with mine.

"So are you working on the film any more this week, Hazel?"

"They want me tomorrow, then Wednesday I have a day off, then I might have more days beyond that but they're going to let me know. I imagine you're busy all the while on this?"

"Pretty much. I'm light on dialogue tomorrow, so I figured I didn't need to do any cramming tonight. There was a self tape I was supposed to do, but I'll fit it in some other time."

It was fascinating to get this insight, little details about the life these high-profile actors lived. He seemed trusting to share this information. For all he knew, I could have been a tabloid journalist.

The curtains in front of the screen closed. The final trailer had played, and now the main feature was about to begin. How had that gone so quickly?

"Enjoy the film, Hazel," Eddy said.

I sure will, Eddy Partridge. I sure will.

The Shop Around the Corner (1940)
Directed by Ernst Lubitsch
Film Review by Hazel Nightingale

Director Lubitsch knew exactly what he was aiming for with this romance set in Hungary. Even before the film had been edited, he predicted audiences would find it a quiet little story, resplendent with charm. The production is less a grand cinematic spectacle and more a cosy flick to watch on a dull winter's day with a mug of hot chocolate. Indeed, there is more a feel of theatre to this film, it actually being an adaption of a stage play, but that only allows the expert cast to shine, drawing you closer to their characters.

James Stewart would go on to make another Christmas classic on the other side of the Second World War. In-between these two films, he would be drafted into the US army, rising to the rank of colonel as he took part in combat missions in Europe. An acting career alongside military involvement even beyond the war only underlined his amazing versatility. And as an actor he could effortlessly switch from screwball comedy to Hitchcock thriller. Hands down Stewart is one of the absolute greatest of cinema.

In *The Shop Around the Corner* he plays Kralik, a shop clerk, the everyman, the persona that proved such an effective component of the winning formula in *It's a Wonderful Life* (perhaps to even greater effect on that occasion). Yet with his tall and slender frame Stewart literally towers over his fellow cast members. His co-star Margaret Sullavan comes to the department store seeking work, but the two don't get along. This despite the fact that, unknowingly, they are pen pals. If the plot sounds familiar, then you might be thinking of *You've Got Mail*, the Tom Hanks / Meg Ryan flick that updated them to keyboard pals as email became their medium of choice.

Sullavan was no stranger to romance at Christmas time, having married Henry Fonda on Christmas Day in 1931. Sadly, it didn't last, and tragically she was only fifty-one when she died of a drug overdose on New Year's Day 1960.

But Christmas 1940 was a sweet and heart-warming occasion in the shop where her character is working. The magic in this tale was all handmade, no ghostly or angelic interventions. Through the correspondence of the two leads, their real selves and the depths of their characters are unveiled. At once, the dimensions of humanity can involve the shallow salesperson steeped in consumerism, and also the tender spirit that is moved greatly by art, as many viewers of this picture are.

Much like Jimmy Stewart, the film rises above all others with its warmth and sweetness, its wittiness and, of course, its charm.

Verdict: 9 / 10

Chapter 12

THE CREDITS ROLLED AS EDDY turned to me and said, "And I bet you didn't know the director was German."

"I did not. And he makes a film set in Hungary during the war? They were on the other side, weren't they?"

The old couple next to me remained in their seats, waiting for the people behind us to clear the aisle. Not that I minded. I could have sat there with Eddy, talking films all night. It seemed so surreal being in the company of a film star as the auditorium lights faded up, illuminating the beautiful trompe l'oeil painting of the Lincolnshire landscape on the walls.

"Didn't exactly have its finger on the pulse of the politics of the time, right?" Eddy commented. I wondered if the film had been an effective means of escapism for the audiences of 1940. In the early days of the coronavirus pandemic when it was all doom and gloom on the news, those Mark Strong government messages on the radio, closure signs on shop windows, wash your hands posters on bus shelters, an edgy Boris Johnson broadcasting a to-camera appeal for the public to remain at home in lockdown, there sure was plenty of anxiety and uncertainty. I desperately needed a distraction, switching off from the chaos outside as I watched things like *Fawlty Towers* on Netflix, immersing myself in a period decades away from a killer virus sweeping the nation.

"Still, I do adore this film," Eddy said. "What did you think?"

"It was great. I'll give it top marks in my review." He peered at me questioningly. "Oh, I write film reviews, by the way. Well, used to, until recently."

"How come you stopped?"

"Thought I'd have a crack at filmmaking, of course." I

didn't really want to explain my current fortunes. *Yeah, Eddy, I don't have a regular job anymore, seeing as my career derailed. Don't even have a place of my own these days.*

He pointed beyond me to indicate the row was clear, so I got to my feet before I gave the impression I intended to trap him here. There were hardly any other folk left in the auditorium. In fact, we were the last two to exit.

As we stepped outside into the chilly December night, Eddy said, "Let me walk you to your car."

Wow. What a gentleman. I'm being escorted by Eddy blimmin' Partridge!

"Oh actually, I left my car over in the village." It was quite likely I didn't mask the disappointment in my voice. "I walked down here."

I expected that to be that, Eddy shrugging his shoulders before heading in the opposite direction to his room at the Petwood, but then he said, "Well, let's go that way then."

"Really?"

"You never know who's about this time of night."

"Oh totally. These Lincolnshire villages, they're like Gotham City beyond dusk."

"Can't have one of my fellow cast members getting into trouble with no Woodhall ghetto punk."

"Now, I realise I found myself on your side of the camera, but I'm pretty sure I'm not going to find my name on the credits at the end of our film."

We headed away from the cinema grounds, walking down Coronation Road through the trees. Outside, he'd pulled his mask down under his chin. He seemed a little shorter than I would have expected, but then, filmmakers often make these stars look so tall on the big screen. He still had a few inches over me.

"So what do you review films for?" he asked.

"I worked for a network of community magazines down

in London, *The Londinium Local.* We sent them out once a month to all the households, mostly advertising local tradespeople and services, and intermixed with that we had editorial consisting of seasonal articles..."

"So the December issue you talk about making eggnog, which type of Christmas tree you should pick?"

"Exactly. That sort of thing. My nan makes a killer eggnog, you know. You just reminded me of that. Anyway, I had the idea of writing film reviews. Near where I lived was the Ritz, this independent cinema, all art deco inside, so I'd go there every month to see whatever was on."

"But you've left this magazine now?"

"It went under. Last year it took most of the knocks. With so many people furloughed, our advertising revenue dried up. The tradespeople didn't have such a great need to advertise when they couldn't get out there to do any work. Meanwhile, the owner moved on to other ventures but he kept the magazine afloat until the end of this year. We all took a pay cut to see it through. Last week was our final publication."

"Sorry to hear that. That sucks. But the big question... Did you ever review any of my films?"

I absolutely had reviewed one of his films, this summer just gone. Did I really want to tell him about that?

"Yeah, there was at least one. The picture you were in recently."

"*The Caretaker*?"

"That's it, yes. Really good film, by the way."

"Five stars?"

"A solid eight out of ten, I think it was."

"I'll take that."

I was so glad that edition had come out months ago, and Eddy could *not* get his hands on a copy, if he might happen to hang out in the capital during his trip to England and pick it up in a dentist's waiting room or somewhere. In that particular review, I may have gushed somewhat about him. He'd played a vampire that travelled in time, and let me just say he made one very sexy vampire. So if he were to read that review? Well, it probably wouldn't quite make an *Alan* Partridge moment, like that episode where he found himself in the home of a superfan who had posters and memorabilia of the hapless television presenter decked out everywhere, but the article I'd penned may have been seen as the start of such an obsession. It certainly revealed a little too much. In my defence, though, I really had not envisaged me going to the cinema with the very actor in question a few months later!

But that review was now dust. Thank goodness.

"Shame you won't get to write one on *Flying Colours*," he said.

"I can always give you my personal reflections once I've watched it at the Kinema."

He grinned. "Please do."

We'd already arrived at my car park.

"So," I said. "That's Clarence over there."

His eyebrows raised slightly, his back straightening up. "Oh, is that your boyfriend? Husband?"

For a couple of seconds he'd lost me, until I realised I'd said my car's pet name out loud. "Oh no no, Clarence is my Clio. Sorry, I have my former room-mate Annie to thank for that. She was always naming everyone's vehicles."

"Ah," he replied, nodding. "I see. A car."

"Definitely no one waiting for me. Except my grandmother. Who's actually asleep in bed as we speak. Or she's.... playing around with a ouija board or dancing a jig with her bells on or something. Whoever can predict? Anyway. I'm rambling. I should stop talking now."

We stood there in silence for a moment. Eddy was smiling.

"It was nice meeting you, Hazel."

"Likewise."

"So, tomorrow. *The Christmas That Almost Wasn't*?"

Was that him asking if I was intending to go to the Kinema again? And if so... *why* was he asking me that? I mean, I assumed it was a question. His voice seemed to inflect on the last word, but maybe it was just part of his foreign accent and it had confused my Lincolnshire ears.

"It's definitely worth going to see," I stated.

"All right," he replied, stroking his mask-covered chin. "These critics know what they're talking about. You should listen to them. Till tomorrow."

"Yes. Tomorrow."

Did I...? Did I just arrange a date with Eddy Partridge?

"Goodnight, Hazel."

"Night." I reached for my door handle and tried opening it up. The thing about Clarence was he could be rather highly strung at times and it was very easy to set off his alarm, which is exactly what I did, his indicators flashing, the siren going, waking up the entire neighbourhood. I cursed as I dug into my purse for my car key, realising I hadn't even unlocked him yet.

"Sorry. I'm definitely not attempting a carjacking here. I am indeed the legal owner of this vehicle," I rambled, pressing the button on my fob and killing the alarm.

Awesome. Very elegant, Hazel. That was all going so well.

Eddy grinned. "Drive safe."

As I sat down in my seat, I caught him in the rear-view mirror, presumably checking that I was capable of driving a car after struggling to open it. He waved as I drove out of the car park and I gave a brief flash of my hazard lights in return.

"So, Hazel," I told myself. I felt I needed to say this out loud to make it sink in. "You've just spent the evening with Hollywood actor Eddy Partridge. Just another day in the

Shire."

I didn't know how in the world I managed to coordinate my feet and hands to drive myself home. It was almost like I floated there.

The indelicate sound of snoring greeted me before I'd even stepped through the front door. That was one way to come back down to earth. Once inside, I popped my head into Nan's room just to confirm it was her making the noise and not one of her visiting spirits. She was alone, of course, a glass of water beside the bed containing her false teeth.

In the kitchen, I checked the evidence of her earlier activities. All the pills I'd laid out for her had been taken, the sandwich in the fridge devoured. Excellent. As Hannibal from *The A-Team* used to say, I loved it when a plan came together. I had to remember to set it all out again tomorrow morning.

There was another long day in front of me, and what I wouldn't give for it to end the same way this had ended, my mind aswirl with the thoughts of a certain American film star as I drifted off to sleep in my bed.

Had that fantastical evening really happened? Or was he a figment of my imagination, the sort of fabrication my grandmother experienced in her saudade for her husband? It wasn't like I had any evidence of it, no selfies of me and Eddy. Would anyone believe me if I told them?

And would I believe my memories when I woke up tomorrow, or would I dismiss them as a dream?

Despite the evening's excitement, I soon became drowsy after my head hit the pillow. Basking in Eddy's presence had made me feel rather mellow, and a deep and peaceful sleep swiftly found me.

Chapter 13

MY HEAVY SLUMBER CONCOCTED A vivid dream that thrashed around my head, leaving an imprint as pronounced as something from reality would. We were in a Lancaster, flying over the Channel after a raid. One by one, my fellow passengers were evacuating the plane until it was down to me and the pilot, a role my brain had assigned to a certain American actor. He was pleading with me to jump out too, but my heels were firmly rooted, hoping we would make it back home to England.

We were in the middle of that argument, the aircraft losing serious altitude, when my 5:45 alarm mercilessly shot that dream out of the clouds. Waking up felt like ripping off a plaster from a wound that was far from closed up. I scrolled through whatever notifications my phone had collected in the night, the dream fading as I slowly woke and tuned into the now. The memory of last night flashed into my brain and suddenly I was very much awake. What an awesome evening that was. And would we repeat it later?

The muffled din of the living room television fought its way to my earholes. Nan must already be up. It was hardly surprising given she'd gone to bed so early. I sat up, reaching for my dressing gown, which I wrapped around me before sliding my feet into my slippers.

"It's freezing. Let's get the fire on," I said as I entered the room. She was on the couch flicking through the channels as she searched for *Good Morning Britain*, but she was making a poor attempt at that, accessing the television's system settings. I took the zapper from her, found ITV, then turned down the volume.

"You're up early," she said as I knelt down to light the gas fire in the hearth.

"Yes, I'm working again today."

"Oh," she replied. So soon into the day, I didn't expect her to recall that I was resuming my role as a film extra. "Do you want me to make you any breakfast?"

With the flames burning, I perched on the nearby single-seater, holding my gown tight to my neck. "I'm good, thanks. I'm just going to have a coffee. Fancy another cuppa?"

"Please."

She watched me closely as I crossed the room. I had no idea why. Who knew where her mind was, what was going on up there? As I returned with two steaming mugs, she again gazed up at me, a strange fascination in her eyes.

"Good day yesterday?" she asked.

"Yes, it was great. What did you get up to?"

"Oh, nothing much. This and that." Her answer translated as: *I can't remember.*

I sat down once more, trying to wrap my body round the lovely hot mug of coffee on my lap.

"Someone's got a twinkle in their eye this morning," she said, her gaze still fixed on me. "Meet anyone?" Seriously, how did she see this stuff? Maybe an ability to perceive ghosts wasn't such a stretch.

"Ah, you know," I replied, shrugging my shoulders and avoiding her eyes. "I seemed to hit it off with someone." She smiled to herself and turned to the television, a satisfied look on her face.

"I'm pleased for you. What's he like?"

It didn't really matter what answer I gave her. It would slip from her brain soon after.

"He's an actor, from America." There was no point explaining he was a figure steeped in fame, a cultural icon in the making, the dapper young prince of cinematic royalty. I already knew that the name Eddy Partridge would mean nothing to her.

119

"Ooh, America," she cooed, her eyes lighting up. "I've been there. What part is he from?"

I couldn't believe what happened next. Suddenly, the man we were talking about was there in the room with us. I succumbed to the instinct to grab the remote from the coffee table, my finger hovering over the channel-up button, but I resisted pressing it. I really needn't have worried, but I still felt exposed, like my diary had been removed from my drawer and was opened up on the desk, ready for anyone to come read it. How surreal to have the guy you were thinking about right there on the television.

Although I may have just told an old lady with dementia that I'd met someone, Eddy remained my little secret of which no one else would have an inkling. I wanted to keep it that way for now.

They were interviewing him on *Good Morning Britain*, and by the looks of the backdrop I guessed they had filmed this at the Petwood. The elegant surroundings just made him come across as even more handsome, more debonair. He was talking about the film, of course. The piece was about the role that personnel from the West Indies had played in the war, and they were leading on to relate it to current race issues before making some reference to *Bridgerton*.

I peered over at Nan to see if she was taking any of this in, but her gaze was now on the window, her mind some place else, the unanswered question she'd just asked forgotten about. I returned the remote to the table and watched the rest of the interview, hiding my spontaneous smile as I took a swig of my coffee.

"You'll have to look after yourself again tonight as I'll most probably be late home."

"You go and enjoy yourself," she replied. "Don't need to worry about me."

The morning in Woodhall Spa involved plenty of waiting around, even more than yesterday, it seemed. Or perhaps I was simply impatient, looking forward to being on set again, being in the presence of my cinema buddy from last night.

Once wardrobe had attired us in our same costumes, they sent the extras to the holding area to await further instruction. There were no mishaps as I climbed aboard the correct vehicle this time. I claimed the first free seat and sipped on the coffee I'd sourced from the catering wagon. The sound of chatter filled the air as new friends talked about themselves, speculated on what we might film today, shared stories of other films they'd worked on.

As I activated my kindle, I heard music behind me. I popped my head up to find my friend Seymour sitting with another chap in RAF uniform.

"Oh hey there, Hazel," Seymour said. "Check this out. My mate here makes his own Christmas music videos. Where are you from did you say, Alexander?"

"Sleaford," the man replied before looking up at me and saying, "Hello."

"Hi there. I'm a local, too. My brother lives in Sleaford."

"Alexander made this video last year when we were all in lockdown," Seymour explained. His friend held his phone against the window, angling the screen so we could all see.

"That's right. Roped in all my kids and even the wife on this one."

We watched as a young blond-haired boy sat in a lonely wooden cabin as the snow fell outside. Various other children drifted into the scene in bubbles as they sang about being in a 'Christmas bubble'.

"Who are all these kids?" Seymour asked. "They can't all

be yours."

"These were from a local youth group. When Boris announced the second lockdown, we had to race against time to record the vocals and film something so I could put them in the video too."

"It's great," I said. "Really catchy tune. So how many children do you have?"

"Five of them now."

"Wow."

"Sounds chaotic," Seymour chuckled.

With interesting characters around like these two, it sure made the hours pass quicker. It was midmorning when they called us to set, the shuttle bus on hand to ferry us to Edrow House, or we could make the short journey on foot if we preferred, as I opted to do.

The function room was in the same state as I'd last seen it with its festive decorations. As I stepped inside, I felt my stomach fluttering, the thought that Eddy might be in there ready for his next scene. I fantasised us sharing small talk, everyone else gawping at me as he gave attention to one of the humble extras. There was no sign of him yet, however.

The ADs placed us in the same spots as yesterday, which seemed to imply we were continuing with the same sequence of scenes. Or maybe this was another party a few days later, and who would know the party-goers were still wearing the same clothes and sitting in the same place because who actually pays any attention to what's going on in the background? With the way these film people fussed over details, I suspected that the former scenario was most likely.

My on-screen companions arrived a few minutes later, the elegant Gale and the diffident Franklin. I resisted the urge to share with Gale what had transpired at the cinema. She seemed the type I could have a girlie natter with, but Franklin's presence dissuaded me. Besides, who would rightly believe me?

With no fanfare, an elegant performer in uniform entered the hall, as though he was just another guy who happened to be working on this film. But this was Eddy, and the sight of him brought about a thumping in my chest, a churning excitement and a strange serenity somehow fused together. All was right with the world when I was in the same room as this star.

I tried to keep it to a minimum, my eyes being drawn to him. I didn't want anyone to notice, to suspect that I might be going weak at the knees with this guy. Oh my, was that what was occurring here? How could I fall for someone like Eddy Partridge? People talked about punching above their weight, but this was a disparity of the highest proportions, a titch and a titan.

I continued to monitor his eyes, waiting for that little moment where he might search the sea of faces, cast his gaze over those players at the opposite end of the hierarchy, searching for me. But, much like yesterday, it was as though none of us supporting artists were even there. Perhaps he was simply so focussed on the work at hand, in character, not thinking about some random girl he'd sat next to in the cinema. He was a professional, a multi-million dollar production on his shoulders. Of course, he couldn't let himself get distracted, not by a nobody like me.

"I was hoping they might move us around a bit today," Gale said to me. "You know, place us closer to the main man over there."

I nodded. "Yeah. Wouldn't that be something?"

As the day's filming went on, I began to wonder if last night had really happened. Might I, at a mere thirty years of age, be experiencing some sort of early onset dementia, my mind muddled like my grandmother's?

The scene today took a romantic turn, but whatever arrows Cupid may have been firing in that room were all misses when it came to me. This was all about Eddy Partridge and Janice Daniels as they disclosed their burgeoning feelings for each other before taking to the dance floor for a gentle sway. I couldn't tell you what number they were dancing to. That was something they would pick up in post.

They both looked so in love, a distinct 'chemistry' going on between them, as us film reviewers might say. Was this simply because they were both so good at their jobs? Or could there be a little truth mixed in with the fiction here? What would I know of what went on between these two individuals when they weren't on set, other than getting an involuntary snapshot by bursting in on their private trailer?

What I would have given to be the one whose body was in his arms. I had to force my eyes off them. What if this was captured on film? What if someone might spot that weirdo loser in the background gawping at the pair, a sad, vicarious longing on her mug?

But right after the final take, it happened. Eddy's eyes met mine. For an entire two seconds that moment lasted, before his focus returned to someone else on his level.

There'd been nothing in his face. Nothing at all. It was merely as though he'd looked at a remotely interesting painting on the wall, before forgetting it as swiftly as my nan could forget anything.

"Are you walking back to the hotel?" Gale asked me.

"Yeah, let's get out of here."

124

It was an earlier finish today, barely gone four by the time we'd de-frocked and signed out. I was just about to leave the changing area when an AD came up to me.

"Hazel, are you interested in doing another day with us on Thursday?"

"Uh..." I didn't really have any reason not to. It would most probably entail being blanked by Eddy Partridge again, but at least I'd earn some extra pennies. "Yes, I'm up for that."

"Great. I'll mark you down. You'll get a message from your agency, so just click accept."

"Will do."

"Thanks. See you Thursday."

I couldn't help but feel the day had been an anticlimax. But then, I don't know what I had been expecting, really. Last night had been such a cool experience from my perspective, unexpectedly hanging out with a movie star, one so chivalrous to walk me to my car afterwards. But for Eddy Partridge, perhaps he had thought no more of it. What was I thinking? Obviously, he hadn't. I was Hazel Nightingale, a name unknown across the globe.

Should I really expect to run into him again this evening at the cinema? Was he realistically going to spend any of his valuable time going to see an obscure B movie when he had lines to learn, rehearsals to attend, self tapes to record?

As I sat inside Clarence, I glanced at the Kinema flyer on the passenger seat. The showing wasn't for another three hours. As much as I enjoyed hanging out in Woodhall Spa, it seemed like a lot of time to kill, a temporal massacre. Plus, after two busy days, I was feeling a little fatigued. It made sense to head on home, to check on Nan and make sure she'd taken her pills, feed and water her, listen to her *Sixth Sense* ramblings.

Yeah, that's the only romance you're going to get tonight, Hazel. Necromancy!

What if she'd fallen over or was bothering the neighbours? How would I explain that one to Martin, given I was now meant to be her primary carer? *Sorry, I went to watch a Christmas movie no one's ever heard of, and one I wasn't in a rush to see again, all on the off chance I might repeat an unlikely meeting with a famous actor after we'd made some nebulous plan the night before.*

I started Clarence up and headed back to New York. I would soon wish I hadn't.

Chapter 14

"YOU'LL NEVER GUESS WHO'S VISITED me tonight," Nan blurted the very second I stepped foot inside the bungalow.

I sighed as I exaggerated the thoughtful expression on my face, my thumb and forefinger stroking my chin. The mood I was in, it meant the mischievous imp within was surfacing. "Um... was it Dwight D. Eisenhower?"

"No," she replied playfully, and as though I'd just given a totally legit answer. I had no patience for going along with her guessing game, however.

"I don't know, Nan. Who visited you?" I removed my coat and kicked off my shoes. This was classic behaviour from Dora Nightingale, bombarding you with questions or recounting her day the second you returned home, when you just wanted a moment to decompress.

"He's still here. Hasn't gone yet."

"Are you telling me I'm going to find an invisible Grandad in the room again?"

"No, it's not your grandfather tonight. It's Maddox."

My eyes closed as I shook my head. I couldn't believe her. "Are you moving on from dead relatives to dead romances now?"

As I opened my eyes again, they rested on an incongruous object on her telephone bureau. Laying on the seat was a crash helmet.

Oh, no. Anyone but him.

The one time you actually *want* your nan to be having another of her delusions...

"Hey babe," Maddox said as he appeared at the living room doorway in his leathers. How had I not spotted his motorbike as I'd parked up outside? "Miss me?" He opened his arms wide as though his natural charm would act as a tractor beam and compel me towards him for a reconciliatory hug.

"What are you doing here?" I asked, tossing my coat over his helmet before folding my arms. "You're a long way from Sumpton, aren't you?"

"I came to patch things up, hon."

"Oh, this is so exciting," Nan said, completely misreading the room, or rather my side of the room. She headed for the kitchen, announcing, "Let me put the kettle on."

"Well, at least one Nightingale is glad I'm here," Maddox said, grinning.

I barged past him.

"This one sure isn't singing."

I plonked myself down on the single-seater, waiting for him to follow me in there.

"Tell me, sugar, what do I need to do to fix this?" he asked as he sat on the other sofa, as close to me as he could get. His leathers creaked each time he bent his limbs.

Babe, hon, sugar? Are you going to throw every pet name in the dictionary at me in the hope you'll melt my heart?

"I thought I was clear enough about this. It's over."

"You say that, but it wasn't quite over only a few weeks ago, was it? You came back to me."

"And that was a mistake."

"No, it wasn't. You still want..." His phone interrupted him with a notification. "Sorry, give me a sec."

I sighed as his meaty digits dabbed away at his screen, my eyes on the rug at my feet, looking at anything but him.

"Who are you messaging?" I asked him.

"It's just work."

I snorted. "Work? Does that mean you're *working* someone?"

"What can I say?" he replied, as he hit send on his text.

"I've been totally clearing up the last two weeks. The recently widowed sure make easy pickings."

My lip curled into a snarl. I didn't want to enquire further, but I suspected he was getting on the bandwagon of romance fraud, befriending people who'd recently lost a loved one and were emotionally vulnerable. Emotionally *pliable*, Maddox might describe it.

Around the back of his neck, I noticed a green strip of fabric decorated with sunflower heads. He still had that damned thing, presumably coming in need if he'd stopped at a service station on his way here. It was his lanyard, what asthmatics or disabled people would wear to signify their exemption from wearing a mask in public.

And what was his disability? Nothing but a pathological compulsion to game the system, whether or not he had a genuine reason to. The guy had nothing wrong with him at all. He merely did not want to play ball. He probably didn't even find mask-wearing to be an irritant. All that irritated him was society telling him to conform.

"Come on, babe," he went on, laying it on as he leant towards me. "I've travelled all the way here to Lincolnshire to make things right."

"Not exactly a trek into Mordor. It's only up the A1."

"Come back with me," he said, reaching out a hand. He could only press his fingers to my armrest. That was close enough. "Why did you come here? Your life ain't here no more, Haze."

Don't call me Haze! It's hardly extra effort to enunciate one more syllable!

"There's nothing down in London for me anymore. I came here because my nan needs me. I'm all she's got."

"Your nan, who doesn't know her backside from a mardi gras parade?"

I threw him a sharp stare. That was so typically Maddox, dissing someone who'd only just been rooting for him.

"Besides, I thought your brother was taking care of things with her. If she's that bad, put her in a home or something. Don't waste your life on a lost cause."

"Funny, I'd give the same advice to you."

He'd lowered his voice when he'd mentioned about a nursing home, not that it was necessary. The old lady in the adjacent kitchen wouldn't have even heard if I'd struck up a chainsaw and howled in delight as I went all Leatherface on my ex.

Nan entered the room carrying a tray and singing a song. I think it was meant to be *Well, Did You Evah!* but I couldn't be certain. Something about a 'swell party' was distinguishable amongst a lot of freestyle vocalising when she didn't know the other lyrics.

"Here come the cuppas," she said.

She placed the tray down on the table and handed Maddox a cup. She'd got out her finest bone china. I couldn't help but smirk as I watched the brute next to me in his motorcycle leathers, blackwork tattoos crawling up his neck, the tip of a tribal sleeve on the back of his hand. There he was sipping from Nan's dainty vessel with its floral pattern. As I received my teacup from her, I noticed the drink within was more akin to rats' urine.

Maddox said, "Thanks, Dora. That's a pukka brew." He then turned to me. "Me and Hazel were just working things out. You wouldn't mind if she came back to London with me, would you?"

"No, of course not," Nan replied. "I keep telling her she needs to think about herself, not me. She doesn't want to be stuck with an old one like me."

"There we go, babe. Dora says herself she doesn't need you."

Unconsciously I took a sip of the tea, but the ensuing grimace was not because of the brew, despite it genuinely tasting like a rodent's discharge. How did she manage to do a simple thing so wrong? What turned my stomach was the idea Maddox was attempting to feed me.

"I think you should get back on your bike," I said. "Where is it anyway? I don't recall seeing it on the drive."

"It's a few houses down. I couldn't remember which one was your nan's."

"If you set off now, you'll be home by eight. Seven, if you ride like the maniac you usually are."

"Hazel," Nan said in her parental voice. Somehow, it was like I'd become an unruly child and the grown-ups were sorting my life out. "You're not sending him back out, are you? It's perishing out there tonight."

"Well, he's not staying here, so he can get lost."

"Stay here?" Nan asked. They were the only two words she'd heard, transforming my marching orders to Maddox as an invitation for him. "Of course. We've got another bed he can have."

"Thanks, Dora," he said. "That would be great."

It was all feeling like a bad dream. How much worse could this day get? The landline interrupted us, bleating a ringtone set to the highest possible volume. Nan rose to answer it. I listened out to check if she'd managed to pick up properly, the ensuing conversation from the hall suggesting she had. It sounded like a friend was on the other end of the line, or it could have been Grandad's last living sister who frequently called.

"You're not staying here, Maddox."

"Really? The lady of the house says differently."

"Would you like me to explain to her exactly what you're about, how you earn a living bamboozling people like her?"

He gritted his teeth, his cheek muscles flexing. His 'career' had been a frequent topic of conversation for us, so I knew my question would press his buttons.

"How many times have I got to tell you?" he muttered. "You know, I tried getting by being the nice guy, but it

131

doesn't pay, doesn't get you anywhere. The straight and narrow didn't exactly work out for you with your job, did it? I was thinking about *us*, babe, trying to make a life for us we can be comfortable in."

"Great. So it's my fault you're a con artist, is it?"

"Most of these fogies have got more money than they need with their free bus passes and TV licences. All I'm doing is some wealth redistribution, freeing it up for people that really need it, the ones struggling to get by."

"Maddox Morales, the modern day Robin Hood," I spat, rolling my eyes. His surname was such an irony, the only *moral* he had in him. "If it's any consolation, Maddox, it's not the only reason I left."

"Well, I'm pretty sure one of those reasons isn't because you met someone else. Don't see you getting cosy with any yellowbelly rube up here."

Somehow I'd drunk all of my cuppa. The caffeine had focussed my brain.

"Am I right?" he asked, tilting his head.

Why don't you tell him about your 'accidental' cinema date last night, Hazel? Speaking of which, are you conceding it was just a one night sitting? Not going to go back there tonight? Is this guy in front of you, who chased after you all the way from London, in fact, the best you can do?

"I'm sorry you wasted your time coming up here," I said as I rose to my feet.

"Where are you going?" I heard the creak of leather behind me, china rattling as he placed it on the table.

"Anywhere but here."

"Haze..."

"Don't call me that."

He grabbed my arm, and I span round, his bulky form towering over me.

If a naked cyborg travelled from the future and met

Maddox, he would have been the perfect donor in supplying Arnie with snugly fitting clothes and boots, before that terminator then made off with his motorcycle, too. Naturally, I'd seen what was beneath the clothes countless times before, not only the times we were intimate. Maddox was a complete poser, showing off his ripped form whenever he could, his body packed with concrete muscles. He hadn't slowly built up this physique with a strict regime at the gym. No, he'd gone the steroids route.

"Please don't go, babe."

Nan reappeared on the scene, her phone conversation finished. I glanced towards the bureau to see she hadn't seated the handset properly in its cradle.

"That was Iris. Have you two sorted things out yet?" she asked. Maddox casually released his grip on my arm, standing up straight, a cocky smirk appearing on his mush.

"It's all settled, Nan. Maddox is about to set off for London and never come back."

I stomped into the hall, making my dramatic exit, but before I did that I suffered a twinge of OCD as I felt compelled to reseat the phone handset properly. With that distraction dealt with, I put on my shoes and grabbed my coat.

"Where do you think you're going, Hazel?" Nan asked.

"I'm meeting someone," I said. I didn't know if that was actually the truth or not, but either way, it didn't matter. It sent Maddox a clear message. Although, judging by the scowl on his face, perhaps I should have kept shtoom. I knew what he was thinking. The guy owned a motorbike, a flashy one, and so keeping up with a humble Clio was easy.

By my knees I saw the helmet. I grabbed it as I stormed out of the bungalow, Maddox yelling my name after me.

The moment unfolded just like the movies, just like a *trope*. I was Sarah Connor running from the cyborg who just wouldn't quit, or I was the 'final girl' fleeing the monster, rushing outside to my car, hoping it would start right away and I could escape. Clarence was still warm as I sat behind the wheel, my pursuer's helmet in my grasp. A security light at the front of the bungalow threw some convenient light on me after I'd triggered its motion sensor.

My faithful vehicle obediently started. I knew he wouldn't have let me down. Maddox stood in the headlights, his palms tilted to the skies as if saying, *'What do you think you're doing?'*

I crunched into reverse and manoeuvred out onto the road. Fifty yards away, I wound down my window and hurled the crash helmet into the ditch. That should slow him down enough, having to find it again before getting on his bike.

A voice inside told me that Maddox was exactly the sort of idiot to ride without his helmet, especially on these country roads, and especially when his emotions were running high, but as I reached the junction at the end of the main road, I saw no headlights in my rear-view mirror.

Is that ex of yours crazy enough to ride without a helmet and *lights?*

If this movie trope was about to live out like it should, then my success was assured. I just hoped that when I made it to Woodhall Spa, the evening would take on a much different genre.

Chapter 15

I WAS LATE TO THE showing. The auditorium lights would have been dimming as I sped out of Tattershall, but at least the pre-movie trailers gave me something of a buffer. I just hoped that Eddy hadn't given up and gone back to the hotel, having assumed I'd abandoned our sketchy little rendezvous. Not that this was an official date, was it? He probably hadn't even turned up at all, had thought no more about going to see this strange film he'd never heard of.

Parking up in the Kinema's new car park, I hastened my pace as I trotted up to the building.

"One for *The Christmas That Almost Wasn't*," I said to the chap in the kiosk. "I'm a little late, I know."

"Plenty of seats still," he replied. That didn't surprise me, knowing this film.

"Ooh, is it possible to have the same seat I was in last night, H8?"

He checked his computer, but then frowned. "Sorry, those are the only ones that were reserved."

"Okay, no worries," I said as he handed me my ticket. I made my way into the foyer and paused. Was I really going to find famous actor Eddy Partridge in there once more? Did lightning ever strike twice like that?

Wasn't a lot in his eyes when he looked at you on set earlier, was there? You really flatter yourself if you think he gave you that much thought.

What if he was the one to have reserved those same seats, bringing along his co-star Janice Daniels here on an *actual* date? And what kind of loser would I look like turning up here on my own? Didn't Eddy himself describe those people as sad sacks?

I dispensed with getting refreshments, seeing as I was in

a rush, although not in too much of a rush that I avoided taking a moment to pluck up the courage to step into that auditorium.

Stop hesitating, Hazel, and get in there!

I took a deep breath and headed into Kinema Too. I'd imagined the main feature to have already started, but I walked in just as its classification was on the screen. Right on time.

The rows of seats were indeed sparsely populated, but the heads of those present turned to look at the latecomer. Sheepishly, I tiptoed to the stairs, trying not to distract them too much and ruining the show. Was Eddy among them? I hadn't spotted him yet, but with the lights down, it was difficult to see. I headed up towards the back, subtly sweeping my gaze left and right as I climbed.

As I reached row H, I noticed one person sitting at the far end. He wore a mask with a dragon design on it, a baseball cap on his head, his eyes fixed on me. Eddy Partridge.

"Hey," I whispered, giving him a stupid little wave.

Great. So he must be with someone if he booked those two seats, and his date is presumably in the bathroom powdering her nose? What's the betting he's here with Janice?

"Hazel," he replied. He beckoned me over, lowering the seat next to him.

For a moment I stood there like an idiot, my brain struggling to compute, but after an interminable three seconds I shuffled down the row and sat down beside him.

Right, so maybe he is on a date and that person he's with is me?

He leant across and spoke under his breath, "I was beginning to think you weren't going to turn up."

"Sorry I'm late. Had a stressful evening."

"You okay?"

"I am now."

"Great. Let's enjoy this peculiar film of yours, Miss Nightingale, film critic. Jelly baby?"

He held up a bag of them. I was sure my eyes lit up.

"Please." He tossed it onto my lap. He had a bag of his own.

I settled into my seat, although my heart continued to leap around in my chest as though I'd just run a marathon.

"I reserved the two seats in front of us too," he said. "So there wouldn't be any heads in my way."

"Good thinking."

I desperately wanted to keep chatting with him, but I was conscious of being *that* person at the cinema who disturbed everyone else, so I munched on some sweets and kept quiet. There was always the intermission. Until then, I would sit next to him, soaking up his glittering aura.

"So, I'm feeling a distinct *Miracle on 34th Street* vibe going on with this," Eddy said at the half-time break. Some of the audience got up to source more concessions. The two of us stayed where we were.

"It's like its strange Italian cousin, right?"

"Definitely a strange one." I didn't know whether that was his way of telling me he thought the film totally sucked, and that I'd ruined his evening by recommending it to him. "So how would this score with Hazel Nightingale in *The Londinium Local*?"

He remembered the name of my magazine.

"Six out of ten? Maybe seven if I'm in a good mood. I realise it's an acquired taste, not box office-busting material. A cult film. Sometimes comparing and rating films is a bit of an apples and oranges thing. Like, how do you compare

Avengers: Endgame with *The Seventh Seal*?"

Shut it, Hazel. You're rambling now.

"The guy out front told me tomorrow night's Christmas movie is on the main screen," Eddy said. "That's where the wurlitzer is, yes?"

"Yeah, it might make an appearance."

Did that mean he was... possibly planning on coming back tomorrow night? Was that the subtext here, his way of implying he wanted to see me again?

I was just opening my lips to say something when he asked, "So, what was the stressful business before you came here?"

"Oh, you don't want to know about that."

"You settled it though, I hope?" Softly-softly he was picking away at it.

"Yes. I mean no." I sighed and then added, "I had a run in with the ex."

"Ah. I see. Did you tell him...?" His voice trailed off.

"Tell him...?"

The lights faded, ready for the second half of the showing, the question left unfinished.

Did I tell him I was coming here to the cinema because I had arranged a date with Eddy Partridge? Does that mean this is official then?

We put our attention back on the screen, watching Sam Whipple helping Santa Claus to pay off the meddling Phineas Prune in order to save Christmas. I wasn't really taking it in, my mind elsewhere. I'd seen it before, though, the strange lip-synched performances, the offbeat castings, the garish sets, the tawdry costumes, the occasional break-out into song. All its quirks were more creepy than amusing. Despite the unsettling feeling that it might morph into a surreal horror at any second, conversely, it displayed all the ingredients of a Disney movie of its time, albeit on a much lower budget. A poor man's Disney. That was exactly it:

Everything about it was *almost*. But that was the critic in me talking. The context of my viewing of this film would trump anything on that screen, even if something perfect like *Citizen Kane* were playing. I was there with a movie megastar.

"There we are; you made it to the end," I said as the credits rolled.

"Not an experience I will forget easily."

There was no one else on our row, and no one behind us either, so we immediately got to our feet and trickled towards the exit. The frigid air greeted us outside, and our lungs became smoke machines, sending out plumes of mist that lingered around us. After feeling all Christmassy from watching two festive films on consecutive nights, what would have made this moment perfect was the magical touch of falling snow. But this was England. Snow was more likely at Easter. Besides, you didn't get fairytales in this country, but *if* you did they definitely wouldn't be in this county. The stars might align to put our footballers in a Wembley final, the script written for their victory to provide us all with a much-needed fillip after everything we'd been through, our nation high up on the covid death toll. But our boys would not get to lift the trophy, and the night would be remembered for a drunken fan sticking a flare up his backside. How terribly English of us.

"Where are you parked tonight?" Eddy asked, pulling his mask down beneath his chin. I stole a look at him now he'd revealed the rest of his face. "In the village again?"

"Over here," I replied, pointing to the car park. I followed the other cinema-goers returning to their vehicles and, saying nothing, Eddy accompanied me. I ambled along, savouring each second with him.

"So how far away do you live?" he asked.

"Just down the road in a small village on the fens. Where do you live when you're not making films in Limey

Land?"

"I'm mostly in LA these days, but I'm an east coast guy originally."

"New York," I said. I knew that fact long before I'd read up on him for the magazine film review I'd penned. The second of three children, he was raised in the Bronx, his father a record producer from Jamaica, his mother a second generation Hungarian, and by Jove, I suddenly twigged why *Shop Around The Corner* would be his mother's favourite film.

He was twenty-six years of age, a whole US presidential term younger than me, and yet, with the life he'd led, all the experiences he'd gone through on such a high platform, it all gave him the aura of someone older than me.

"I bet you didn't know I'm a New Yorker too," I said.

He cocked his head at me.

"That's the name of the village I live in."

"Oh right, is that like a Boston thing where you guys ripped us off?"

I smiled. "Yeah, it totally happened that way round."

"Wow. Another New York. I have to see this place before I leave."

"Really isn't much there, you know. No park, no *Perk*, no police department. Once you've seen the village sign, you've seen everything."

"Still have to see it," he insisted. "Think you can pull off a guided tour?"

"Shortest tour in history."

"What's it like living there? Must be something to do there."

I needed a moment to engage my brain to answer that one. "Um, we sit at home watching television, transported to much more exciting locations, like Albert Square or Winterfell, or even Button Moon. Actually, I do enjoy going for walks, wandering off into the barren landscape. If you like bowls, archery or classic motorbikes then there's all that going on in the village hall, or if you want to do something more interesting you can rent the venue for seven quid an hour but you might have to purchase tokens for the heating as well, so make sure you budget for that. Oh yes, and in the summer we have our flagship event, the annual Wheelbarrow Racing Championship."

"And is that as thrilling as it sounds?"

"In all honesty, I found watching guys trotting across a field with a wheelbarrow full of potatoes something I needed to see only once in my lifetime."

"Is there, like, a hall of fame somewhere? Who's the current champion?"

"You may have to check their website, but I think Benjamin Thwaites holds that distinction, since 2018, I believe. Although last year he didn't need to do much to retain his crown as they sadly cancelled the event."

"Fascinating."

"No. No, it really isn't."

"So does your place have any famous residents?" Eddy asked.

"Nope. Not now, not ever. In fact, prime ministers are more likely to come from your New York rather than mine. At the moment, we're actually losing one nil on that matter."

He laughed. "Sorry about that. So what was it like round there during the pandemic? Anything like what happened in my New York?"

"Let's see... my nan's neighbour Kitty had quite the panic, thinking she'd come down with covid. After cooking the Sunday roast one weekend, she had a distinct change in taste. However, it turned out she'd used coffee granules instead of gravy granules. Then there was Clive at number 26, who said the father of his darts team captain had tested positive, but he was asymptomatic. And he didn't even live in New York. So, no, not a great deal, on reflection. Nothing like your New York. That was on the news a lot over here."

"I was back home when I came down with it."

"Oh no, you caught the 'Rona?"

"I had long covid, and it sure *did* seem to be long."

"Yikes. You're okay now, yeah? Or do I need to keep my distance?"

I wondered if this perhaps accounted for the little hiatus in his career. Even when productions started up again following lockdown, Eddy had laid low for a while, not rushing to finish the uncompleted film he'd abandoned in the first wave. I'd often heard it mentioned on the news that the virus prevailed in black hosts. Race aside, it hadn't mattered who you were. Leaders of nations were just as susceptible as anyone else, a thought I'd found so chilling.

"You're fine. I had a lingering issue with my taste," he explained. "This carried on even after I was through the worst of it. And I kept getting this strange smell that I'd never experienced before. I can't begin to describe it. When I had the vaccine it all suddenly stopped."

"Glad to hear. I caught it too, but it didn't hang around, thankfully. Didn't have any trouble with my taste." Although, weirdly, contracting the virus had coincided with my initial split with Maddox, so perhaps I'd had a change of my taste in men?

We'd already reached my car, both of us pausing by the boot (or the *trunk,* as Eddy would call it). He stood between me and the vehicle.

"Anyway," I said, trailing my fingertips through the thin glaze of ice that was forming on the back window. "Here's Clarence." The frost was soft. The wipers should remove it easily, so I didn't bother digging into my purse for a credit card to scrape it off.

"I recognised him." He raised his palms and added, "I'll make sure to keep my hands off him. I've witnessed his prima-donna tendencies."

For an awkwardly long beat, we stood there in silence. Me because I didn't want this moment, this evening, to end. Him? Who knew what was going on in his head? As enigmatic as usual.

"It was nice to see you again, Miss Hazel Nightingale."

I lowered my gaze to my shoes, wrapping my coat tighter around my body, biting my lip. "You didn't seem so thrilled on set earlier. Looked right through me."

He nodded, his blue eyes going out of focus. In that moment, I wasn't sure I'd ever noticed it before, the unusual colour of his irises.

"Sorry. Didn't want people to notice anything. You've seen what these shoots are like. You have to keep focussed, not screwing up your lines and everyone having to reset and go again when there's a whole bunch more shots to get through."

Am I that much of a distraction then?

"Well, I'm not there tomorrow you'll be relieved to hear."

"Nope. No SAs tomorrow. Would be kind of weird given the scenes we're doing."

"Is it something a little more intimate? Surprised you're not getting an early night, going over your lines instead of coming out here with me."

"I should be doing that. You're right, Miss Hazel."

"Tomorrow evening, then. Stay home and pass on whatever's playing here; I can't remember."

"*Last Christmas.*"

"Right, that was it; *Last Christmas.* You'll just have to catch it on Netflix."

"But..."

"But?"

He paused, scratching the back of his head before saying, "You don't get a live wurlitzer with Netflix."

"You might not tomorrow night either, it being a

143

Wednesday. I think it usually pops up on the weekend showings."

"No, I have it on good authority it'll be out tomorrow. Tomorrow is a sell-out."

"There we go then. That settles it. Our run of festive films comes to an end." I zipped open my bag and fished for my car keys. I desperately needed to organise this thing.

"But... if you did want to make it three for three..." He reached into his back pocket and pulled out a pair of tickets.

"Are you... inviting me out, Mr Partridge? Again?"

"I'm counting two tickets in my hand, and there's two of us."

"Um... well, I'd be delighted," I said.

"Great."

"Great."

I finally found my key amongst all the receipts and antibacterial wipes and hand gel. I took it out and zipped the bag back up. We continued to stand there as though we didn't know whose line was next, or even how this story went. Any director would have yelled 'cut' at us by now.

"I like spending time with you, Hazel Nightingale. I like it very much."

I couldn't say what came over me next, stepping into his personal space, my lips searching for his. Perhaps I just wanted to know exactly what was going on here, what his feelings were underneath his guarded demeanour. Perhaps it was something to do with what happened earlier, the devil-may-care mood I'd found myself in. But his lips gratefully received mine, his hand reaching behind my waist. We swayed backwards slightly, but that was all that was needed.

Clarence started off on a fit again, the horn blaring, the lights flashing.

"Well, that's one way to kill the moment," I muttered. Fortunately, with the key clutched in my hand, I soon shut him up. "Sorry."

Eddy chuckled. "I think your car might have jealousy issues."

"Until tomorrow, Mr Partridge."

"Laters." He handed me one of the tickets. "Just in case it's the date that almost wasn't again because you're held up."

I took it, before getting inside the car. On the reverse of the ticket, I noticed a string of digits that confused me momentarily before I realised it was his mobile number, his *cell* number.

Holy moly. What was happening here? I just kissed Eddy Partridge. As I drove home, that magical moment on repeat in my mind, a few flakes of snow fell from the heavens.

I spotted no motorbike parked on any of the neighbours' drives as I approached the bungalow, and there was none standing on Nan's drive. I really hoped he'd buzzed off, didn't want another appearance from him, spoiling what had been an amazing evening.

As I stepped inside, I was relieved to find no crash helmet anywhere, just the sound of Nan snoring, emanating from the lounge, almost vibrating the glass in the door. Before checking on her, I peered into the spare bedroom. Empty. And there was no one in my room either, just to be doubly sure that Maddox wasn't here. And while I was at it, to make triply sure my life wasn't getting *too* ridiculous, I checked Nan's bedroom too. Thankfully, that was also empty. My neck muscles eased.

In the kitchen I discovered her pill dispenser, still full with the evening's tablets. I could forgive her for letting it slip from her mind tonight, what with the earlier excitement. At least I was on hand now. Picking them up and filling a glass with water, I stepped into the lounge.

The television was off. I seemed to recall it would automatically switch itself off if you hadn't pressed any buttons in the last few hours. Nan began to stir as I sat next to her.

"Need to take your pills."

"Oh yes. Must have nodded off."

Once she'd taken them all, I asked, "So Maddox isn't stopping then, no?"

"Maddox? Did you see him?"

I shouldn't have mentioned him. Usually, anything about that chap would stick in her mind.

"He popped round earlier."

"Ooh, do you think you…"

"No," I snapped, cutting her off. "He and I are finished. If I had any modicum of doubt before, I have absolutely none now. We are done."

"Oh. Shame. He's a nice man, he is. He's been good to you."

It wasn't worth discussing it with her.

"Come on, Dora McSnorer, I think it's bedtime."

Once she was settled, I soon turned in as well. Lying in bed, I held the cinema ticket in my hands before entering the handwritten number into my phone. I sent Eddy a quick text to open the digital doorway between us.

Goodnight Partridge. Thanks for a lovely evening. From that other bird. X

And yes, I'd ended it with a kiss. For a few moments, I lay there staring at the screen, waiting for a reply. Perhaps he was already asleep, given he had more scenes to shoot tomorrow.

Eventually, the drowsiness became too strong and I drifted off into a much-needed sleep.

Chapter 16

I COULD SCARCELY BELIEVE MY bleary eyes when I checked my phone. It was almost ten o'clock. Boy, I must have been tired. Not even the blare of the television from the living room had woken me.

Among the various notifications my phone had curated during my slumber, was a reply to the last text message I'd sent. Once I'd read it, I realised it had generated a Cheshire cat grin on my lips, after catching my reflection in the mirror. Surely this message was convincing evidence that I had not dreamt what happened last night, that I was not stumbling down a rabbit hole. I had indeed gone out with a Hollywood superstar, and I had *kissed* him. My brain was positively bathing in one hundred percent proof serotonin today. I couldn't imagine anything souring my mood, not even if Maddox were to rear his ogreish head again.

As I drew back my bedroom curtains, I gazed at the dusting of snow outside. The light bounced off it, giving that celestial feel as ice crystals twinkled in the rays of the morning sun. It would probably melt by the afternoon, but right now it looked pretty, defining each branch on the trees, telling the story of each vehicle that had driven through it, each person and creature that had disturbed its pristine arrangement with their footsteps.

On the far side of the road, I noticed a tyre track running along its dead centre. That whispery voice inside my brain apprehended the unsavoury truth: a motorbike must have created that. So the spectre of Maddox continued to haunt me, erasing a tiny amount of that happiness chemical before I forced him out of my mind.

"Good afternoon, Sleeping Beauty," Nan said as I appeared in the living room a few moments later. "You do get up sometimes then."

I couldn't help but smile. Back when I was a young girl, that was a line Grandad always gave me when I made my first appearance of the day, something that often took place beyond midday.

"Morning. Cup of tea?"

She handed me her empty mug as her way of saying 'yes'.

After a drink and some breakfast, I ventured up into the loft and dragged out Nan's artificial Christmas tree, and much to my delight, I also found those tune-playing bells. Pulling them out of the box of decorations, I switched them on, the cheap and cheerful electronic arrangement of *Rudolph the Red-Nosed Reindeer* instantly taking me back in time twenty years to the magical and wonder-filled Christmases of my childhood. Before too long, the notes slowed, then distorted to a fuzz. New batteries needed.

After placing the tree in its stand in the corner of the room, I set Nan on the task of decorating it with tinsel and baubles. I then wrapped up in a hat and scarf before stepping outside to explore the wintry landscape.

I headed down the glamorously sounding Dogdyke Road this morning, another long straight route that went on forever. The barren fields stretched out on either side of me, and my mind drifted as my feet roved. If those loopy flat earthers really wanted to prove their theory, they ought to visit the Lincolnshire fenland. Trekking along this byway gave the impression one might eventually fall off the end of the world into the abyss. Either that or you'd arrive at somewhere like Grantham, which to some was more or less the same thing.

At a break in the trees bordering the lane, I came upon someone in a flat cap making the most of the altered landscape. The artist noticed me in his peripheral vision and raised his hand.

"Hazel, good morning," he said.

Montgomery was rather talkative today, tripling his word count. Although, I supposed this time he didn't have a brush clamped in his teeth to impede him.

"Morning Montgomery," I replied. "Don't sit there too long. You'll catch a chill." He was already immersed in his landscape painting once more. The conversation was over.

I glanced back the way I'd come and realised I'd covered quite some distance. Time to head home. I'd barely retraced fifty of my steps when a distant sound caused me to clamp my teeth together, the serotonin flowing through my blood suddenly curdling. Behind me came the unmistakable whine of an engine, its revs far higher than they should be with these driving conditions.

There was no point running, no point hiding in the bushes. I knew the rider of that motorbike would have spotted the figure in the crimson coat ahead of them, its hue standing out clearly on the colourless scenery. All I could do was carry on marching until the roar of his sport bike increased in volume and he was pulling up alongside me. He kicked out the stand and killed the four-cylinder engine.

"Hey," Maddox said as he removed his helmet, stomping towards me.

"Knew I should have thrown that thing further away." I continued my march, and he grabbed my arm.

"We need to talk, Haze."

"No, we don't. We're not in *Eastenders* land here. Up here we don't talk."

"I'm in love with you, Haze. Please. Let's get back to where we were."

I sighed, my head drooping on my shoulders like an unwatered rose. For a moment, we stood in silence before the thunder of the Coningsby jets in the distance complemented the atmosphere of seething emotions.

"Where did you stay last night?" I asked, changing the subject. I was really hoping he'd buzzed off back to London.

"Checked in at a bed-and-breakfast in Tattershall, and there I'll stay till you see sense."

"I told you, Maddox. It's over. I... I've met someone else."

Whatever was going on between me and Eddy was something I couldn't resist using as ammo against my ex. The romance was embryonic, of course, and who knew what was to grow from our secret cinematic meetings, whether a walk into the sunset was in the future. Probably not. How could that follow? We were from different worlds, where the fusion of the words 'New' and 'York' evoked deeply contrasting images. But despite that disparity, what was absolutely true at that very moment was that I was falling for him.

Maddox's head shook, his grip on me releasing as he ran his hand over the nape of his neck. He cast his gaze back along the road and snarled. "Don't tell me it's that weirdo Montgomery. What, was he the last one in the barrel?"

"God's sake, no, it's not him."

"Who is he then? Come on, I'll find out, eventually. Can't be that special a romance if you're uncomfortable talking about it."

"He's an actor. I met him working on that film shoot nearby."

Maddox snorted. "An actor? So he doesn't have a proper job."

"Oh, like you're in a position to talk about having a proper job. Which poor pensioner did you con out of their money so you could afford that bike? Seriously, how do you even sleep at night doing what you do?"

"Quite easily, actually, knowing all my bills are paid. And what's this about a film? Are you Frederico Fellino now?"

"*Fellini.*"

"That's what I said."

I shook my head. "And it's Federico. Whatever. Maddox, I'm just sorry that we got together in the first place. It was a mistake from the start."

"How can you say that? We had something, babe. You can't throw it away. If you want me to change, then I will. I'll make this work for you."

I took a deep breath of the frigid air as my brain composed another retort, but movement in the corner of my eye distracted me. "Oh no, what's he doing?"

Maddox turned to see the peculiar artist lurking behind him down the road, a pad and pencil in his hands, evidently sketching the performers of this melodramatic scene taking place in this usually barren spot.

"Oh, don't mind me," Montgomery called over to us. "Carry on as you were and pretend I'm not here. *Easy Rider* chap, you were facing the other way."

"Yeah, I think you should face the other way as well, pal," Maddox shouted back at him before stomping towards him. "Want me to ram that brush up your backside?"

My fellow New Yorker wasn't the tallest of fellows, and had about as much aggression as Peppa Pig, so with the sight of this leather-clad hulk storming his way, he soon abandoned his latest muse and returned to his chair and easel. I took the interruption as my cue to leave, resuming my hike back to the bungalow.

Behind me, Maddox started up his bike once more and swiftly caught up with me. He shouted something to me, something muffled by his helmet and drowned by the engine. I replied with a shake of my head. Thankfully, he then sped off, at far too great a speed for these untreated roads. The squeal of his increasing revs carried through the air even when he was far beyond me, that attention-seeking sound that prats like him got off on.

Hey entire neighbourhood! Stop what you're doing and look at me. I'm riding a motorised form of transport with only two wheels!

When the peace returned, I filled my lungs with the frigid air and shivered. Okay, so maybe Maddox could kill my mood.

Silence greeted me when I stepped inside. In fact, it was *too* silent, no sound of a television turned up to a volume that a Spinal Tap guitarist would be proud of, no snoring from a geriatric lady having her midday nap.

The tree was half decorated. Not a bad effort, all things considered. She'd also laid out the strings of fairy lights across the floor. Tinsel draped over the furniture and mantle piece.

"Do you think it's time for some lunch?" I called out to Nan as I peeled off my coat and kicked off my shoes. As I peered through the doorway, I noticed the television was off, probably having gone into powersave mode once more from being idle.

"Cooey. Do we have a Dora McSnorer in the house?" I shouted, increasing the volume a notch. Again, my question was met with silence.

Inside the room I found Nan sprawled out on the sofa, her mouth hinged open like a flytrap as her head leant against the headrest, her feet up on her camel-shaped footstool. There was a bowl of warm water nearby, along with some nail scissors. Before cutting her toenails, she would always soak her feet first. Why she didn't dispense with that faff and just snip her nails like the rest of the population, I did not know. Perhaps old folks' nails were so tough and gnarly and in fifty years' time I would understand for myself what this process was all about.

"Who's the Sleeping Beauty now then?" I asked, again

pressing 'up' on my internal volume switch.

The recumbent elderly lady before me did not stir.

"Nan? Are you going to wake up, Nan?"

My mouth was dry, my heart shuddering beneath my rib cage.

Oh my God.

I peered ever closer. Why was she not snoring? Why was she not waking?

Oh please wake up.

"Nan!" I shouted, but the sound would not shake her awake as she continued to lie there like a stone. I couldn't detect any movement from her chest, couldn't hear any breaths being drawn into her lungs.

Please no, please no.

I was reaching for my phone when her eyes flicked open and she drew a garbled gulp of air down her throat.

"Oh hello," she said. "I wondered where you'd got to."

I collapsed onto the other sofa, my runaway pulse still pounding.

"Oh. My. Goodness. Talk about a *Bad Santa* moment."

"Say what?" she asked, before peering out the window. "Well, blow me, it's snowed."

"Right, I think I'm going to celebrate your prolonged existence by fixing us some sandwiches, and then I have the perfect film for us to watch this afternoon."

Bad Santa (2003)
Directed by Terry Zwigoff
Film Review by Hazel Nightingale

It's natural to view this black comedy and
wonder just what on earth is going on. Billy
Bob Thornton plays Willie, a safe-cracking
crook who works as a Santa in the shopping
mall that he and his cohort, the elfish Tony
Cox as Marcus, are planning to rob. Scene
after scene goes by of Willie's lousy
existence, his womanising, his drunkenness,
his foul language. He's a complete lost
cause, and that doubt begins to nag you: is
this film somewhat pointless too?

It's a deft move from the storytellers,
one you'd long given up on. Our bad Santa
befriends a bullied youngster who rescues him
from an attack. The kid rushed to the rescue
when he witnessed his beloved Santa in peril,
and Willie was quick to exploit his charity,
first robbing his house and taking off with
his father's car, and later even moving in
with him. With the kid's father in jail, his
only guardian is his elderly grandmother, who
is sadly no longer of sound mind. But now
he's got Santa looking over him.

We've seen the trope done so many times
before, the transformation the main character
undergoes in the festive season. Dickens
started it, and every other Hallmark movie
does it to death, the cold soul who's only
interested in money or building a new ski
resort or leaving their wife (or overcharging

Santa on his rent as in *The Christmas That Almost Wasn't*). But Christmas makes these characters change their ways. Christmas *saves* them.

And that's what happens here, but the lead-up is the antithesis of a Hallmark movie. It even turns model mum Lorelai Gilmore (Lauren Graham) into a breezy chick with a fetish for guys in a Santa costume. Along with this and enduring Willie's immoralities in technicolour detail, you'd be forgiven if you thought a part of you had been corrupted in the process too when you chuckle at him.

But even Willie's soul can be saved, and by the end the film pulls it around as he discovers some good, some meaning, within himself. And then you get it, then you realise where we were going this whole time, and you're grateful we did it without the schmaltz.

If you're a fan, you may be tempted to watch the sequel, *Bad Santa 2*, that came thirteen years later. All I would say is, don't bother. Have you ever wondered why Dickens never made a sequel to his beloved Christmas book? It's because it would have been pointless, because a follow-up that reuses that winning formula at the same time as properly *understanding* the original story is impossible.

In fact, *Bad Santa 2* only serves to make part 1 look even better. The first one worked so well because the film itself *knows* that, however indecent Willie gets, what he's doing is inappropriate. The sight of the drunken sleaze contrasts with the normal folk around him, regular upstanding mothers going shopping with their kids, appalled by the dishevelled and sweary Santa. Humour is built from that awkwardness.

The sequel, however, is more a juvenile celebration of Willie's badness, a pedestrian exercise in trying to be as crude as possible, and everyone else seems to join in with it. Yeah, he's back to his old ways, doing the same things he did before his redemption, rendering that whole journey pointless. It's a subtle ingredient, but without the fabric of decent folk and innocent children in Willie's world, you don't have that contrast, don't get that awkward feeling as he swears and shouts in front of them, for instance. Without that diversity of character, you merely end up with screwball nonsense.

Verdict: 9 / 10 (for part 1 in case you were wondering).

Chapter 17

THE ROLES HAD REVERSED. I arrived at the Kinema a good ten minutes before the start of the film. Hovering outside the entrance for a few moments, stomping my feet to generate some warmth (the snow had largely sustained throughout the day), I wondered if Eddy had turned up before me and was in his seat again waiting for me. Should I send him a text? There had been no more from him since the one he'd sent last night. Perhaps he'd been so busy today and just didn't have the time.

Seeing as I had a ticket, and this was exactly the sort of eventuality he'd prepared for, I decided it made sense to head on inside. I got myself a hot chocolate to defrost myself, along with some more candy, wondering why I'd mentally called it *candy* rather than *sweets*. Two evenings spent with an American and I'd already picked up the lingo.

Eddy wasn't here yet. I took my seat on the back row just as the Pearl and Dean trailers were beginning. I again checked my phone to see if there were any messages, but there was nothing, so I switched it to silent and left it upturned on my thigh. He'd reserved the two seats on the end of the row. Had he suspected he'd be held up tonight?

We were about fifteen minutes into the film when a man in a dragon mask appeared.

After swiftly sitting down next to me, he leant his head close to my ear, almost as though he was nuzzling me.

"Sorry I'm late. Crazy, crazy day today."

"That's okay," I whispered to him. "You made it in the end. Emilia Clarke is a screwup, nowhere to live, then she met a nice chap called Tom."

With that catch-up, I put any more conversation on hold until the intermission. Cinema visits were perfect for first dates where chatter may stutter and awkward silences occur. But tonight I just felt frustrated, like I had to rest my tongue and wait for these fictional characters to work out their own romance first.

So there we sat, our mouths closed, our eyes directed at the screen rather than at each other. Eddy rested his hand on my hand as it lay on the armrest, his thumb slowly caressing my skin.

I couldn't help but wonder what he'd been filming today. Evidently, this film we were making was a wartime love story, but I didn't know if it was PG rated or what. What words had been manufactured from his lips earlier, what tenderness had he displayed to another woman? Was it easy for him to switch from that fiction to this reality?

Come the mid-point of the showing, Eddy clenched his fist in an exaggerated display of triumph as the wurlitzer appeared from the centre of the stage. Appropriately, the organist kicked off the performance with *Winter Wonderland*.

"How did filming go today?" I asked.

"The snow messed things up for us."

I hadn't anticipated that. One just expected these Hollywood filmmakers to wield some sort of divine power over everything to make it precisely as they wanted, prepared for anything. A simple change in weather could cause a headache. If there's one thing you can't rely on in England, it's the weather.

"Is that what held you up?"

"Yeah, that and the agent. He phoned as I was walking over here. Sore with me because I still haven't done that tape."

Oh my goodness.

It suddenly struck me, what an influence I was playing on his life, on his career. Without me around distracting him, he could have recorded that blasted tape by now. And who knew what it would mean for him, maybe his first Oscar award? But no, he'd sneaked off to the cinema with Hazel Nightingale, unemployed film critic from the Lincolnshire wilds.

"What film is it for, anyway?" I asked.

He shook his head, his gaze still fixed on the wurlitzer. "Nah it's TV. Some new series Ricky Parkinson is making."

"Oh my giddy aunt. Ricky Parkinson?" Earlier in the year, the man in question had released a film on one of the streaming services, *Cyber Conversion*, nicely timed for the April Oscar nominations. It had been a massive hit, creating an exciting buzz much like Tarantino had created when he first emerged. Parkinson was just *cool*.

I sensed underneath Eddy's mask he was grimacing. "I haven't even seen that *Doctor Who* rip-off he made yet."

"That's no excuse. Right, you need to sort out this tape as soon as you get in. I'm not seeing you again until you've done it."

"Do you want to help me with it, then?"

"Help you... like read the other lines against you?"

"It's a monologue. I was thinking you holding the camera."

"Sure, yeah. I'm no Federico Fellini though, apparently."

"As long as you frame it reasonably and tap record. You're a film critic, so I assume you can discern what constitutes a good shot."

"And do you have a camera?" I asked.

"I have an iPhone."

"And that's what you normally use?"

"I'm an actor, not Stanley Kubrick."

"Right. Sure. Let's shoot this."

Wow. If I wrote Christmas letters to friends and family, this past week would certainly have provided the ingredients for an epic. As we resumed watching the rest of *Last Christmas*, I couldn't stop thinking about it.

Presumably we were going to record this at the Petwood? Perhaps up in Eddy's room?

The cloud of Maddox continued to lurk in my mind, like I knew exactly what he'd say to me.

Right, you fell for the old I-need-to-make-a-self-tape routine? Come up to my bedroom why don't you, pretty lady, and we'll make some magic together.

Surely if he'd wanted that groupie kind of lifestyle, Eddy would have opted for a career in rock 'n roll rather than acting. A guy like this wouldn't spend his time watching that offbeat film last night if he was just trying to get me into bed. And if fate *did* have in store for me being used by someone, then you'd want to have someone like Eddy Partridge doing that, right?

"So what location are we using for our little production?" I asked him as we shuffled outside amid the throng of cinema-goers, a feel-good spirit in the air after watching that bittersweet romance.

"I'll need to head back to the hotel. I had my lines printed out and I need another look at them."

"Do you want me to drive us up there?" We continued to follow the crowd towards the car park. The Petwood grounds butted with the cinema's, but to traverse between them you would take the road round.

"Nah. Found a shortcut."

"Right."

I'd seen enough horror films to recognise that heading into the woods at night was how it always started, but Eddy seemed to know what he was doing. He activated the torch app on his phone as he hurdled over the car park barrier, pausing to hold my hand as I swung my legs over it.

160

"Are you sure we can get this way?" I couldn't resist asking him.

"We'll be there in seconds."

It was eerie, but also exciting. In that moment, I realised the frisson Eddy brought to everything, that larger-than-life quality. Even something as trivial as walking up the road to a hotel could have a little excitement injected into it, transforming it into a mini adventure. I supposed things like this were second nature; Guys like him wouldn't get through life by going by the beaten path. Before we knew it, we emerged into the walled garden in the corner of the Petwood grounds.

"Ooh, this is where my friend got married," I remarked, remembering that summer's day from years ago. They'd filled the area with chairs covered with elegant satin sashes, beautiful arrangements of pink flowers that echoed the in-bloom rhododendrons of the gardens. It was strange to see it empty and blanketed with snow, the moonlight bouncing off it like a magical glow. Celebration was in hibernation, fairies and sprites the only residents, besides me and Eddy.

"Cool. What friend was this?"

"Yes, I know you might find it hard to believe, but I actually do have some real friends, all non-imaginary. Mostly. She was an old classmate."

"Still see her?"

"No, she moved away. You know what it's like when people get married. They change."

We paused on the platform beneath the pavilion where the wedding aisle would end and vows would be made.

"So tell me more about yourself, Miss Nightingale. I hardly know much at all. Don't have the benefit of checking you out on Wikipedia."

"Have you been cyber-stalking me, Mr Partridge?" I asked in playful accusation, my eyes narrowing.

"Come on, you're at a distinct advantage over me."

"What would you like to know?"

"Well, why we're on the subject of marriage..."

"I think us getting engaged is a *tad* premature. Come on, we need to go on at least four cinema dates before that."

Now he was no longer wearing his mask, I could see the smirk.

"And previously...?"

"Nope. Never been married. Or engaged, although I suspect the ex was planning it."

"You grew up round here, yes? And you live with your grandmother, right? No parents on the scene?"

"They're both gone," I said, staring at my shoes.

"I'm sorry."

I perched down on the steps while Eddy leant against one of the pavilion columns.

"Gone in different senses, that is. Dad left when I was four, cleared off back up north. I haven't heard from him in years. He could be dead too, for all I'm aware."

"So your grandmother became your guardian after your mother passed?"

"That's right, both my grandparents. I spent my first nine years in Boston, but me and my little sister Phillipa went to live with them in New York. My brother was old enough to get his own place by then."

"I assume these were your mother's parents."

I nodded.

"So what about this ex? What..."

"He's a twit," I said, cutting him off. "I'm a Gemini, my shoe size is six, I'm double-jabbed with Pfizer, only three points on my driving licence, and I've never seen an episode of *Line of Duty*. Think that's about everything. Oh, and those points expire soon."

Nodding as though that was *exactly* what he wanted to know, he asked, "What were they for?"

"Running a red. I lived in London. Everyone has points

down there."

"Sorry, it's second nature for me, asking questions. Comes with the job. Us actors, we like to get under the skin, to really understand people, getting our grasp on characters."

"Well, I wouldn't say you were *getting under my skin*, Mr Partridge," I said. "Not *quite* yet." The little imp inside was making her appearance again.

"All right, I'll stop with the third degree."

I didn't mind, really. It was rather humbling that someone like him would take such an interest in my life, especially when I hadn't lived the exciting kind of life he had. Nothing happens in my New York. Our theme song could have been that record by Del Amitri, but even in *Nothing Ever Happens*, with its secretaries switching off typewriters and its billboard advertisements, there's way too much happening. The music video did feature morris dancers, however, which hit the mark when it came to my nan.

"Come on," he said, trotting down the steps and extending a hand to me. I grabbed it and he pulled me to my feet. "Let's get in the warmth."

We trailed across the lawns, still hand in hand, reaching the cherub in the frozen fountain. A small icicle hung from the trident he clutched. The path beyond him leading up to the hotel had been cleared, so we made a gentle stroll along it.

Once we reached the terrace, Eddy tried the door to the lounge, but it was locked. I didn't study it in great detail, but through the window, I noticed the room was filled with familiar looking flight cases. Maybe this was where the crew stored their stuff at night. We walked round the building to the main entrance. Stepping past the empty front desk, Eddy pointed up the stairs to indicate the direction we were going. I caught glimpses of the Lancaster paintings and aviation relics within the glass cabinets as we walked along.

On the first floor, we encountered a hefty figure in a high vis jacket as he sat there in the hall watching Netflix on his phone. As soon as he heard our footsteps, he turned round and got to his feet.

"Hey there, Bowman," Eddy said to him, exchanging a fist bump.

"Hey Eddy," the security guy replied, his eyes darting to me, his brain immediately computing that, although I was a stranger, I was evidently in the company of the man he was protecting. I was certain that, unaccompanied, the guy would have swiftly evicted me.

"Calling it a night now," Eddy said.

"Sweet dreams," the guard replied before getting back to his phone.

"Wow. You got the honeymoon suite then," I said as we entered Eddy's room. He illuminated the chandelier hanging from the ceiling, throwing light on the elegant four-poster bed in front of us, an emerald chaise longue beside it.

"I guess." He tossed his key onto a cabinet and picked up a sheet of paper.

I sat down on a chair by the window that must have offered a wonderful view of the garden in the daylight.

"Just need a few minutes to walk these in," Eddy said as he read the lines of his audition piece, pacing up and down the room, silently mouthing the words.

I nodded in reply, afraid to distract him. His eyes looked sharp, despite the late hour of a long day. I felt as though I would fall asleep the moment I closed my eyes.

After about ten minutes, he said, "All right," before reaching into his pocket, activating the camera function on his phone and handing it to me. "Tap that button to record."

"Got it." Like the rest of the world in the 2020s, I'd held a mobile phone in my hand countless times before, yet this time it was as though I was holding a powerful weapon. I gulped. If I were to scroll through its address book, just who else's numbers would I find? I was a couple of screen taps away from being connected to the likes of Tom Cruise or J.J. Abrams. And what about his photo gallery? I proper felt like Michael McIntyre with the power to execute another embarrassing Send To All routine.

"Where are you going to be?" I asked, swiftly trying to put my mind into filmmaker mode, summoning some aesthetic appreciation as I analysed the shot before me, when really all I perhaps needed to do was to stop my hands from shaking.

"I'm going to walk around so keep up with me."

"Okay, move a few paces back, let's get some more light on you."

Another moment I did not see coming before the end of this year, or indeed at any point in my life; I just totally directed Eddy Partridge!

It all ended so soon. Somehow this was a one take deal, Eddy content with his performance off the bat, or perhaps he just wasn't feeling this project, wasn't too bothered about securing this role. Perhaps the asking for help was his way to lure me up to his room. If that was the case, someone really needed to tell him he needn't have weaved such a ruse.

"Want to watch this?" I asked him, feeling like a school kid looking for affirmation from the teacher about her work. Eddy didn't seem too fussed about viewing it, but anyway, we both sat back on the bed as we watched the playback, me scrutinising my rudimentary camera skills, he his world class craft.

"Yeah, that's great," he said halfway through, fluffing up

his pillows before stretching out and finally relaxing for the day. We weren't far off midnight now. I should have got up to go home, but, the truth was, this bed was too comfy.

"I accept it wasn't quite..." I began, trying to think of a film, any film, to compare it to, but my mind was flagging.

"*The Christmas That Almost Wasn't?*"

"Well, nothing can be quite like that one."

"It was just what I wanted. Thanks, Hazel."

"You're welcome. I work on a modest five percent commission."

"Five percent? Sounds like a bargain." His words were slurring, his eyes were heavy.

My car was still parked at the Kinema. Was I going to retrace my footsteps through the garden and the woods? Or would I walk back along the road? Either one seemed like a long trek, and I was sure Eddy would be asleep before I opened the door. Staying where I was seemed so much more attractive a proposition.

Staying there on that bed was exactly what I did.

Chapter 18

THE SOUND WAS SO CONFUSING, beginning in the dreamscape I was lost within, continuing as it dragged me into reality.

Although I didn't know what was creating the clamour of that electronic beeping, my eyes swept round my surroundings, searching for the source. I felt a tickling on my arm, a vibration emanating intermittently.

You're still in his room, Hazel. On his bed!

Next to me was Eddy, and it seemed he was only a few seconds behind me in reaching consciousness. Between our prostrate bodies was his phone laying on the duvet, having a fit.

Luckily, it had woken us so I could get on home. I wondered who might be calling him. Someone from America, perhaps, who hadn't realised he was in a time zone five to eight hours ahead?

His eyes coming into focus, Eddy muttered something before grabbing the phone and killing the noise. His head fell straight down again.

"Who was it?" I asked.

"It was my alarm," he spoke into his pillow.

"Alarm?"

I felt so confused. Surely we'd both just nodded off? It felt like only a few minutes ago that we were watching his audition tape. It was still so dark outside too, as though it was the middle of the night. But when I snatched the phone from his hand, I saw it was half five in the morning.

I'd been there all night! Suddenly feeling much more awake, I sprang from the bed, my head spinning from rising too quickly.

Had we..?

No. We were both still wearing the clothes we'd gone to

the cinema in. Any 'sleeping with' that had transpired in this honeymoon suite was literally just that, a suspension of our consciousness in a mutual location. But still... I had to admit, it was rather cool. I could brag without lie that I had slept with a Hollywood superstar.

The circumstance seemed to ring a faint bell in my brain. Had I seen something along these lines played out in a television show, two youngsters out on a date perhaps, and they'd fallen asleep instead of coming home? If so, I really needed to stop plagiarising other people's narratives. Not that I would return to an angry guardian in my case. At thirty years, I was a big enough girl to have the right to do this sort of thing. And besides, it was highly unlikely Nan had even noticed my absence.

"Eddy, I'm going to have to go."

It looked like he'd fallen back asleep, although he managed some sort of indecipherable groan.

I had a nagging worry I needed to check on Nan, that she was in trouble having tripped over, and had been calling out for me for the last five hours. Yesterday's plan had been to get her to bed and ensure her pills went down her throat. Instead, I'd spent the night in a hotel room. With a guy. Boy, I really was the worst carer in the world.

"I've got to be back here for seven," I told him, conscious of every second going by. I had to return to New York and reset, make sure all was a-okay at base.

Eddy muttered something again.

"What?"

He turned his head round and said, "I'll walk with you."

"Come on, then."

The security man Bowman remained at his little station in the hall, continuing to gaze at his phone like he'd been binge watching *Bodyguard* or *Brooklyn Nine-Nine* or whatever. As we reached him, I caught a quick glimpse of the screen, a figure in a red jumpsuit in frame. Of course.

Squid Game.

"Morning Bowman," Eddy said.

"Good morning," I said to the man, too. I'd never had the luxury of a guard looking over my quarters all night. I proper felt like royalty. And no wonder I'd slept so soundly.

I'd seen *Notting Hill*, so I knew the intrigue this scenario conveyed, Eddy Partridge emerging from his hotel bedroom with a young lady in tow. I had the sense, however, this Bowman guy was a professional and would not be selling the story to the tabloids. Hopefully.

Damn. *Notting Hill*. That was yet another narrative I'd stolen.

After descending the staircase, I took a deep breath before we stepped outside. To my relief, there were no flashes, no mass of paparazzi waiting for us, no cameras thrusting into our faces. This was still mine and Eddy's little secret. Well, and Bowman's too.

"You won't forget to send that video to your agent now, will you?" I asked as we scooted across the lawn, crusty snow covering it. It seemed we were taking Eddy's shortcut. Made sense, really. "Get it sent before you get to work."

"I sure will, Miss Nightingale."

"So... am I going to see you on set today?"

He turned to me, looking me over to gauge exactly what I meant by that.

"Can't make a love story without a love interest."

So... yes?

"And afterwards?"

"They're playing *Elf* tonight." He'd put extra inflection on the title.

"Do you mean to imply you don't like that film?"

He squinted. "It's o-*kay.*"

"Well, I'm sorry, Mr Partridge, but that is a total deal-breaker right there. Don't like *Elf;* How can anyone say such a thing?"

"Fancy getting something to eat instead?"

"Okay, that might make it up to me, but I want you to think about what you said, mister."

"You got it."

We'd reached the trees by the walled garden and he switched on his torch app to guide us through. There was only one car in the cinema car park.

"There he is," Eddy said. "Clarence, right?"

"Well, let's not dwell on that," I replied. "Thanks for walking me here. I'd better go."

I turned to leave, ever conscious of all I had to do before returning here for my 7am call time.

"Wait," he whispered, grabbing my hand.

I twirled around and he dragged me closer, my body colliding with his, before his lips connected with mine. All of a sudden, I was in absolutely no rush.

The reflected light in my rear-view mirror dazzled me. Pulling out the keys, I climbed out of the car onto the drive and turned round to investigate. A motorbike had pulled up behind me, the rider flicking out the stand as he removed his helmet.

"So where have you been, you dirty stop-out?"

I shook my head. I had no time for this, and certainly not without any caffeine in my system.

"Get lost, Maddox. Have you been stalking the village all night looking for me or something?" I turned from him, searching out my door key. The Christmas lights that I'd put up in the living room window were on. I doubted Nan had switched them on first thing after rising; most likely she'd left them on overnight.

"It's getting serious then, is it?" he asked, opening my

car door to have a peek inside, perhaps looking for evidence of what I'd been up to, as though I'd reverted to being a jejune teenager fumbling around on the back seat. The guy was acting way too creepy now. I'd never seen anything like this in him before. What was he trying to achieve? I pushed the door shut again and clicked the clicker to lock it.

"None of your business," I replied, swinging round and marching away.

"It's true then. You really have gone from Claudia Winkleman to Claudia Cardinale."

"What are you on about?"

"I've been reading about your little film venture," he said, producing a copy of the local newspaper, *The Lincolnshire Echo*, from his backpack. "What's it called? *Memphis Belle Episode 2: The Third Reich Strikes Back*?"

"Oh, whatever."

"It's got Janice Daniels in it, I see. And Eddy Partridge."

I felt a flutter in my stomach on hearing his name uttered out loud, shaded with unease at it coming from this Neanderthal. It was like he'd sullied the name just by spitting it off his tongue. Had he worked it out? Had he possibly spied us at the cinema?

"And then it mentions," he went on, "that some locals have been working as extras on it. So that's you, right? And that's how you met your new flame, I presume, and he's apparently a *thespian* now, not some ten-a-penny background loser."

I opened my mouth to reply, but stopped myself. It made sense for him to believe this mistaken theory. Besides, he surely wouldn't believe me if I told him I'd just been kissing the leading man.

"Well, it's nice to know that's how you see me," I said, folding my arms. "Which begs the question, why are you so intent on wooing me back if I'm merely a *background loser*?"

"This isn't you. You've lost sight of everything. You were someone down in London. Don't become some Lincolnshire deadbeat."

I rolled my eyes. Being able to see through his attempts to manipulate made him look such a sad case.

He sighed, switching the tone in his voice, putting on the tenderness, but it all sounded so fake. "Come on, Haze. What more do I need to do to prove it to you? I love you, babe."

I didn't believe it. The only person he loved was himself. Maddox had demonstrated his tenacious ability to persuade others, what with that 'job' of his, tricking victims over the telephone as he fleeced their bank accounts. He knew how to put on the act, and so you couldn't accept a word he said.

Never trust an actor, eh, Hazel? Unless he's a famous movie star, right?

"You think this is endearing? It's barely six in the morning and you turn up on my doorstep like this. Let it go, Maddox. Please, just let it go."

I expected him to continue with his not-so-gentle persuasion as I span away and strode up to the door. As I unlocked it and stepped inside, I glanced back to see him standing there silently, the rolled up newspaper clutched in his gloved hand, a photo of Eddy on the front page. I slammed the door shut.

"Hazel? Hazel, is that you, duck?"

"Yeah, it's me," I shouted towards the living room, but I doubted Nan had heard me.

"You're up early," she said as I walked into the room. "Sleep okay?" I was sure she hadn't realised I'd only just arrived home, believing I'd risen from my bed down the hall three seconds ago.

"Slept rather well, actually. How are you? Had a good evening?"

"Oh, well, you know." And by that she meant: *I can't*

remember.

"Let me fix us a brew."

In the kitchen, I discovered untaken pills. Ah crap. I absolutely was neglecting my duties, allowing the hormones to cloud my judgement. Maybe Maddox was right. Maybe this thing with Eddy was turning me into something else.

I heard his bike starting up, the ensuing roar as he zipped away down the road. My shoulders eased, the knot in my stomach loosening.

After a coffee and fulfilling my catering and nursing duties, I whipped on some clean clothes and got ready for another day of being a loser extra. Somehow I'd completed all that in time, and set off with a whole twenty minutes to get back to the Petwood.

As I turned round in my seat to reverse, I spotted a figure at the end of the drive, someone walking their two border collies. He waved at me and walked up beside the car.

"Now then, Hazel, I'm glad I caught you." It was Mr Baker, the local busybody. He wore his usual tweed blazer the colour of dishwater, a pin badge of the county flag on a lapel, Hunter wellies on his feet, a flat cap on his bonce. Everything about his look screamed *stereotypical Lincolnshire,* and he had the Yellowbelly twang in his voice to go with it.

"Hi, Cliff. Sorry, I'm in a bit of a rush..."

"Oh, well, I just wanted a quick word. Won't be a second."

I swallowed back my sigh.

"You see, being on the committee for Best Kept Village, you appreciate how we're keen to keep the neighbourhood looking spick-and-span, everything in order."

"Oookay..." I replied, trying to fast-forward him on.

He peered back along the drive. "And I couldn't help but notice, with collection day yesterday, you're yet to fetch in

173

your recycling wheelie bin."

He was right. There it stood by the roadside. Was that really it? *That's* what he was holding me up for? A flipping wheelie bin?

"You know what, Cliff? Let me get onto that this second." I left the car running as I got out.

"The council guidelines state that you should return it from the front of your property the same day it's collected."

Why the heck was everyone so *on* at this unsociable time?

"Absolutely. Understood."

There you go, Hazel. Your standards are slipping yet again. Can't even employ basic wheelie bin etiquette.

"I don't mind it being out the evening before, because I realise they sometimes come early, so I'll let that slide. But we'd really like to avoid a row of bins lining up the streets like some council slum. You appreciate how that doesn't look so good."

He continued prattling on as I strode up the drive to gather in my offending waste receptacle.

"I will make sure this doesn't happen again next week," I shot at him as I carted the bin away. There were other shots I could have fired that would have caused more damage, like airing out loud the vicious rumour concerning the Bakers: *You're not actually a native New Yorker, are you, Cliff? In fact, weren't you born somewhere over the border in Leicestershire?*

"Thanks, Hazel," he called out. "Lovely to see you back again, by the way. And don't forget the changes later in the month. We have a different collection day the week before Christmas."

"I will make a note in my diary."

Already I was disappearing up the side of the bungalow, wheeling the bin away to sit with the others beside the 'scrapyard' of the back garden. Dominating that area was a rusty old camper van that hadn't moved from its spot in twenty years.

Once out of sight of him, I clenched my fists and growled through my gritted teeth.

"Why were you late for work this morning, Hazel? Ah, I just had to make sure my wheelie bin was positioned correctly."

This village really had the knack of bringing you back down to its flat earth.

Chapter 19

"FEWER OF US TODAY," I remarked to Melissa as we joined the short queue for the refreshments van. I couldn't see my fellow extras Gale or Franklin anywhere, no seasoned professional Leonard either, but one couldn't miss Seymour, who was full of energy as ever, his chuckle carrying across the car park.

Our costumes differed from the ones we'd worn earlier in the week, swiftly put on us first thing. I was in a casual yellow dress with sharp shoulder pads, Melissa in a tan playsuit. Presumably we were still the same village characters, but this would be a different day and possibly a new location.

"That's a good thing, though," she replied. "Won't be lost in the crowd so much. Be easier to spot ourselves."

"Good point. But best of all, we get to the drinks quicker," I said as we reached the barista, who prepared us some lattes.

"Hey, did you hear on the radio this morning?" Melissa asked me as we sat down on the bus. "They were talking about Eddy Partridge. Word on the street is he's been going to the Kinema all week."

"No, didn't catch that one," I replied casually, pretending not to be too interested, even though my pulse was instantly racing at the mention of his name. "I'm tuned into the BBC station."

"This was on Begley's show. He had some local on the line who reckons she saw him, said he wore his mask all the while, not because it's a covid thing, but so people wouldn't recognise him."

"I suppose it's possible," I answered, employing some fake scepticism in my tone. *Just as well we weren't planning to go there again tonight!* "I wonder if he might pop to your dad's place for a pint some time."

"Oh, that would be so cool. I could like proper *talk* to him then. Wouldn't be breaking any rules. You know, it's going to seem really boring round here when they all disappear. Wish this would go on for longer."

"Yeah. Me too."

I hadn't allowed myself to think that far ahead, so caught up in the exciting moment I was in, but she was right. Before I knew it, and presumably before Christmas, they would up sticks and fly back to the States. What then? What of me and Eddy? Was there even enough time in the amount fate had handed us to turn our thing into something tangible? How could I even consider that a possibility when we were from such different worlds? Sure, it had worked out for Hugh Grant and Julia Roberts in the end, but I couldn't tell if we were headed in a similar direction. A famous actor and a film critic? Shouldn't we be mortal enemies?

Not with that review you wrote on his film, Hazel!

"One of the assistants told me we're filming here at the Petwood today," Melissa said.

"Yeah, last night they looked like they were setting up in the lounge area," I replied, recalling what I'd seen as we'd strolled up to the hotel.

"Oh, right..."

Oh no. What had I just said?

Melissa frowned. "How did you..?"

Come on, Hazel. How are you going to answer this one? Think of something!

My mouth opened as I took a deep breath, but no words came off my tongue, my head empty.

"Good morning, Rosie Riveters," Seymour greeted us with bubbling enthusiasm, derailing that conversation. "We ready to kick some more Nazi backsides today?"

"We absolutely are," I replied, my brain now working

again.

Nice one. Saved by the Seymour.

When not being used as a film set, the Squadron Bar at the Petwood hosted a range of Dambusters memorabilia. I didn't know whether Eddy's character was part of the squadrons that were based in this building, but I suspected the location was doubling for somewhere else.

Whatever, it was a much more intimate atmosphere compared to the Christmas party of my other scene. As usual, they arranged the supporting artists around the set. They separated me and Melissa, her at the other end of the room again, me sitting at a table beside the crackling fireplace.

"Hi there, I'm Bruce. Ground crew," an extra said to introduce himself, smiling in amusement at the make-believe of portraying a member of the wartime RAF. He sat down opposite me.

"Hazel. Hi," I replied.

He seemed a spunky chap, full of smiles, but I could detect the *type* of smiles he was flashing my way, the ones you get when someone suspects fair game and sets out to chat you up.

Bruce, please, you have to be way further up the echelons to stand a chance with me, darling.

Eddy was the first of the 'foreground performers' to appear on set, along with two other young chaps who walked with a swagger that suggested they, too, were *proper* actors with lines to deliver. I didn't recognise either of them, so wouldn't know if a gig like this was small fry for them or the pinnacle of their careers so far. Good old Seymour was positioned amongst them, but more to the back seeing that his participation in this production was somewhere between background extra and main cast.

Bruce was trying to impress me by reeling off the myriad productions he'd been in. "And then there was the *David Copperfield* film we filmed up in Grimsby. No, Hull, that one was, sorry. If you pause the video when Micawber first stops outside the pawnshop at about thirty-three minutes in, you'll see me on the edge of the screen in a top hat and red coat."

Bruce, my dear, have you ever been on the front cover of Rolling Stone magazine? Did you ever go on The Late Late Show with James Corden? No? Just a smudge of pixels, then? I'm feeling a Shania Twain song coming on, so why don't you save your breath?

"That's cool," I said, or rather, I *acted*.

I glanced aside. Eddy stood within his group of aircrew as they limbered up for the first take. He caught my stare, gave me a quick wink that was unnoticed by everyone else in the room.

I was certain Bruce hoped he was the cause of the smile that blossomed on my face. This only seemed to spur him on to convey more impressive facts to me.

Gazing around the set, he said, "It's quite remarkable the integration you saw within the RAF in the war. Do you know much about Gerrick James?"

"Who?"

He pointed to the airmen. "Eddy Partridge's character. One of the *pilots of the Caribbean*."

"Oh, is that his name?"

"The Yanks brought their Jim Crow over here and kept their black GIs separate. Poor chaps were fighting it on both sides, quite literally if you were up at Bamber Bridge. The Royal Air Force, on the other hand, eventually realised it was best not to tolerate that nonsense. They lifted the colour bar so you saw the West Indians integrated with our own boys. Our country gets things right sometimes. Only fair when they volunteered to help us."

"I think if I lived in the Caribbean I'd be rather inclined to stay there rather than..."

"Coming to fight the master race from snowy England? The book I'm reading on Gerrick said how he wanted to stand up to the bully. They were afraid that once Britain fell, they would be next, and slavery would be back in fashion."

I leant a little closer to him. Perhaps I was taking a shine to this fountain-of-knowledge guy after all. "So, do you know the story of Eddy's character? Like, what became of him?"

"That's the fascinating thing..."

An AD interrupted him, approaching our table. "Sorry, Bruce, we're going to have to move you."

"Blast," he said in mock disappointment. "You had my best side from this angle."

"The director wants you over here."

"Right at the back? That's showbiz. Cold and brutal sometimes. Anyway, nice talking to you, Hazel."

"And you."

I expected the ADs would direct someone else over to my table, but for whatever reason known only to the film producer gods, the seat remained empty and I would be the lonely lady in the corner. I would have liked Bruce to sit with me so I could continue picking his brain. His nerdy nature was actually proving to be rather useful. At least I had a front row ticket to witness whatever information this scene had to reveal.

An operation was imminent, another bombing raid, and I suspected from their performances that this was a significant one within the narrative of our film. Eddy was on edge, or rather Gerrick James was. He didn't have a good feeling about this one, his sixth. The number six had always been an inauspicious number for this man, so he confided in his amour Polly, played of course by Janice Daniels. But Gerrick would do his duty. He would enter the theatre once more. That's why he'd sailed across the Atlantic after seeing that recruitment poster. The motherland needed help.

His Most Gracious Majesty King George calls on the men of his Empire, of every class, creed and colour, to come forward to fight.

I made a mental note to ask Eddy if he had many scenes to shoot with the Lancaster in flight. I remembered reading in our local papers about a film shot by some independent filmmakers in Sleaford involving that particular bomber. They'd built their own replica, so presumably this production would follow the same principle, filming in a studio rather than a real Lancaster. There was only one airworthy plane in England, based with the Battle of Britain Memorial Flight at Coningsby, but this was a treasured relic, not a toy for filmmakers to borrow. Maybe they could get shots of it taxiing at least.

The props department had handed me a newspaper dated December 1942. Although there were genuine articles on it from the time, I only pretended to read it, my mind's focus fixed on the action taking place nearby.

With several takes captured from their initial camera angle, the crew began to set up for another.

The actors at ease, a figure sat down in the empty chair opposite me, and as I raised my head, I saw him doing up a shoelace that didn't need doing up.

"You'll be glad to know I sent it," Eddy muttered under his breath, his eyes still fixed on his shoe.

"The audition tape? Pleased to hear." I fixed my gaze on the newspaper on my lap, mirroring his body language in not suggesting we were in conversation with each other, our secret connection going under the radar. Janice had stepped off set. It felt like we were conducting an affair here, me stealing her man.

"So, are you not coming back from this mission?" I asked him.

"No."

It's just a film, Hazel. It's not real, not for Eddy.

I could not help the feeling of loss, however, my fortune having some weird dependency on someone else's story from eighty years ago. My rational brain told me this moment in the narrative was only what was taking place today. I realised it was highly unlikely this would be Eddy's final scene. They typically shot films out of sequence, although, granted, they did shoot in sequence sometimes. But even if he had more scenes slated, at an airfield or within his Lancaster, it was a certainty they wouldn't require my anonymous villager character decorating the background.

But what if this *was* his last scene on location in Lincolnshire? If only Gerrick had a longer story to tell and then Eddy would stay here longer. But because some random Nazi pilot or some flak gunner had shot him down, it could well spell the end of this thing we had going on. My love life was at the mercy of whichever scriptwriter had penned this film.

"Are you flying back to America soon?"

It was a blunt question, but I needed to ask it.

"Not yet, no," he replied, the words carrying faintly on his breath like he was talking to himself. "There's something else I need to deal with." He stepped away from my table, submerging himself back into the fray of film production.

Chapter 20

"WHAT'S THIS?" EDDY ASKED AS I handed him a small gift wrapped with a foil bow.

"I have it on good authority that people may be seeing past your disguise, mister Hollywood superstar."

He immediately unwrapped it as we stood by the Dambusters Memorial in the centre of Woodhall Spa. Earlier, he'd warned me he might be held up, so I'd been waiting at our rendezvous point for over fifteen minutes. It was far from being a dark and deserted village tonight though, the villagers milling past as they investigated the stalls and activities of the Christmas Fayre, excited little boys and girls holding onto the hand of a parent as they made their way to Santa's grotto. Fairground rides filled the car park of Melissa's pub, their flashing lights complementing the strings of lights across the main road. Carol singers sang *O Holy Night*, one of my favourite festive tunes. You couldn't help but smile, seeing the community being able to do the things we used to do before, a distinct magic in the air.

"And again, what's this?" A frowning Eddy held up a face mask.

"That there is the Lincolnshire flag." It was embroidered on the material. "Now you'll blend right in with all of us."

"Right, because every third native round here wears one of these."

"And later I'll teach you the lingo. Tates and mizzling and gettin' frit."

"*More* words to remember?"

"Ditch that dragon mask, mister. They're onto you."

"All right, all right." He was willing to play ball, wrapping the new one over his face.

"Perfect. Suits you. Now we can check out the Fayre. Or maybe grab a pint in *The Mall*? You never know, you could be an answer to a question if it's quiz night there."

"You hungry?"

"Not really." I hadn't been hungry all week, my stomach full of butterflies. Actually, that seemed too tame. More like a stomach full of bats.

"I did eat quite a lot at lunch, actually. Were those Lincolnshire sausages today?"

"Yes, a superb choice of local cuisine. You should be grateful they didn't pick chine."

We were already making our way towards the stalls, as though they'd caught us in their gravitational pull. As we melted into the crowd, we mooched along the road past artisan food stands and tombolas.

"Mulled wine," Eddy said as we walked by a stall selling drinks. "Sounds nice."

"Yes. If you enjoy drinking your own vomit, then it would certainly be up your street."

"So that's a rain check then."

The hook-a-duck stand next piqued his curiosity, and we paused by the trough of ducks as he observed someone else having a go. A girl hooked a plastic yellow duck, whipping it from the water, the man on the stand then presenting her with the prize of a small teddy, something that looked more expensive than it probably was.

"This I need to try," Eddy announced, handing the man some coins.

I experienced a flashback, recalling that time Maddox and I had visited a fete down in Sumpton, and he'd won that giant orange bear that I couldn't bring myself to part with. It certainly wasn't because it was my unconscious way of holding on to our relationship. The more time I spent with this American, the more I realised I was completely over him.

Eddy chose his duck, hooking it with his fishing rod (or ducking rod?) then hoisted it into the air. The flat cap-wearing carny checked the underneath of the waterfowl, but it was unmarked. Eddy tried again, producing the same result. His third and final try was a success, however, the carny presenting him with a knock-off teddy in the form of a carrot-nosed snowman character.

"Jeez, I wonder what this is ripping off," he remarked before offering his spoils to me.

I placed my palm on my chest, my eyes and jaw opening wide. "For me? Why, thank you, brave hunter." We walked on from the river of ducks. "I think I shall call him Ol*eg*."

Eddy chuckled.

Farther up the street, on The Broadway, I could hear the unmistakable sound of bells jingling and wooden sticks clanking.

"Now here's a perfect taste of English eccentricity," I said to my foreign companion. "Morris dancing."

"I don't even..." he muttered, his head cocked.

"My nan does this, you know?"

"Awesome. I have to meet your nan. You speak so fondly of her."

"Yeah, I suppose she ain't so bad."

Something took Eddy's attention away from the folk dance as he peered across the street.

"As much as I love my new mask," he said. "I'm doubtful it quite has the efficacy you'd hoped for."

I followed his gaze to see a bunch of teenaged girls gawping our way, or rather Eddy's way. They stood by a cart selling roasted chestnuts, munching sweets and drinking hot chocolate.

"Blast. It could be that cap of yours, you know. What is that, a New York football team or something?"

"I guess you'll have to get me a Lincoln City hat for Christmas."

"Want to split?"

"Hey how about you show me New York like you promised?"

"I promised that, did I?"

"I'm certain that's what you said."

The adolescents nearby were getting more and more excited, a girl with a hairdo half Amy Winehouse, half Marge Simpson, taking some snaps on her phone. Great. That meant we would be appearing on someone's Facebook page soon. When I'd observed this same thing happening to him at the Lincoln Christmas Market, Eddy had seemed happy to oblige his fans and so I wondered what was different now, why he wanted to remain anonymous. Perhaps because he had no entourage with him, no security. No one besides me.

New York would be quiet. It's just that the two did not compute. Hollywood heartthrob Eddy Partridge in a remote Lincolnshire village? Those two things didn't go together. It was against all natural laws, surely.

"We'll have to drive there," I said. "I'm not sure you and Clarence have sorted out your differences."

"I'll sweet talk him," he replied, giving me a wink.

More onlookers were peering at us, Eddy transforming into the main attraction.

"I may have to channel the spirit of Harrison Ford in a second," he said. "Wag my finger at them and plead for some space."

"I can't imagine you ever being *that* grumpy."

I recalled the news story he was referring to, the Hollywood legend spotted up north in Tyneside earlier in the year as he'd been filming another *Indiana Jones* flick. Thinking about that fact brought a synchronicity to my mind; I'd once read there was yet *another* New York, somewhere up near Newcastle. Had Harrison checked out that one during his time over here? A stroll through New

York to get him back into shape after his on-set accident?

"So, New York then?" Eddy asked.

Can't ignore this little co-inky-dink, Hazel. A subtle nudge from the universe!

"All right. Let's do this."

After the classic confusion of Eddy instinctively approaching the driver's door before remembering we drove on the opposite side of the road, we took our seats inside Clarence and set off down the country lanes to my home village.

What on earth was I doing? Taking him to my humble little bungalow, taking him to meet my nan? She'd have no sense of his social standing, of his fame, just another chap to her. Except that Eddy kind of stood out, even when he was wearing a face mask.

I wondered how many times Nan had seen a person of colour in her life. Probably very few, besides what she'd seen on television. Lincolnshire was one of the most monochromatic regions in these isles. And as for using sensitive language? I had no hope for her at all on that one.

Oh my lord. What am I doing?

The closer we got to New York, the more unsure I felt. What if she was having one of her bat-crap-crazy dos? Prancing round the house in her Morris getup? What if she was all dressed up, her face lathered with greasepaint, heaven forbid? That would *just* be my luck.

Oh no...

Perhaps seeing those morris dancers in the village was meant to be a sign! A warning not to take him home to see Nan.

No, no, no and no some more.

Why did my brain have to think of this? There was no way out now, though. I hadn't even advanced out of fourth gear as I trundled towards the village sign.

"Here we are then," I announced. "Welcome to New York, the village that never wakes."

I pulled over by the Catchwater Drain. Eddy looked at me questioningly.

"No doubt you'll want a photo of yourself by the sign."

"Yeah, yeah, let's do that."

Nice one, Hazel. The perfect distraction. Maybe once he's done that, he'll forget about visiting your home.

We got out, and he handed me his phone as I became a camera operator again. He grinned as he held up both his thumbs, and I suspected no one else had exhibited such enthusiasm for being in this remote hamlet. He giggled as he thumbed through the photos.

"So which one's your place?"

I sighed. "Can I just say something first?"

"Shoot."

I took a deep breath as I delicately composed my answer. "My nan suffers from dementia, so she may exhibit some... peculiar behaviours."

"Oh sure, yes. I understand."

Still I hesitated, standing by the roadside, bathed in the glow of Clarence's red taillights.

Red light, Hazel. You know what that means. It means it's not a green light. Move on the red light and you'll be eliminated! Stay where you are!

"Are you sure?"

"It'll be fine."

"Okay."

We returned to the car and concluded the rest of our journey. Thank goodness there was no motorbike outside the bungalow. Boy, I hadn't even thought about Maddox.

Yet another big reason not to have come here, Hazel!

"Looking festive," Eddy remarked as I pulled up on the drive, the ropes of multicoloured illuminations in the front window greeting us.

"The lights may be on, but there's definitely no one home!" I said, before erupting into a laughing fit. It was most probably down to my nerves rather than my lame attempt at a joke. Eddy peered at me out of the corner of his eye, an eyebrow raised.

Do these things run in the family, Hazel? You might be displaying a degree of that peculiar behaviour yourself here!

"You seem a little on edge, Miss Nightingale."

My laughter dried up, and I took a long breath. "Let's just get this over with."

Nan would most probably be sitting on the sofa with one of the soaps on. She would watch them religiously, even though she was incapable of keeping track of the storylines, not recalling what had happened the day before.

"Nan," I called out loudly as we entered. "I've brought home a guest." I motioned to him to step into the hall and I closed the door. Nan had already appeared. "Eddy, this is my nan. Nan, this is Eddy."

"A pleasure to meet you, miss," he said.

Her eyes opened wide. I knew exactly where her mind was. I could see the surprise on her face.

"Ooh. You're Hazel's friend, are you? I'm Dora. Dora Nightingale. Hazel never told me you were a..."

"Let's not even finish that sentence, shall we?" I blurted over her.

She looked at me as though I'd bitten her head off, which I supposed I had. I knew all this was a bad idea.

"What?" she protested. I closed my eyes, shaking my head. "I was just going to say..."

Please... Please don't. Each syllable seemed to slip out in slow motion.

"... that it looks like he's a New York Yankees fan."

I could not help but sigh in relief. Talk about a heart in mouth moment.

Sorry, Nan. Seems I underestimated you.

"Right," I said, once I'd opened my eyes again. "That's what your cap is all about, yeah? I can make out the N and the Y now."

"Oh, you know about the Yankees, huh?" Eddy asked Nan.

"I saw their stadium once," she proudly bragged.

"You did?"

"Oh yes. Years ago, I went to America on holiday with my husband. You weren't even born then, Hazel."

"I've heard about this infamous trip," I said. "What was the incident on the streets of Manhattan again?"

"Now don't embarrass me, ducky."

It was an easy mistake to make, much like Eddy had made earlier. But crucially for Nan, she was getting *out* of the taxicab rather than getting in, and had not appreciated that the traffic would go past on her side of the car. Another cab swerved out of the way of her open door, careering across the road and smashing into another vehicle. According to Grandad, after causing this calamity, Nan had done what only Nan could do in that situation; She ran.

"At least no one died," I said. "Come on, let's have a sit down. Can I get you a drink, Eddy?"

"Coffee would be great."

I felt a lot more relaxed as I sorted out the drinks. It sounded like the two of them were getting on well in the other room as she chatted him up. I should have had more confidence in this, that Eddy would know how to handle such a character as my nan. He was an expert when it came to people, understanding what made them tick, how their cogs operated. I was absolutely positive that this wordly man from the other side of the Atlantic would never have met a yokel from Lincolnshire like Dora Nightingale, though. In fact, I was sure there was no one else quite like her anywhere in the world. Her mannerisms and the wiring of her brain did not really match with the currents of characteristics that ran in communities or on the television, but simply went its own unique way. She was so unique that she may as well have been an alien from another planet, and yet Eddy could charm her with ease.

I entered the room with a tray of mugs.

"So how did you meet my Hazel then?"

"We're both working on a film."

"Ooh," she cooed. "What do you do on it?"

"I'm an actor."

"Whereabouts have you been filming?"

Oh no. Here we go again.

My heartbeat instantly accelerated. If he mentioned Woodhall Spa, she would think about the Dambusters. And if she thought about them, she'd think about that dog! Oh no. This was another car crash. Now I understood *exactly* how Basil Fawlty felt when those German guests stayed at his hotel.

"Well, we've been filming over in Woodhall Spa."

"Thought so. That's where the Dambusters were," Nan remarked. I had to nip this one in the bud pronto.

"Look, let's not go down this road."

She scowled at me again for cutting her off.

"I realise this is unusual for you, Nan. You're not used to seeing people of different races round here."

"Whatever do you mean?" she asked, trying to piece some understanding from whatever words she'd pulled from my comments.

"You know what I mean."

"Oh Hazel," she said, disappointment dripping from her words. "Why are you being so small-minded?"

Eddy turned to me, a crooked smile appearing on his

lips as he gave me a faux telling off. "Yeah, Hazel. Get in the twenty-first century, why don't you?"

I really needed to just shut it.

"Stop *busting my chops*, mister," I shot back at him, repeating a phrase I'd heard many times in American films but that had never passed from my lips before.

"Your grandfather was good friends with a chap from Barbados during the war. Charlie Dunlop. They stayed in touch for years. All their lives actually."

"Oh," I replied. "News to me."

"He's the one he organised the charity cricket match with over in Sleaford, England against the West Indies. Not an official international, of course, although your grandfather was an excellent player."

"Grandad played cricket?" I asked. I'd heard nothing about this before. Was this another one of her delusions?

"Yes, they all had a little trophy afterwards."

She pointed towards her cabinet behind the sofa. It was full of trinkets and things, stuff that had *always* been there, all my life, but stuff I hadn't questioned, just took their existence for granted, like the sun rising each day. Sure enough, there was a trophy in the shape of a cup, Grandad's name engraved on it, dated 1943. I'd seen this a million times before, but right in that moment, it was like I was looking at it for the very first time.

I couldn't imagine there being time or even an appetite to play sports during wartime, everything focussed on that one aim of defeating Hitler. But perhaps such a cricket match was important for morale amongst those who served. Perhaps it helped keep them fit. Charities wouldn't have gone away, despite there being a global conflict monopolising the headlines.

"Well, I'll be," I muttered. "You learn something new every day."

I supposed it wasn't beyond the realm of possibility that

my grandfather could have known Eddy's character, Gerrick James. Wouldn't that have been weird?

We sat back down, back to our drinks. Once we'd finished them, I should have suggested we made our exit, got out of there while the going was good.

But no. We stayed. And plenty more awkwardness awaited.

Chapter 21

"Did you live round here during the war then, Dora?" Eddy asked.

"Oh yes. Lived in Lincolnshire all my life."

"What was that time like for you?"

"I was still a girl when it started, so I was living with my parents. My father was part of the home guard and my mother looked after evacuees from London. I helped her with that. Margaret and Anna were the two girls who stayed with us. Sisters."

Eddy turned to me. "So, just to clarify, Dora is your maternal grandmother?" He had a photo album on his knee that Nan had dug out for him. There weren't too many embarrassing ones of me in there, thankfully. Not many of me anywhere.

"That's right."

"And once your father disappeared, you ditched his surname."

Oh no. Not this. Eddy, why do you have to be such a sharp one?

"Well, yes and no, you know."

He nodded politely, then paused. "No. Not really. Is Nightingale not your real name?"

"Uh yeah. It's my real name."

"And it's the only surname you've ever had?"

"As I said, never been married."

I could practically hear his brain whirring as he tried to work this one out.

"You're going to have to help me out here."

I sighed and said, "Okay. You understand how fate springs up these little quirks of fortune sometimes?"

"Like when someone sits down in the movie theatre and

they recognise the person they're sitting next to?"

"Mm-hmm. Yeah..."

I took a second. Did I really want to tell him this? It wasn't like we were in the school playground here. We were sensible adults. I hadn't thought about this matter for a long time, and yet those old feelings were still there. Seemed those scars persisted.

"Well," I said, "it just so happened that my mother and my father... they had... the same surname. Pure chance. Please let me stress that they were absolutely not related at all, in any way. They weren't brothers and sisters, not cousins. He wasn't even from round here. Came from up north."

Listening in on our conversation, Nan nodded sympathetically. "Glasgow."

"You sometimes find this in our county, people *keeping it in the family*, if you know what I mean."

"I get you. See, over in New York state, there's this town called Oriskany Falls. Can't be any worse."

"Anyway, when the kids at school discovered my little secret, I was the butt of jokes for years. And I don't even know *how* they found out. Dad was long gone before I started secondary school. But yes, me and my sister were known as the inbreds of the fens." I held up my palms, my fingers fanned out. "Ten of them. Yeah?"

"Relax. I believe you. Hey, they didn't go easy on me either. Do you know how many pear tree jokes got thrown at me?"

"Trust me, if you'd grown up in England it would have been much worse, all thanks to Alan."

"Alan?"

"Google him."

He reached the last page of the album, closed it up and leant forward to place it on the coffee table.

"Oh, is this your London magazine, Hazel?" he asked,

spotting the unopened copy of the December edition.

"Indeed. That was the final one. *A Boy Called Christmas* was the film I reviewed for it."

Already he'd picked it up and was flicking through it.

"Hazel sends me one every month," Nan said.

"Not that you ever read it," I muttered, so only Eddy's ears would pick it up.

"Say, Dora, I'd really like to read the one from a few months back," he pondered before turning to me. "I think the August edition?"

I put on a frown. "Can't remember what was on then."

"You don't recall a film called *The Caretaker*?"

I carried on playing dumb. "Rings a faint bell, maybe."

"You ought to look through my collection," Nan said.

Your what?

"I store them all in that cupboard next to the settee. Help yourself."

Oh no. No, no, no. Nan, why did you do that? You never told me you saved them! How could you do this to me?

Sure enough, as Eddy slid open the door, there they all were, every single edition I'd ever sent to her, including the August magazine where I'd reviewed a certain film starring a certain film star. This was bury-the-needle embarrassing. I got to my feet, stepped into the kitchen and sat down by the table, hiding my head in my arms with every intention to remain where I was for the rest of time and have nothing to do with anyone ever again.

I couldn't believe Eddy Partridge was in the other room reading my review. Fate really needed to stop with all this mischief! I'd practically proclaimed my love for him in this piece.

And just when I thought this evening couldn't get any worse, next I heard a fist hammering on the front door, causing me to sit bolt upright. Three thuds were followed by someone shouting my name.

My eyes came back into focus. "Maddox."

Darting outside before anyone else got to the door, I discovered my bad penny once more. He held his helmet under his arm, his bike parked on the drive beside Clarence. What did I need to do to get rid of this nut?

"What now?" I asked.

"He's here, isn't he?" His words erupted in a growl.

I shook my head. How did he know this? Was I under surveillance? Knowing Maddox, he'd probably persuaded one of the villagers to act as his spy. There was clearly no point lying to him.

"Yeah. He is."

I saw him peering into the back of the Clio, at the new passenger, the snowman with the crooked carrot nose. A sneer formed on his face. It was like this stupid stuffed toy was a symbol that underlined how someone else had come along to furnish me with silly gifts, Oleg usurping the place of the big orange teddy that Maddox had won for me. I hadn't even named that bear. Should have left it in the bin.

He swung his head towards me.

"Meet the family time, is it? Are you going to introduce me then?"

"What for, Maddox?"

Already he was barging past me in the direction of the bungalow, but he didn't get as far as the door. Standing on the doorstep was Eddy.

"Well, I'll be," the American said. "That is the GXA-5000. Check out that bad boy."

Maddox's jaw dropped open, all his aggression tamed by the sight of a movie star emerging from my home. Eddy strode past us to the motorbike, crouching down to admire the pistons or fenders or the exhaust system or whatever it is that guys find so sexy about motorcycles but produces nothing more than a shrug of the shoulders from me.

If he hadn't reeled off the particular model of Maddox's

197

bike, I might have assumed he was just pretending to be in awe of this vehicle, just acting. Right then, it struck me how both men shared the same talent. They each knew how to put on an act, masquerading as someone else, Eddy portraying war heroes or vampires on the silver screen, Maddox slipping into the role of a bank worker, or a Microsoft expert, or a vaccine distributor, or a Nigerian prince, whatever scam he was employing that day. However, I would have much preferred that they didn't bond over their similarities or their appreciation for two-wheeled modes of transport.

"Nice pair of wheels, dude," he went on. "How long have you had it?"

You are acting now, right, Eddy? You're not really interested in having guy-talk with him?

Maddox's mouth was moving, more like twitching, trying to come up with a response. Never in my life had I seen him so dumbstruck.

"Had it on order, so... uh... got it when it came out. Uh... July second. Or... perhaps it was the third."

"What kind of speeds have you had out of it?"

Maddox said nothing for a moment, staring vacantly at the film star, who continued to scrutinise the machinery before him.

"I've uh... I... What was the question again?"

"So," I said, grabbing the reins of this conversation. "Maddox, this is..."

"Yeah, I know his name." He had no problem finding the words for me.

"Great. And Eddy, this is Maddox."

"Take it easy, man," he said, prodding his fist against Maddox's arm. "Time we split, Hazel?"

"I'm pretty sure it is, yes."

We took one step towards my car, but then Eddy paused.

"Oh, I should say goodbye to Dora."

"Don't worry," I replied. "She's already forgotten you came round."

"Right."

We both got in the car, leaving my crazed ex standing there on the drive. As I reversed onto the road, the security light faded, plunging that bulky figure into darkness.

The Caretaker (2021)
Directed by Kit Tinsley
Film Review by Hazel Nightingale

There has been a lot of time travelling of
late. As nations have shielded themselves in
the sanctuary of their homes while that covid
storm raged outside, Netflix and the like
have provided escapism for them, taking
viewers back to a time when a certain virus
was nothing but a twinkle in mother nature's
eye, or in some mad scientist's eye as they
manufactured it in a laboratory, whichever
narrative you subscribe to.

Production on *The Caretaker*, the latest
Eddy Partridge flick which will surely raise
his star as far as it can go, began way back
in 2019. Filming halted when the pandemic
hit, the finish line tantalisingly in reach
with only a handful of scenes still unfilmed.
When better days returned, the studio was not
too hasty in resuming with the schedule. A
completed production would merely have joined
the queue of films for the theatres once they
reopened, headed by that postponed outing
from James Bond.

Indeed, *The Caretaker* is worthy of the big
screen rather than being demoted to one's
television via a streaming service. Watching
the film in segments on one's mobile phone
screen while making a commute to work would
have been a travesty. This is a visual
spectacle that takes a spin on the time
travel genre I have never seen done before,

one that finds the right balance between storytelling, character portrayal, and visuals.

And Eddy Partridge is, already at his young age, a master in his field, here playing a regretful vampire called Nemo who is offered the chance to go back in time to fix a mistake. Even as a vampire, Partridge is rather easy on the eye, perhaps more so. This reviewer certainly wouldn't object to being compelled by him or having his fangs sunk into her neck.

The ever dependable Ewan Mude plays the title role, a mysterious caretaker of an abandoned hotel built within an anomaly in the space-time fabric. But the star of the show is most definitely Partridge as he undergoes a journey that has echoes of the temporal travelling Scrooge makes in *A Christmas Carol*. Being a self-confessed fangirl (if I wasn't so far beyond my teenage years, sure, I would have his poster up in my room so he could perpetually watch over my bed), I had been looking forward to his film ever since I heard its announcement, and Partridge certainly makes it worth the wait. *'Oh Eddy', I utter as I swoon over his beautiful face. Please don't let it be so long till your next release.*

Verdict 7 / 10

Chapter 22

THE FIRST HALF OF OUR journey back to Woodhall Spa took place in silence. It wasn't until we'd passed through Tattershall that I mustered the courage to put the question to him. Perhaps I was fretting needlessly. I hadn't been in the room, so I did not categorically know if he'd read that review. Maybe Nan had distracted him.

"So did you read it?" I kept my eyes ahead. There were no streetlights out here on these roads, but still you'd find other vehicles tearing along it.

"Sure did."

Crap.

"And now you want to run a mile?"

"Still here, aren't I? Although, in all fairness, I wouldn't be able to remember the way back to my hotel, so I have little choice but to take your ride."

"I could have called you a taxi."

"And how would Clarence take that? We've only just bonded."

The silence returned as I pulled up to a junction, and I waited for a couple of cars to clear.

"What do you make of me now?" I asked.

"I'm disappointed, Hazel."

"Oh?"

"You lied. You said you'd given the film an eight. It was actually only seven. Seven? Really?"

"Must have been a typo. Those numbers are pretty close to each other on the keyboard. But at least it means I don't sound too much of a crazed fangirl."

"Oh no, that came across."

"Great."

"But you didn't know me in August. You had no idea

about what films I like to go see at the movie theatre, my favourite baseball team, my talent for hooking ducks. It was only the smoke and mirrors you had to go on back then. But now you've been up close and personal with the real Eddy Partridge, you've seen the true me."

"That you're actually just another jackass? Totally."

"Absolutely, Miss Nightingale," he replied, smiling. "And now you've shown me your home, I can see that..."

"I'm nothing more than a racist inbred?"

"I'm glad we've made this progress."

"It's like we've undergone the reverse journey of *Shop Around the Corner*, starting off liking each other before we discover the ugly truths underneath."

He nodded. "Exactly."

We passed the pub, doglegging up to the village outskirts. The streets looked empty, everyone back home after visiting the Christmas Fayre, excited kids tucked up in their beds hoping they remembered to tell Santa all the presents they wanted in two weeks.

"You know what, Eddy?"

"What's that, Hazel?"

"Yes, I may have spent a lot of time with you this week, but I still don't really know much about you. I don't even know..."

"Know what?"

"What... we're doing."

"I thought that was obvious."

"You did, did you?"

"Yeah. We're running away from your ex. But then he does have a brand new GXA-5000, so keeping up with a Renault Clio is a can of corn." He placed a tender hand on the dashboard. "No offence, Clarence."

I glanced aside to see Eddy cocking his head as he peered into the wing mirror.

"He's *behind* us?"

I hadn't noticed the bright single headlight in my rear-view mirror this entire journey.

"What's he *doing?*" I said. "How much more embarrassing can this evening get?"

"You shouldn't be embarrassed, Hazel."

"Easy for you to say. You're not the one whose entire pitiful life has opened up here."

"And yet everything just makes you even more endearing."

Oh. Well, that doesn't sound so bad.

"What are we going to do about Maddox?" I asked.

"Nothing."

"I have a bad feeling, Eddy. You thought Clarence had jealousy issues? Wait and see what Street Hawk back there is capable of. Did I mention he's into kickboxing?"

"It's okay. We got backup."

"We do?"

"I believe you've met my good friend Bowman."

"Oh. Right. Yeah, I'm sure he'll keep him off you. He seemed like a decent bodyguard. Shame he can't escort me home again."

"You don't have to go back, you know."

"No?"

"It's really safe up in my room. I can guarantee you won't get any bother from anyone."

"Is that so?"

"In fact, I insist on it."

"You do, huh? Well, that sounds like the most sensible course of action."

Maddox followed us into the drive leading up to the hotel. We swiftly got parked before hopping out. Eddy grabbed the clicker from my hand and jabbed the button. I heard the thunk of locks activating as we made a beeline for the entrance, Eddy's hand around my lower back as he ushered me towards safety. I didn't even look behind myself to view my screwy ex hot on our heels, but there was no mistaking the sound of his voice bellowing as he called my name.

"Mr Partridge," the security guy said to greet Eddy as we crossed the lobby to the stairs. I was sure his ears must have pricked at the roar of the motorcycle, and he was already on his way downstairs to check it out.

"Bowman," Eddy replied. "Take care of him, will you?"

The guard nodded. "Sir."

I peered over my shoulder as we scooted upstairs, glimpsing Maddox remonstrating with poor Bowman, his voice deforming into a growl. And there we had someone else's true colours unveiled as we witnessed a snapshot of the monster that lurked within.

"Hazel! Hazel, come back here!"

"Don't worry," Eddy said, taking my hand and encouraging me on. "Bowman's got this."

Swiftly walking down the corridor, Maddox's adrenaline-inducing voice became fainter in my ears, and by the time we stepped into Eddy's room and closed the door, it was like we were shut off from everyone. Eddy filled up his kettle as I took a seat by a dresser, staring at my reflection in the mirror. What a crazy evening it had been.

Although my transatlantic companion exuded an air of confidence after fleeing from my ex, my feelings weren't quite following suit. What if the thug was making a nuisance of himself down there? What if Bowman wasn't the ninja Eddy thought he was? Looking back over our relationship, sometimes I'd witnessed flashes of aggression from Maddox, giving me faint suggestions of what he might be capable of. Certainly they were enough to sow tangible doubt in my mind as I sat there in Eddy's room, chewing on my thumbnail.

"What's with the little gargoyle dude?" Eddy asked, dispersing my worrisome thoughts. The kettle came to a boil.

"The what?" I was still miles away.

"Near the entrance, there's a carving, a little creature with a leg crossed. First time I noticed him."

"Do you mean the Lincoln imp?"

"Maybe?"

"One day the devil set loose his minion demons, and for some reason they descended on Lincolnshire to get up to some mischief, because that's the go-to place for a swell old time evidently. But the angels turned up to sort them out, or something, turning one of them to stone. If you go inside the cathedral, you'll find him somewhere up in the rafters. I spotted him on a school trip once when I was like eight, but I couldn't tell you exactly where he is. There was a whole trail of giant imps in the city earlier in the year, by the way. Not sure if they're still there. I think they sold them off for charity, the ones that weren't vandalised, that is. Huh. Rather ironic really. I wonder which imps did *that*? Making mischief-makers really invites mischief."

Boy, I sure could ramble sometimes. It was usually a sign I was tired.

"So have I got this right?" he asked. "Any evildoers planning on coming to the Petwood might notice that stone carving and it would scare them away?"

"Yes. Especially if there's a heavyset bodyguard on the door called Bowman."

"Coffee?"

"No, thanks."

"Oh."

He abandoned the drinks station, sitting on the end of the bed as he wrapped his arm around one of the columns. With my back still to him, he viewed me via the mirror. "Are you certain you don't want a drink? Not sure what to do now."

"How you can put caffeine in your system this late in the

day? I'd never sleep."

"Never do anyway."

"Well, you wouldn't if you keep necking espressos." I focussed my eyes on my reflection, running my fingers through my hair, which turned into a stretch as I held my arms out. After all that excitement, I sensed a post-adrenaline crash coming on. "The other guests are going to start talking. Two nights in a row you've brought a lady up to your room."

"What scandal."

"You never did answer my question."

"Which one was that?"

I didn't want to have to say it again. It seemed it was only me who was trying to articulate this. "Why haven't you kicked me to the kerb yet?"

Eddy got to his feet, a ponderous look on his face. He stepped towards me, my reflection blocking his. He sighed.

"Ever since that moment when you burst into my trailer, I haven't been able to get you out of my mind, Hazel Nightingale. And then again, at the cinema, you appear, the universe continuing to throw us together."

"I'm relieved you look on those incidents as cute quirks of fate, not that you've got a loony stalker."

"Well, in truth, I haven't completely ruled that out, but even if that were the case, I doubt it would change things."

"What things?"

"I mean the way I feel compelled to see you. I don't get what it was when you first came along, but it felt like I already knew you, that you were meant to be there."

He appeared in the mirror once more, standing right behind me. God, he was so easy on the eye. I could never tire of gazing at him, and now Eddy was aware of this very proclamation, seeing as I'd written it in my film review for the world to see.

"No, I definitely wasn't supposed to be there. You ask

Janice Daniels."

"I hope you understand I would never have kicked you out."

"I still feel like the other woman," I said as I got to my feet, turning round to face him. "Like I'm stealing you off her."

He edged ever closer to me.

"Want to know a secret? She's not really my type."

"And what is your type, Mr Partridge?"

"Ah, you know. From a tight-knit family, webbed toes. Can't operate a car clicker."

"Hey, you saw my hands. I proved this to you."

"Think I need to see the rest of you."

"Is that right?"

"'Fraid so."

He leant forward to kiss me. I was absolutely sure there would be nothing literal going on in his room tonight.

Chapter 23

I SEEMED TO ERUPT INTO consciousness from a sleep that was deeper than Snow White's, my lungs gulping down air, my heart racing. I'd been practically comatose. No alarm had woken me this time, any kisses from a handsome prince had been on the other side of my slumber. It was more as though my dream itself had revived me, leaving its impression in my brain. It hadn't been like the humdrum dreams I'd get any other day, not when I lay in bed beside a cultural icon. In the presence of such an exalted figure, it was like my mind had been handling raw archetypes, its narrative involving a devilish imp trying to lead me astray. I had been mistaken for the ringleader by the avenging angels and was the one to be turned to stone. And at that point, I could feel my paralysis as I tried to move my limbs from within my dream. Eventually, I dragged my eyelids apart as my brain switched into reality and brought me to freedom.

I was naked alongside a bare-chested Eddy who had his arm draped over me. Despite my fidgeting, I had not woken him. Perhaps he was wired so that he only woke to the sound of his alarm. It was yet to go off, so it must have been early, assuming the alarm was still set for the same time as yesterday. Beyond the windows there was a thick darkness, but this meant nothing in these short winter days. Three o'clock or seven o'clock, they were both the same.

Recollections of last night dispelled the weird aftertaste of my dream. They produced a smile on my lips, too.

Sure wouldn't object to doing that again.

I pressed myself up by my elbows, glancing over the bed as Eddy rolled onto his back. He was still sleeping soundly. On his bedside table, I spotted his phone, but I couldn't quite read the time on its screen. I thought about reaching across him to grab it, and suddenly it was as though I genuinely did have a mischievous imp inside my head whispering bad thoughts to me.

Take it, Hazel, and have a little look through it. See all the messages he's been writing to his lassies back home.

Did he have someone else in New York? Or Los Angeles? Heck, this was the 2020s, so maybe he had two on the go. Or three, rather, given the port he was in here. He'd never seemed edgy in those brief moments when his phone had been in my hands. I hadn't picked up on a guilty aura with him, certainly not last night.

These actors are masters of illusion, Hazel. He can make you believe he's anything you want him to be.

Even though we were where we were, I realised it didn't necessarily mean happily ever after, that we would live out that trope of walking off into the sunset. There were so many complications, the biggest one of all being the Atlantic Ocean. I say tomato; he says toe-*may*-dough. He says New York, and I say that's a no man's land where nothing happens and dreams don't come true.

I simply had to make the most of it while I could. So far, I'd been taking this whole thing a step at a time, expecting it might end at any second. For all I knew, yesterday could have been Eddy's final filming day, his flight back to New York booked for this evening.

Illumination flashed in the corner of my eye and I turned my head to see that Eddy's phone had lit up.

Another message from his girlfriend, his real *girlfriend? Why else would it light up in the middle of the night, unless it was a communication from someone in a different time zone?*

I slowly emerged from the silky linen cocoon, Eddy turning over again as I gradually slipped the top blanket from the covers and wrapped it round me.

Tiptoeing to the foot of the bed, I came to a stop, my

curiosity grinding me to a halt. Was he definitely still unconscious? Would it hurt to take one peek at his phone, at least just to get the time?

Wonderful justification, Hazel. You can check your own phone for that as it's only over there on the table.

Perhaps it was later than I thought, and Eddy had overslept because I'd distracted him last night, and without doing a little detective work, he'd be late for filming. So really, this was for his own good.

I crept up to the bedside table, reached down with my left hand as my right held the blanket to my body. Pressing the button, I found notifications cramming the screen. Several emails had come in overnight, one from someone with a flashy name, one from Amazon. The most recent, which had landed a moment ago, was some spam rubbish about bitcoin. Wow, he may be a worldwide superstar, but he still suffered the same trivial annoyances as all the rest of us, couldn't even stop those infuriating unsolicited messages filling his inbox. Digital junk was the ultimate leveller.

There were a few WhatsApp notifications, but they seemed to have landed in groups rather than to him personally. This guy got more messages in one night than I got in a month.

Scrolling past all the other swipe-worthy notifications, I eventually discovered the reason I had turned into some insecure girlfriend, my first step towards boiling his bunny; His alarm was set for half seven. Late start today then. The time was fast approaching the hour. I decided I would perch by the window as I waited for him to wake, keep myself out of any more mischief.

As I sat down, I noticed a sheet of paper on the table so picked it up. My phone was laying there too, so I grabbed it to use its screen as a reading light. I may have had more success translating hieroglyphics, but after a few minutes, my morning-fuzzed brain eventually determined this was today's call-sheet. Eddy wasn't required in make-up until nine o'clock, hence the later start time. There were four scenes listed for him today, the last of which wasn't until eight in the evening.

It came like a cold, smothering wave, life getting in the way, drowning this great thing we had going on. They would steal away Eddy from me tonight, our run of dates ending. Until this point, I may have spent every evening this week with him, but that had just made me want him more. How dare those film producer gods not take me into consideration! At least there was the weekend, though. Surely these Tinseltown folk had the Saturday and Sunday to rest and recharge their camera batteries? That was when I noticed there was another call-sheet with tomorrow's date. Okay, maybe just Sunday then. If I was lucky.

"What time is it?" Eddy's voice startled me, a flash of guilt washing through me as I held his private documents.

Could have been worse, Hazel. He could have caught you looking through his phone!

"It's a little after seven," I replied.

He rubbed his face, stretched, then sat up in bed.

"I had the weirdest dream," he muttered.

"So did I. What happened in yours?"

It was like he hadn't heard me though as he grabbed his phone and thumbed through the notifications that had only just been thumbed through. After reading one of his messages, he stood up and approached the table in nothing but his boxer shorts. I couldn't help but gaze at his toned frame, a perfect ridge of muscles on his belly, broad shoulders, the exact sort of biceps you saw on your average hero on the cinema screen. And all of those features I had been running my hands over last night.

"The agent wants me to buzz him."

"Is that...?" I began, recalling the Mr Flashy McFlashpants name I'd read a moment ago, Troy Austin the

Third. I was just about to blurt it out when I stopped myself and backtracked. "Is that the agent you mentioned the other day?"

And, like, how many agents is he supposed to have, Hazel? Spreading his net out wide because he's short on work?

Fortunately, he didn't react as though it was a stupid question.

"Yeah. I should really phone him. Eleven o'clock in LA. He's probably in bed right now."

He continued dabbing away at his screen.

"Busy couple of days for you," I said, placing his call-sheets down.

"Tell me about it."

"However will you fit in time for any private matters?"

He raised his eyes to me to see if I was looking at him, then pulled up the other chair and sat beside me.

Was I merely another facet of his life that drew demands on him? Wanting a piece of him. Wanting him *here*, when others wanted him *there*. I was sure he didn't need Hazel Nightingale adding to all that, the poor guy endlessly trying to solve his own *Lament Configuration*, desperately trying to find the right arrangement before he found himself raising hell.

Hazel, why are you comparing your relationship with him to a device from a horror film? That's not the genre we're doing here!

The question was on the tip of my tongue, though. *When am I going to see you again, Eddy?* I needed to know *now*.

"Saturday is my last day of filming. After that I'm pretty much done for Christmas."

"And how long are you hanging around in old England?"

He cocked his head at me. "Until I wear out my welcome?"

And heaven forbid you give me a straight answer for

once!

"Is this a star-crossed romance, then?" I asked, locking eyes with him, deliberately giving a sense of ambiguity until I picked out a couple of sheets of script from his papers.

He remained silent for a moment. "Aren't they all?"

"What happens? This is all in the history books, surely. Or on Google. What became of Gerrick James and Polly from the fens?"

"It was all down to that fateful sixth mission that gave me bubbles in my blood, just days before Christmas. The Germans shot me down as I flew home. I ran and hid in some farmer's shed, the Nazis scouring the area looking for me and my crew. There I light up the cigar I'd been saving for when I got back to England, and the smoke from it gives me away."

"They catch you?"

He nodded solemnly. I didn't ask what happened next. It seemed too obvious.

"I can't help the feeling that..."

"What?" he prompted me.

... That once you get on a plane to go back home, I'll never see you again either.

"Never mind," I said, leaving it unsaid, thinking of something else to change the subject. "So have you got to go to France or Holland or somewhere to film your cigar in the cowshed scene?"

"France, not that we actually filmed there. We already did that sequence, right before we came to Lincolnshire."

"So you don't have much left to do?"

He shook his head. "Tomorrow I'll be done. They're still filming for the next couple of weeks beyond that, but for me it'll all be in the can."

"I rather like you, Eddy Partridge."

He turned to face me. "I don't know whether you gathered, but I'm kind of fond of you too, Hazel

214

Nightingale."

"Think I've become accustomed to seeing you each day."

I stood up, the blanket slipping from me. He ran a hand up my body as I leant forward and kissed him.

Chapter 24

MY TIME WITH EDDY THAT morning seemed so fleeting. The closer we got to his call-time, the more his mind was switching to a different compartment. After coffee and breakfast-for-two delivered by room service, it was time for me to say goodbye. He kissed me, told me he'd message me later, and then I schlepped off downstairs to Clarence. Eddy accompanied me to the car park, just in case. I didn't spot any motorbikes across the tarmac, however, and there were none on my route to New York, none like Maddox's swish model, at least.

Parking on the bungalow drive, I cast my gaze up and down the street. Still there were no bikes to be seen, no sound of an engine zooming along the fen adding to the noise pollution, only the Coningsby jets which my brain was starting to filter out again now I'd been back a couple of weeks.

Had Maddox finally got the message and returned to London? I had been expecting a blazing row with him once I'd exited Eddy's hotel, my jealous ex having stewed on it all night, laying in wait to ambush me. The silence was almost unsettling. Was Maddox the type to give up, even after seeing me with someone way above his 'weight' class? I just hoped that was so.

I discovered Nan asleep on the sofa when I walked inside, the Christmas tree lights twinkling, an untouched tumbler of whisky on the table. My instincts told me she'd nodded off in front of the television and remained there all night. She was still wearing the same clothes as when I last saw her. In the kitchen I found untaken pills and suddenly I felt so guilty. I was supposed to be her chief carer, but I'd been neglecting my duties, drunk on hormones and my perceptions dazzled from being up close and personal with a Hollywood star. I was really putting my surname to shame here. What irony. Florence would be turning in her grave.

Nan didn't have the capacity to tell me I was doing such a crap job of this. She didn't even realise she needed the help in the first place, and the thought that she wasn't able to make me feel guilty just made me feel even more guilty.

Today would be different, and I would make it up to her somehow, especially as my American distraction was otherwise occupied. It was time I took her out somewhere, and perhaps tomorrow we'd go to *Sherman's* to replenish the kitchen cupboards. I really needed to think about my Christmas shopping too, and now that I was Nan's carer, I would no doubt be in charge of her gift-buying and sending out cards, keeping up the pretence that she was still capable of observing these festive customs by herself.

"Are you doing any more work on that film today?" Nan asked me in a flash of lucidity as I placed a cup of tea down for her. It seemed that one was now sticking to her impermeable brain, just as it was coming to an end. Typical.

"I did my last day yesterday. So you're going to have to put up with me being around a lot more. Do you fancy a trip out somewhere today?"

"That'll be nice," she replied before the idea instantly shot out of her mind as she focussed her attention on the television. The presenters were wearing their ironically twee festive jumpers on *This Morning* this morning. Christmas was fast approaching. It would be here before we knew it. I supposed I hadn't wanted to think too much about the holiday because it would inevitably mean that Eddy would have returned to spend it with his loved ones in the States. By the twenty-fifth of this month, I feared it would all be over.

"Shall we go to Boston?" I asked her. "Do some shopping?"

217

"Can if you like."

Another of those surreal moments occurred, but it took a moment for my brain to clock on to the fact, like the sonic boom that blasts towards you several seconds after the explosion. A VT played featuring an interview with Janice Daniels, Eddy's co-star. Undoubtedly, she would be talking about the film to build more hype. It was so odd seeing something I had recently been involved with on the television so frequently. It felt as though the lines were blurring.

As Nan had only just mentioned it, I pointed to the television and said, "Look, this is the film I've been working on." The crew had taken some shots at East Kirkby airfield, and again I saw that twinkle of recognition in Nan's eyes as she viewed the Just Jane Lancaster.

"I'm looking forward to seeing this," she said. "Ooh, is that your friend there?"

The report was now talking about the leading man, playing a clip from his other film, *The Caretaker*. She really was on a roll this morning.

"Yes, that's Eddy who came here last night."

"He was a nice chap. You two looked good together."

"I don't think there'll be much of that *together* stuff going on," I muttered. She didn't hear me.

"He reminds me of your grandfather's friend... Gareth Jones." The name hadn't rolled off her tongue as it had last night, and neither did it match.

"I thought you said he was called Charlie Dunlop or something."

It was hardly a million miles away from Eddy's character's name, was it? Gareth Jones. Gerrick James. My eyes narrowed.

Huh. Another strange quirk of fate, Hazel?

Might it somehow be possible that my lover was portraying a real life character who was personally known to my grandfather? Sure, Nan had said the wartime buddy was from Barbados, whereas Gerrick James came from Jamaica, but Barbados and Jamaica were basically the same place to her.

Oh my goodness. How weird would this be? Except that it appeared Gerrick James didn't make it out of the war alive. That was the end of his story, right? Captured by the Nazis in the cowshed.

"Did you ever meet him yourself?" I asked.

"Who?"

"Grandad's West Indian friend."

"I did, yes. Met up with him on our trip to the States in '74."

Maybe it wasn't him then, not if Eddy's character had been apprehended and dumped in a concentration camp.

I gazed across to the sideboard, to that little wartime cricket trophy. "Did Grandad have any photographs from back then?"

"If you want photographs, then you ought to have a look in that old suitcase of his, up in the loft."

"I may just have a look for them after some breakfast. Now then, what are you having this morning?"

After some porridge and marmalade on toast, I ventured into the attic for the second time this week. I shivered as I reached the top of the ladder, the air so chilly up there. Thankfully, with it being an awkward place for my nan to get into, not to mention it being *out of sight and out of mind*, she hadn't cluttered it up with too much junk.

I soon found the suitcase in question, a vintage item, leather straps holding it together, patchy stickers covering it, all of them now impossible to read. The only legible marking was an inscription on the case, giving his name and service number. Fragments of string dangled from the handle, what once held identification tickets from voyages past that Grandad had taken.

It was very heavy too, full of books and documents and photographs, whatever he'd collected over his lifetime and felt compelled to keep on to. I dragged it down to the hatch, and with all my strength, I manoeuvred it down to the ground floor. Once back down, I quickly closed up the loft before all the heat from the bungalow escaped, and then lugged the suitcase into the spare bedroom.

Placing it on the bed, I carefully opened it and proceeded with my detective work. On top of the contents, was a collection of old books from way back when. I held up one with the title *Bunty*, feminine images on the cover. On the first page, I found an inscription that caused the water to well in my eyes. This had been my mother's. Not from a period when I knew her. This was from when she was a young child. It was a sudden peek into a part of her life I had never known.

There were plenty more books, their spines damaged, the pages falling out. There didn't appear to be much order to the rest of the suitcase's contents, photos of forefathers I'd never met, Nightingale generations whose lifetimes had not overlapped with mine. In one photo, a trio of men were dressed in army uniform, but their style seemed more First World War than Second. None of them was smiling.

Along with some medals, I discovered Grandad's discharge papers from leaving the RAF in 1947. With the Nazis and the Japanese Empire defeated, I imagined the armed forces at home were soon deflated, my grandfather leaving only two years later. It wasn't like the nation had immediately got over those six years of conflict, part of the document giving instructions on remobilisation. In fact, the papers stated he had only been released, capital letters stressing that he had not been discharged.

The document gave his role, his years of duty, and all his other basic information, such as his height. One section seemed more like a school report, describing his RAF character as 'very good' and his proficiency as 'superior'. It concluded with a statement of any special aptitudes or types of employment for which recommended, written by his commanding officer, but the handwriting was almost completely illegible. I deciphered the word 'conscientious', which brought a smile to my face. My teachers often used that same adjective in my school reports.

I put the document aside to read in closer detail later. Digging into the case again, I found a scattering of photographs, some from the war, some from years afterwards. There were sporadic scribblings on the reverse of these images. I recognised Grandad's handwriting on some of them, but it said little, perhaps merely giving the name of the place he'd taken the picture.

Some portrait photographs were in the form of postcards, 'for correspondence' marked one side, 'address' on the other. So that's how they did selfies back in olden times.

I came across a bunch of sepia images tied together with an elastic band which snapped the moment I pulled it. A cricket match was in progress, a bowler hurling a ball to a black batsman. Was the bowler my grandfather? Was the batsman Charlie Dunlop, otherwise known as Gareth Jones, potentially known as Gerrick James?

There were no inscriptions on the back of these photographs, nothing to indicate on what date they'd been taken, no names, nothing to give them any context, snapshots of occasions that had been lost in time.

Our generation had really been spoilt. With Google at our fingertips, we could bring up random information in seconds. But this suitcase was effectively a primitive search engine of my grandfather's life, orphaned documents that came with no 'metadata' to categorise them, to organise them, little to explain their meaning. Sure, I could ask my nan, but what authority did her explanations carry? She hadn't known him back then. It was so frustrating to think that the universe had given me an opportunity, a window that was many years in length, but a window when I was so young that I didn't even appreciate one was there.

The war wasn't without an abundance of stories, but how many had been taken to the grave?

Chapter 25

"OH, THERE'S MONTGOMERY," NAN REMARKED as I drove us out of the village. I glanced over to see the artist in question by the Catchwater Drain, a feature he'd quite possibly painted a hundred times before. I raised my hand to wave to him and he mirrored the gesture.

"Painting again," I said. "Does he ever do anything else?"

"His mother wants him to move out, get his own place, so Kitty told me."

"Like that'll happen."

Kitty probably had mentioned this to Nan, but it may easily have been a decade or two ago. At this stage, I reckoned Montgomery's mother had given up all hope of him ever moving out.

We headed to Coningsby for a food shop at *Sherman's*, the cupboards in the bungalow looking bare once more. It had been two days since I'd been with Eddy. Whenever I was with him, it seemed to be an experience that lived up to his name, a *whirlpool* of romance and emotion. Being without him indeed felt like a static drought. Although our plans for getting together had been nebulous so far, things weren't quite so sine die today; I would definitely see him later and I couldn't wait.

I wondered if his experience with me was true to my name. Did he find being with me much like a *haze*, unable to keep his head clear? Or did he think it an accurate description of me, someone unclear who had no definition to her life? It was funny how people lived up to their names like this. I once knew a Peter whose interest in things always waned. My university ex, who studied Drama, Philip, had the knack for providing a *fillip* to his friends. Was Pep

Guardiola so successful as a football manager because he knew how to inspire his players with such rousing *pep* talks?

These frivolous ruminations weaved through my mind all the way to the convenience store in Coningsby. They were instantly quelled as I stepped foot inside the shop, as too was the air that dispersed from my lungs.

I could not believe it. For a moment, I indeed thought I was losing it. More of that blurring, or at thirty years of age, was I displaying 'early onset'?

Oh no. This can't be happening.

My eyes fixed on that pile of newspapers for at least twenty seconds, my jaw in dire need of my mask to hold it to my face. The photograph of Eddy on the front cover had initially caught my eye. But that was only the start of it. *I* was front-page news. *Me.* Hazel Nightingale, unemployed film critic from rural Lincolnshire. I was the Sunday morning gossip for tabloid readers across the country. And not only this particular publication. As I glanced at the one next to it, I read the headline 'Lovebirds' and knew exactly where that was going, too.

Wow. They must have needed all day to come up with that!

"Are you okay, dear?" Nan asked me as I held my hand against my forehead, slowly massaging it as though I might ease the horrible realisation that had been wedged into it.

"Just a little headache. You go on ahead and pick out some fruit." I didn't want to get into this right now, didn't want to draw any attention to myself, which admittedly was rather difficult when you were in the national newspapers.

I knew exactly how this had happened. Maddox. The snake.

As much as I wanted to scoop up both piles of those tabloids and shred them, I realised doing that was like trying to put out a forest fire by spitting on it.

Everyone up and down the country was soon to know

about my private life, mine and Eddy's little secret. Preventing the chance of the residents of Coningsby and its environs to read this news would only delay the information getting to them temporarily before it was splashed over the internet or even, heaven forbid, on television. I could just imagine us being talked about on some light entertainment discussion show. What exactly had Maddox told them?

I picked up a copy of each tabloid, thinking that this was quite possibly the only scenario where I would spend my money on these rags.

Herding Nan around the shop helped take my mind off it. Not much, but slightly. Actually, I don't think it did at all. The anxiety was building inside. What was Eddy going to make of this? What would he think about being caught out over this, that he was seeing some nobody from the fens? I was hardly on the same level as him. It was so embarrassing.

Once we'd filled our trolley, we proceeded to the checkout. I wished I had some shades on, praying that the girl on the till wouldn't make a double-take when she grabbed the newspapers. Fortunately, she displayed nothing but boredom on her face as she scanned my items. Thank goodness for face masks.

With the shopping stuffed in the car, I raced on back to the bungalow. I left Nan to put the food away as I shut myself in my bedroom and read the two articles.

Hollywood Star's Secret Love Nest was the headline on the first newspaper. How could they take our story and make it sound so sordid and scandalous? Of course, there would be nothing about our rendezvous at the cinema, would there? Watching black and white films from the 1940s was hardly sensationalism, right? No, it's all about what happens in the bedroom.

As I suspected, it was Maddox who'd gone to the paper to tell the story. To s*ell* it, most likely. There he was on page

2, jerking the tears, describing his heartbreak after the girl he loved had ditched him to get in bed with a Hollywood star. To back his claims up, there was a snap of me and Eddy holding hands, taken at the Christmas Fayre, something that had no doubt appeared on social media. Journalism was so easy these days. All you had to do was thumb through your Facebook feed and rehash the juicy-sounding statuses.

"That's utter rubbish!" I shouted at the newspaper as I read a quote from Maddox saying how he and I were about to start a family after a four-year romance. "We weren't together for that long. We never even lived together! Bet you didn't confess to the paper how you did a Matt Hancock during lockdown when you couldn't resist keeping your distance from me."

I really wanted to roll up this newspaper and ram it down his throat, stop him spouting any more lies or attempting any more trickery ever again.

To my horror, there was yet another photograph of us. We were sitting inside Clarence on my Nan's drive, what looked like some paparazzi snap, the image looking so dirty and grainy, but not enough that you couldn't identify the driver and passenger. The weasel had taken a photo on his phone. I bet in that moment he was already planning to take this to the press. I shouldn't have been surprised. That's how his sly brain was wired.

The other tabloid, the *Lovebirds* one, didn't really have much else to add to the matter, just their lame attempt to keep up with their competitor. It was padded with various library images of Eddy, taken by the paparazzi while he was out and about with past girlfriends. They made it seem like he went through them at a fair rate of knots. This one had a cold undertone to it.

It was sickening. I lay back on my bed, feeling as though my life had been violated. Nobody, besides me and Eddy,

226

had the right to know any of this. My rational mind knew that, although this was headline material today, tomorrow it would be fish and chips wrappings, except for the fact they stopped using newspapers for that decades ago. Perhaps, then, it would be part of the bedding in rabbit hutches, or bird cage lining. Or a fly swat.

I had to give Eddy the heads-up, needed to apologise to him on behalf of my scumbag ex, so I sent him a text. My phone soon pinged with a reply.

Hey Miss Nightingale, yeah someone at the hotel told me about it this morning. Don't worry about it. Karma has a habit of coming around for people like him. How did your Christmas shopping go yesterday? Get me something nice? X

"Really?"

Hold it there, buddy. How on earth can you do that, Eddy Partridge? Segue from the horror of being front-page news to a shopping trip in the very next sentence? I don't think I'm done dissecting this!

I fired him back a quick reply, ignoring his question.

Just want this to go away. X

Later on, I would talk to him. With his status, this sort of thing surely happened all the time. But for me, it was all nauseatingly new. In fact, I'd barely ever made the local press throughout my life. Once when Princess Anne had visited our school and we all sang a hymn for her, *Autumn Days* or was it *One More Step Along The World I Go*? Another occasion when I led a fundraiser for a young boy from Coningsby who needed life-changing surgery. In neither report had they also covered my love life. Neither had they driven me to barricade myself in my room and intend never to emerge again.

I was really struggling to come to terms with all this. What was Maddox hoping to achieve? This would bring me back to him? That was the one silver lining, that surely he must have seen this as a kamikaze stunt, any semblance of a relationship between us going out in a blaze of glory. Not that there was anything glorious about this. More like a blaze of disgrace.

I folded up both the newspapers, hiding the front-page stories so only some inoffensive sport story on the back page was on display. How did this guy live up to *his* name then? The 'mad' section needed no explanation. And what I would give to see him in the *docks* so he could be punished for all the crimes he'd committed.

Chapter 26

"I JUST DON'T GET HOW any of them feel they have the right to tell my story, *our* story. How can they be allowed to do such a thing?"

Eddy sat in silence next to me. He was in the driving seat today, following my directions as we cruised along the quiet country roads. I wasn't exactly sure how he'd produced this electric blue Audi R8 Spyder, but I knew for certain it was the most expensive car I'd ever been in.

The sun was already setting on another crisp winter's day, but for me, it was only just getting started. We weren't heading anywhere in particular, simply somewhere that Maddox or today's tabloid readers wouldn't expect to find us, so neither New York nor Woodhall Spa was the place to be. I figured we'd go out driving, maybe show him the hidden little secrets of the area. When one of us was a Hollywood superstar, we didn't need a destination. Eddy could draw the wonder and excitement from any moment.

"You sound like you're just working out for the first time how tabloids work," he eventually replied. "It's really not worth getting upset about. This too shall pass."

He placed a hand on my thigh and I took a deep breath to stem the tears that were threatening to roll down my face. At least I had someone to moan to about this, someone in it with me. And it sounded like he might be around a lot in the coming days. With his scenes on this film now all shot, he had nothing else scheduled before Christmas. I felt so lucky. All that time where I could have him all to myself. Or perhaps I would have him for as long as it took him to get bored with me. What was the betting that would be sooner rather than later? A native New Yorker in Lincolnshire? With the dearth of stimuli round here, surely for him, it was like being on Mars.

"Although, I have the suspicion the topic will be brought up on tomorrow's filming," he said.

"Wait, what? I thought you were done filming."

"Oh, yeah, I am with *Flying Colours*. But as I'm staying on in England, they've piled on some interviews for me to do."

His work really was never ending. Okay, so maybe we wouldn't be seeing too much of each other.

"Is this for *Look North* or *The One Show* or something?"

"All sorts of things. They want some behind-the-scenes stuff too for all the bonus material."

"They still do that now no one buys DVDs anymore?"

"Sometimes I enjoy all that more than the main feature."

"Totally. Same here," I agreed. "So how come you're not racing back to America, Mr Partridge? I thought you'd want to reunite with all those girlfriends I read about."

"Ain't nobody over there waiting for me, fact. Not like that, anyway."

We drove in silence for a bit. Perhaps it might encourage him to open up a little more, fill the void with chatter. I couldn't help but wonder what had happened with all those relationships. Did they all dump him? How could anyone do that to him? Surely it wasn't scientifically possible.

"Have you ever been to New York?" he asked.

"No. Never been to America at all."

"Would you like to? A backwater yellowbelly like you, it would totally make an English *Crocodile Dundee*."

"That's not a spade," I said in a thick Lincolnshire brogue. "That's a spade, *mayate*." I switched back to my regular accent. "Right, yes. I see what you're getting at."

"You guys are into your spades round here?"

"Absolutely. They're our sacred tools. Martin was telling me about a special spade in his home town, one that Prince Philip had used to plant a tree there. They had it on display this year and I'm pretty sure they worship it and have sacrificed the occasional goat to it."

"Fascinating. And I can't even tell where the truth ends and the humour begins."

"You don't want to know."

He chuckled. "So how about it?"

"America? You're actually inviting me over?"

Did that mean this thing of ours was getting serious? But would I really be able to do that? Jump on a plane and leave everyone behind? By *everyone*, all that realistically entailed was Nan, of course. Her dementia would never go away. How she was in this very moment, over this last seven day average at least, was the best she would ever be for the rest of her life as she continued that gradual decline. And as for how long that decline took? A couple of years? Five years? Another decade?

"You've shown me your home. It's only right I show you mine."

"Sure is an appealing proposition, Eddy. It's just..."

"Dora."

"Hmm."

"I would say bring her with you."

"Even if I could get insurance for her, I don't think New York has quite recovered from her last visit."

"I heard about that," he replied. "Anyway, do you have any idea where we're going?"

"Right now or in general?"

"I like to leave my questions open-ended."

"I've noticed." Just as Eddy was happy to get in the car and follow his nose, I suspected too that there was no roadmap to this thing we had going on. We would fumble along, taking it as it came, much like the government. Was he putting on any restrictions on his feelings as I was? Trying to keep his emotions under control? I was failing miserably at that, however. "We're coming up to a village called Anwick. Famous for its chickens and the birthplace of a famous songwriter."

"Hmm," he replied, pondering on who it could be.

"Collaborated with Elton John a lot."

"You mean Bernie? I know him."

"For real?"

"Yeah, he's one of us now. My father worked with him a couple times."

"You'll soon see the building he was born in," I said as we drove past the chicken factory and out of the village. As we approached a lone farmhouse, I pointed a finger. Eddy pulled over and took a few quick photos.

"Awesome. I'll show him these when I next see him. Where next?"

"Well, we're close to Sleaford now, where my brother lives and a certain special spade."

"Tempting."

"Or we can turn off and visit the ruins of a priory."

"Is Sleaford the birthplace of anyone else I know?"

"It's a fair certainty it isn't."

"Then let's check out this priory."

Mere seconds after pulling into the car park, Eddy jumped out of the two-seater coupe as he peered towards the ramshackle remains of Haverholme Priory. Standing across the field from us as precariously as a drunkard on a bender, one could half imagine that if the wind blew hard enough, the building might collapse into a pile of rubble.

"Now that would make a really cool location for a film," he said once I'd stepped out of the car. "That might even work for..."

"For..?"

"My script."

"Script for what?" I asked.

"Something I'm working on."

"You're writing your own film?"

"I'm giving it a go. Got a producer interested."

"Awesome. I'm not sure the priory would be of much use. It's a mess inside." I squinted at the structure as Eddy took some more photos. "And I have the impression more of it has collapsed since I last came here."

"Yeah? When was that?"

My mouth opened to give a knee-jerk reply. *It was only a few years ago* were the words on my tongue. But when I took a moment to reflect, I realised the years made rather more than a few. I was still technically in school on that occasion, camping out with friends in the nearby woods across the river to celebrate the completion of our A-Levels. How did life go by so quickly like that?

That was something I'd noticed with the coronavirus pandemic. Separated from friends and acquaintances you might have seen more regularly in normal circumstances, it tended to highlight the collateral damage of time. When the government relaxed the restrictions earlier in the year and we could meet up again, hug one another, I realised how much people had aged. And with that constant corona shadow and its variants hanging over us, perhaps the fear had only amplified our ageing. Somehow I'd come out of it all in my thirties. I'm still not quite sure how that happened. Even those you occasionally saw on television, B list singers or comedians or theatre actors, with their stages mothballed, they'd had no choice but to disappear from public view and wait for the storm to pass. And once they reappeared, they didn't look like they were when we last saw them.

"So, whereabouts did you camp out?" he asked.

"Follow me," I said as I beckoned him towards the river.

We manoeuvred through a stile, illuminating the torches on our phones as we followed the path into the trees. "So how did you get hold of that car, by the way?"

"The Audi? A guy in Woodhall Spa lent it to me."

"He just *lent* it to you?"

"Yep."

"Why would he do that?"

"So he could brag that a Hollywood actor has driven his wheels?"

"Yeah, I can see where you're coming from. Amazing what doors open for you when you're cinematic royalty. So what's his name? I'm assuming it's a he?"

Eddy was silent for a couple of beats. "You're talking about the car now, right? Not the guy in Woodhall."

"You know me well."

"I'm afraid I forgot to ask."

"He looks like a Clifford. Or maybe we should call him Bernie." My voice raised as we got closer to the lock, the sound of rushing water hissing through the air.

"Wow, this is like something out of Middle Earth," Eddy remarked. "I can just imagine Aragorn and Arwen standing on the footbridge over there."

All trace of the sun had now disappeared, only the light of the moon illuminating the area. We sat down by the lock, our legs dangling into the chamber.

"So over the river there, that's where we camped," I told him. "I hope the kids are still upholding this end-of-year tradition."

Eddy leant back, arching his spine to stare skywards. I peered above too to observe the stars pinging on one by one, a chaotic splattering of dots illuminating on the blank canvas of night like tiny lightbulbs, ready for any intelligent life-form below to join up those dots and create meaning from its randomness.

"Do you think they really guide our fate?" Eddy asked

me. I understood exactly what he was on about, referring to my star-crossed comment the other day.

Didn't he already know the answer? Didn't his exalted status make him privy to such esoteric knowledge, freeing him from the worries and contemplations of ordinary mortals?

"Sometimes they appear to, and then sometimes they don't," I said.

"My mother is into all that stuff, taught to her by my grandmother. Astrology, tarot. She even communes with the dead."

"Snap. My nan has got into that, too, although there is a strong suspicion it's related to her dementia. But who knows? Perhaps the dementia has just lifted the blindfold from her inner eyes."

Eddy stroked his chin as he gazed in wonder towards the heavens. My focus had shifted to the beauty down below.

"I visited my mother right before I came over to Europe," he said. "She's forever divining on me and my brothers and sister, peering into the crystal ball, giving us insights we never asked for. She always knew I would become famous, she told me, destined for all this stuff I do. And when I saw her before I left, she said my trip would be transformative, that I needed to be alert for something that would come along and change things."

Was he thinking of those words in that moment when I'd erroneously stepped onto his trailer? Did I have his mother to thank for him not dismissing me as a random nobody, conditioning his mind to be open to pursuing this thing we had going on, whatever it was?

"Got to listen to mum," I replied. "She knows best."

He caught me looking at him, a moment of silence coming between us before his lips moved closer to mine. We were seconds into a kiss when my phone started ringing.

"Well, it wasn't quite like Laura Linney in *Love Actually*," I remarked. "Could have been worse. Could have been half naked." I read Nan's name on the screen, so I accepted the call. "Yes?"

I put it on speaker for the benefit of Eddy.

"Hazel, it's Kitty. I'm just with your grandmother..."

"Oh no, what's she done now?"

"She's rather unsettled, came knocking on the door, talking about Warren, and wondering where you were."

"Okay. Can you put her on?"

"Will do. I'll leave the phone with her. Must pop back as the tates are on the stove."

"Thanks Kitty."

We heard her speaking to Nan and as the handset passed to her, it sounded like Nan was climbing a mountain rather than sitting on her backside at home.

"Hazel," she said, "your grandfather wants to know if you're coming home tonight."

Eddy raised an eyebrow. It was like she'd been listening in on our conversation.

"Is Grandad there now?"

"He's sitting right beside me."

Eddy manufactured a worried expression, his lips curling.

"Can you put him on the line for me?"

"Wait a second."

We both listened in, Nan getting increasingly agitated as she attempted to converse with the imaginary being in her mind. Her voice sounded so normal, no pretence in it whatsoever, and that just made this scenario even more chilling as we continued to listen in.

"He won't say anything," she said. "He doesn't look very happy at all."

"Of course not," I replied.

"What time are you coming back, Hazel?"

Sighing, I said, "I don't know. I'm out with Eddy at the moment. We were going to get something to eat and then I was hoping to stay with him tonight."

Nan had no prudish side to her at all. She'd never had any, so it was easy to be honest with her like this.

"Warren, Hazel wants to speak to you," she continued to shout at thin air. I rolled my eyes as she spouted something else, and then the line went dead.

"Do you think we should go see her?" Eddy asked. "Make sure she's okay?"

"Yes, that would be the right thing to do," I heard myself say. I really didn't want to move. I'd been enjoying this moment, the serenity of being in this secluded place with Eddy. Even though it was chilly out there, our body temperatures gradually lowering, I would have been content to stay there with him all night.

But I was my nan's carer. This was my responsibility. In *Love Actually*, Laura had ditched her lover with no hesitation so she could attend to her upset brother, destroying her chance for love. Hazel Nightingale, on the other hand? She just lays there, wanting to hang on to a moment that had already gone. It had all been so perfect until that phone call as we stargazed, imagining we were in a fairytale Tolkien world.

Eddy was first to his feet, offering me his hand. Once he'd pulled me up, I kept my grip on him, and we walked hand in hand all the way back to the car.

Chapter 27

"YOU'VE JUST MISSED HIM," NAN said right after we rushed into the living room. Not even with that flashy Audi at our disposal had we managed to get there in time to catch the revenant of my grandfather. I was certain Nan would have greeted us with the same statement if we'd instantly teleported ourselves back to New York.

"Oh well," I said. "Not to worry."

Still she was restless, peeping through the Venetian blinds to see if he might be out there, rubbing her hands together, pinching the little flap of skin between her thumb and forefinger. That was often the telltale sign she was experiencing one of her senior moments.

"He went off in this black car. It pulled up on the drive and he got in the back. Never spoke a word to me about where he was going."

"Let's sit down, Dora," Eddy said, putting on his hypnotic movie star charm. "What about if Hazel makes you a cup of tea?"

"I suppose," she conceded, as Eddy put an arm around her shoulder and steered her to the settee. I didn't think in a million years, even with a fortune-telling mother offering him the secrets of his fate, would he have imagined that on his trip to England he would act as a carer for a geriatric with dementia.

Nan settled in her seat, muttering to herself, "Nobody knows what it's like. Nobody knows." Eddy tiptoed off to the kitchen with me as I made the drinks. He peered back round the doorway as Nan's mutterings dissipated.

"She's not so buggin' now."

"Thanks," I said, throwing him an appreciative smile. This job was so much more manageable with someone else to help you, when you had backup. "So what's the betting this black car that came for Grandad was a hearse?"

Eddy nodded. "Still dealing with the grief? How long ago did he pass away?"

"Eighteen years it must be now," I said, my head cocking back as I reflected. "We were a few years into the new millennium. It was a May day, May Day, in fact..."

I was about to tell him more, how Grandad had been out in the back garden pruning the rose bushes. One moment he was happily clipping away, the next he was lying on the grass. I was at school when it happened, Nan the one to discover him, the one to raise the alarm. He was long dead before the ambulance had arrived.

I glanced towards the window much like my eyes are often drawn to a television screen even though it isn't even on. Despite there being nothing to see, much went through my mind. Eighteen years it had been, and it still felt as though Grandad was out there attending to that rose bush.

"She had no signs of dementia until he died," I said, returning my gaze to Eddy, his sparkling blue eyes a very welcomed comfort. "It was like she just couldn't deal with the new reality of him gone. I know she continues to miss him dreadfully, so that's why she creates these fantasies."

"She really believes it though, doesn't she? She was absolutely convinced he came to her tonight."

My jaw firmed, I nodded in sombre agreement.

"Kind of hope I'll be like this when I'm her age, not knowing what's real, what's your mind playing tricks," Eddy said. "And that's the thing with people with dementia; they don't realise they have it, at least once they get so deep into it."

"Well, I got her genes," I said. "So it's already written as far as my stars are concerned. Something to look forward to, eh?"

"Do you think maybe you should stay here with her

tonight?"

"Oh," I replied as I poured boiling water into the mugs.

"It's not that I don't want you to come back to mine," he said, placing his hand on my shoulder. "What if she goes outside again looking for him, walks out into the main road?"

I nodded. "Yeah. No telling what she might do, I suppose."

But what if she has another do tomorrow night, and the night after, and the night after that? Come on, Eddy. You're the only good thing I got going on in my life!

"Hopefully she'll be settled again by the morning," he said.

"As long as you make it up to me for the evening we've lost tonight, Mr Partridge."

"You can count on it, Miss Nightingale."

We took our drinks into the living room and sat with Nan who, by the time it had taken to make those cuppas, had forgotten we were there. I left Eddy to conduct the dementia therapy with her, seeing as he was such a natural at it. Perhaps he had an advantage from not having been around her as much. He hadn't had to put up with her asking the same questions again and again like I had. Mine had been eroded some time ago, but Eddy's cliff of patience was largely untouched by the tides of her disorder.

I flicked the television on, searching for the channel with all the game shows. That one was always a safe bet with my nan, an effective distraction.

A little later on, Eddy's phone rang. He disappeared out the front door to escape the din of the television. I had the impression it was an important call, fate attempting to interfere with our evening once more.

Back off. You've already messed things up!

Fifteen minutes later, he still hadn't returned, so I popped outside to investigate. I heard no chatter, Eddy

240

sitting on the bonnet of the Audi in the darkness as he dabbed away on his phone screen. The security light triggered again from my movement, bathing us in a harsh glare.

"Sorry, Hazel, I have to go."

"Right. I thought that was coming."

"I'll be getting another call in a bit."

"Well, till tomorrow then, I guess."

"Yeah." He straightened up and approached me. "How's Dora?"

"Enthralled with the hundred thousand pound final round against the chaser."

"Great. I'm sad I'm going to miss it."

He leant forward and kissed me on my forehead.

"Goodnight, my little Berkeley Square songbird."

"Night, Eddy."

He flashed a smile, then hopped over to the Audi. The car sparked into life, Eddy reversing onto the road, throwing me one last wave before zipping off into the night. The security light faded.

Much as my grandfather had allegedly got into a car on that drive, all trace of Eddy was now gone, nothing to prove that he had been here. I could almost believe this ability to manifest one's beloved was something shared by all generations of the Nightingale family, although there was one telltale sign that Eddy's visit was no illusion, the scent of his aftershave on me from kissing him. Unless that was all part of the delusion. Or I had covid again.

I returned to the living room, the two contestants of the final round successfully winning the prize money with only one more question for the chaser to get through. At least this was a lucky night for someone, or rather it was just the *retelling* of someone's fortune, seeing as this was a repeat.

"What's on next?" I asked Nan.

"Do you want to put a film on?"

"Sure. Why not?"

I flicked through the streaming services to see what caught my eye, soon arriving at a childhood favourite. Something with a darker edge seemed fitting with the mood I was in.

The Nightmare Before Christmas (1993)
Directed by Henry Selick
Film Review by Hazel Nightingale

Although he didn't direct it, this
production has Tim Burton written all over
it, a visually stunning tale filled with
weird and macabre characters and a thumping
soundtrack by Danny Elfman. And just imagine
what they can do with all its imagery.
Yogurt, the Yoda parody in *Spaceballs*, would
go crazy with all the possibilities for
merchandise, merchandise!

Indeed, *The Nightmare Before Christmas* is
a masterpiece in terms of its visuals, a
stop-motion animation that took years to
make. If this were a game of Top Trumps, then
nothing is going to beat it in this category.
But pick another category and perhaps it
isn't so indomitable.

The festivals of Halloween and Christmas
aren't so distinctly different when Jack
Skellington, the main protagonist of Burton's
animation, gets his hands on it. A resident
of Halloween Town, he finds a portal to
Christmas Town one day and resolves to take
his own stab at this festival of light and
gift-giving. But Jack can do this in only the
way he knows, beginning with usurping Santa.
As he goes from chimney to chimney in his
sleigh pulled by bone-deer and a ghostly red-
nosed dog, he delivers kids stomach-churning
gifts of swollen heads and killer snakes.

Perhaps these two seasons are closer

cousins than you might have thought. With only a couple of months between them, both falling within the darker days of the calendar year (at least for the Northern Hemisphere), some might suggest they should have been thrust together in the same story sooner. They might argue that they are both horror shows, especially those bah-humbuggers amongst us, right? As Charles Dickens showed, the Yuletide festival can have a dark and spooky edge to it.

But while the masterful *A Christmas Carol* is the indomitable card to have in the narrative category, *Nightmare* could learn a thing or two from its vanquisher. With its many musical sequences, it often feels as though you're watching a… well, music video. So focussed on its visuals, what is neglected is what's underneath it all. Although it's a magnificent film, you have that nagging thought that it could have been so much more.

With a fresh cinematic release in the autumn of 2020 proving a success, it only demonstrated the love that audiences retain for this movie. Or perhaps with a new wave of coronavirus about to crash back then, the title seemed an apt description for the times we were living. *This year, kids, Christmas won't be like any you've known before!* Just as the police car warned the neighbourhood of Christmas Town over the tannoy, it looks like Christmas might be cancelled.

The ending always feels a little abrupt. Perhaps with the monumental effort that went into the film, they simply ran out of steam.

But it's an incredible journey over that seventy-six minutes, one that will please your eyes every time you watch it.

Verdict: 7 / 10

Chapter 28

I AWOKE THE FOLLOWING DAY with an uneasy feeling, but it wasn't until I knocked back my morning coffee that I could get my thoughts in order. There was something in the air, for sure, something causing the nerves in my guts to fire like static, and it definitely wasn't the butterfly-bats this time.

My daydreams drifted down some dark avenues. What if Eddy had run into trouble last night after leaving me? Unused to these rural roads, driving on the other side of the road, operating a *stick shift* as he described it, one he'd never driven before, it wasn't so hard to imagine that something had gone wrong. And how would I have known? If he was bundled into an ambulance, nobody would say, '*Hang on, we'd better tell that chick he's been hanging around with, make her aware he's off to hospital. You know, that local girl who was in the newspaper?*'

Checking my phone, there had been no messages from him overnight. No doubt his agent had kept him up late talking movie biz stuff.

Or he's lying in Pilgrim Hospital on a ventilator.

I fired him off a quick text. There was a really simple way to settle these nerves and then I could put these worries out of my mind and get on with the day.

Hey Partridge, just wanted to say good morning. Find your way to the hotel okay last night? X

Every second that I waited for a reply, did that nagging doubt get louder and louder. *Why hasn't he texted you back yet, Hazel? What's happened to him? Is it time to start phoning the A&E wards?*

Eventually, a message came in. It had seemed a lot longer, but it had taken him only three minutes to answer me.

Hey Nightingale. For sure. Gotta love sat nav. See you later x

There I had it. He sounded absolutely fine. Nothing to worry about. Yet somehow that strange souring of the atmosphere lingered. Perhaps it was residue from the film we'd watched last night, Jack Skellington and his nightmarish Noel. I half imagined the universe had some ghoulish gifts to bring my way.

Once Eddy had filmed all his various interviews, he was going to shoot over to New York to pick me up before we headed towards the coast. He'd mentioned about seeing the Mayflower monument on the outskirts of Boston, and then we'd go on to Skeggie. I really didn't mind where we went, just as long as I was with him.

"Do you want me to make you a pancake this morning?" Nan asked me as she emerged from her bedroom in her dressing gown. I'd heard her snoring loudly in the night. Last night's fuss had taken it out of her.

"You need to think about making your eggnog, Dora. Not long till Christmas now. We can't go without that."

"Oh, I'll make some if you want, add a little of your grandfather's whisky."

"Sounds great."

"So what about breakfast?"

"I thought I'd distracted you from that subject. I'm not hungry, Nan."

"Don't be thinking just because you have a man now you have to be starving yourself."

I raised a smile, but it soon faded.

"I fear I might be punching here."

"Eh?" she asked, the wrinkles beside her eyes even more pronounced. I knew she wouldn't understand the boxing analogy of competing in a class far above one's own.

"I don't think I'm right for him."

Her eyes opened wide. "Don't talk so soft. Anyone would

be lucky to have my Martin."

"Hazel."

She scrunched up her face in frustration at the wrong name coming out of it. "*Hazel.* With looks like yours, you could have anyone."

"Thanks, Nan."

I heard the signal, two crisp, short pips. That flashy coupe even had a tone to its hooter that sounded far sweeter and superior to your average car horn, like an angel sounding a melodic note from a trumpet. I grabbed my coat, shouted goodbye to Nan, and hurried outside.

"You're late, Mr Partridge," I began, the start of a cutesy telling off.

Something with this picture was wrong. Eddy sat on the bonnet, his face angled away from me, his eyes to the frosty stones of the gravel drive, his shoulders sagging. Someone was sitting in the passenger seat, in *my* seat. There were no back seats to the Audi Spyder. It was a motor for zipping around with some speed, for turning you into a poser, enabling you to show off to the girl beside you, but it wasn't a vehicle for three-wheeling.

"Bringing a chaperone this afternoon?" I asked him.

Eddy said nothing, still wouldn't look at me.

"Did you read up on Skegness last night and realise you needed to bring along Bowman for your own security? It's really not that bad, you know."

The bodyguard wore shades even though it was gloomy. He angled his face towards the neighbour's bungalow, but I suspected his eyes were focussed on me.

"I'm sorry, Hazel..."

I nodded, my mouth somehow forming a smile. My

rotten luck the past couple of days was perversely amusing.

"You're leaving."

"I knew there was a reason not to go for that role."

"That self tape you did?"

He didn't reply to my question, which gave me the answer. I'd sown the seeds for this very moment myself, encouraging him to do that damned tape, not realising it would come back to haunt me.

"They want me to do a screen test, first thing tomorrow morning."

"Tomorrow? You're going to get there in time?"

"Actually, I need to be there today. Drinks with Ricky Parkinson this evening. Schmoozing."

"Back home?"

He nodded. "In LA."

Right now he was standing there in the Lincolnshire wilds, an engagement planned on this same day at a place over five thousand miles away, an ocean and a continent between the two. How had he even factored in this time to come to New York to say goodbye to me?

If Bob Geldof could get Boy George to fly his forgetful backside from that other New York to London on the same day to record his charity single, *and* going against the time zone grain, then I supposed it was possible for Eddy to make it to LA, even without Concorde at his disposal.

My mind seemed to fixate on these logistics, as though I needed the distraction, anything but dwelling on the fact that very soon he would not be around me anymore.

"Well, you'd better get moving then. Getting into Heathrow can be a pig, whatever time of day. What time's your flight?"

He just shook his head, unwilling to spend this last moment with me talking about trivial matters like departure times, or what terminal he was flying from, or where to look out for speed cameras.

"Safe travels, Eddy."

I turned round, about to retreat to the bungalow so he wouldn't see me crying.

"Hazel, I'm so sorry. I didn't want this to happen," he said. I heard the crunch of gravel as he made steps towards me.

"You have an important life going on over there. This backwater is no place for you."

"You don't understand. What I feel about you..." He was right behind me now, but I still couldn't turn to face him. "I've never felt like this before about anyone, Hazel."

"Don't, Eddy. You're just making this even harder for me." My voice was breaking. "Just go."

He placed his hand on my shoulder and as I stifled some sobs, I turned to him, burying my head in his chest as I bawled. My arms wrapped round him, as though I might keep on to him if I held him tight enough.

You want him back, Bowman? You'll have to wrestle him off me!

"It's not over," he whispered to me, but my feelings told me differently. The only time I would see him again would be via the cinema screen or on television or in magazines. Or perhaps, by some fluke, his work would bring him to Lincolnshire once more, reprising his role as Gerrick James in *Flying Colours Part 2*, even though he never made it out of the first film alive.

The passenger door opened. Bowman emitted a subtle cough. Time.

"I gotta go now, Hazel."

"Yes. Go."

I pulled away from him, our eyes locking together for the last time, just like they had done in that moment on his trailer, the whole universe flashing between us.

He walked to the car and got in as his companion did the same. Moments later he was gone, the growl of the

Audi's engine fading from the air as I sat down on the front doorstep and stared numbly at nothing. And that was that. The fairytale was over.

I was still there, however long had passed, when a figure lingered at the end of the drive. Although I'd seen him, it took me a few seconds for it to register in my brain.

"Good morning, Hazel." It was Cliff, the local busybody out walking his dogs. I'm sure he timed that activity to coincide with bumping into me, twitching his curtains beforehand to see if I might be around.

I raised a hand to acknowledge him. It was all I could muster.

"Now then, don't think I'm interfering," he began, which meant he was about to interfere.

What have you got to tell me, Cliff? Some sort of dramatic revelation to relay to me? An unlikely twist of fate that will rescue me from the black hole of despair that has swallowed me?

"I couldn't help noticing your wheelie bin..."

Oh my lord.

"Yes. I realise it's out a day early," I spoke over whatever garbage he was explaining to me. "I was planning to be out all day so that's why it's there now."

"Oh no, it's not that," he said, injecting a note of understanding in his voice, which made him sound even more patronising. "Soon going to put my bin out, too. It's just that, you've placed rather a lot of rubbish in yours, so much so the lid is actually unable to close properly."

He crouched down to inspect the gap, as though that chasm needed close examination to comprehend the earth-shattering problem it was causing.

"Right...?" I asked after a pause.

"You know full well what the weather's like round here, the wind whipping in off the North Sea. It won't take much to flip your lid the rest of the way open, and then we'll have soiled napkins and potato peelings and a plethora of unmentionables blowing all over the street. A tidy village is a happy village."

Suddenly my life of romancing a movie star seemed light years away. Eddy had been right here only minutes ago. In fact, in the grand cycle of existence, this was essentially the *same* moment. The smell of his aftershave still lingered on me. Yet somehow, we'd gone from one extreme to the other.

"I do apologise, Cliff," I said as I lifted myself to my feet. Could he not tell this was not the right time to be talking about refuse collections? Hadn't he noticed my forlorn demeanour as I'd sat slumped on the doorstep?

How tone deaf can you get, man? You really want to see me flip my lid?

As I grabbed a wooden cane from the front garden, what had been stuck in the soil as support for one of Nan's summer sunflowers, I strolled up to the bin and used that stick to prod my rubbish down further into it.

"Thank you for giving me yet another lesson in the etiquette of neighbourly waste management."

I slammed the lid shut, tossed the cane aside, then marched up to the bungalow, leaving the wheelie bin-obsessed pillock behind me.

"And stop putting on that fake accent," I shouted over to him. "We all know you're not a true native!"

Before I disappeared behind the building, I glimpsed Cliff looking startled, his head peering around to see if anyone may have heard my scandalous allegation. I entered the bungalow through the back door.

"Has he gone?" Nan asked the moment I stepped inside. She stood by the front window, one of the blinds dislodged from her prising it apart so she could peep at the unfolding drama on the drive.

"Cliff Baker? I hope so."

"I meant your American friend. Eddy."

Not only had she remembered seeing him when he'd been gone a whole five minutes, she even remembered his name. Undoubtedly today she would have been absolutely fine, no confusion, no bothering the neighbours, no arguing with ghosts, no creating at all. The perfect condition for me to spend the entire afternoon and evening away from her on a date with Eddy. As if the universe really needed to kick me so mercilessly when I was down. First Cliff and now this.

"Yeah. He's off back home."

"Oh. I am sorry. He was a nice man. You two looked good together."

"Well, that's life," I replied as I kicked off my shoes and shrugged off my coat. I headed straight for my room where I shut myself in with no intention of emerging from it for the rest of the day, or, with any luck, the rest of the year.

Chapter 29

"Ninety-two years old but she can still prance around the dance floor better than your average *Strictly* contestant."

As Christmas fast approached, I'd emerged from my cave to attend some kind of contemporary market on the grounds of the craft centre in the middle of Sleaford. I was chilled to my bones standing outside, and all I could think about was my warm bed.

The entertainment had been provided by the locals, and Martin made a fair assessment of Nan's performance with her fellow Morris dancers. Fellow fruit loops, more like. Within the pavilion, their bells jingled, rods clacked, ribbons streaming from their outfits that had more colour than a Christmas tree.

"You just see her when she's been on the sherries," I replied. "Michael Jackson didn't have nothing on her."

"Aren't you glad now you came, you grump?" Martin asked, wrapping an arm round my shoulder, either to display some tenderness or because I was looking hyperthermic.

Having heard all about my recent fling with a certain foreigner, he'd been in touch to check up on his bigger little sister. I really had made his life even more complicated. Not only did he have Nan to think about following my woeful efforts to care for her, he also had to keep an eye on me now I'd slipped into this funk.

He was the nearest I had to a father. When Dad had cleared off, my elder sibling had stepped up to the plate, eyeing the crown of patriarch. Thankfully, his constitution had not been confused in receiving two lots of Nightingale genes, his character constructed from the good ones, the ones on Mum's side.

I'd been back in the Shire for a few weeks now, so it was about time to reconnect with him, and especially before I joined the *all-men-are-let-downs* club. Martin was a great ambassador for the male contingent of the species. Typical that the only decent guy I knew was my own brother.

"Yeah, it's refreshing to get out the bungalow," I conceded. "And nice to see you, too. You look old by the way, big bro."

He laughed off my catty comment. I knew, in fact, he liked it. Often we would trade playful insults, attempting to outdo the other. They served well as a release valve.

I felt like I now truly understood what all those England fans had gone through after we'd lost the final of the Euros. Personally, I had little riding on that game, no years of emotional investment that yearned for a silverware return. But caught up in the hype of that tournament and the excitement of my fellow flatmates, it was the first match I'd ever watched all the way through, and it had gone to extra time. The only other times I'd viewed any of the sport was when Dad would come into the lounge to turn off whatever kiddie show Phillipa and I were watching so he could watch the footie before we sulked off to find something else to amuse us. So I'd never had a good association with the game, it mostly reminding me of my dad's tyrannical command of the television remote.

And really, I simply wanted an England victory so that all my friends would be happy. Recalling their crestfallen demeanours that lingered days after England's last penalty was saved, I imagined was the aura I currently conveyed. A feeling of loss, a teasing glimpse of how life could have been so victorious, only for it to be ripped away from me. And the knowledge that it was surely a once in a lifetime experience and that nothing would ever be as good again. I'd been there for my friends to lift them from the gloom, and now my brother was doing the same for me.

'Nobody wins unless everybody wins,' my mother always used to say, quoting her favourite singer.

Someone else would bring our nation unexpected glory a few months later on, however, Emma Raducanu in her unbelievable rise to greatness as she won the US Open Tennis Championship. Now that truly was a fairytale of New York; I heard the commentator say as much. And just another reminder that the New York of America was the only one where they could happen.

With their set over, the dancers cleared away as a bearded guitarist then began setting up for his bit. He sported a long scarf, reminiscent of the one Tom Baker wore in *Doctor Who*. As I peered over, I had the feeling I recognised him, but my brain was like fog and I couldn't place him. He continued the festive theme, singing lyrics that invited the audience to picture a snowman with a big carrot nose.

Beyond the craft centre, I'd earlier mooched around the giant marquee on the green, mustering some admiration for the various handmade items on sale, jewellery and ceramics and expensive tat that in other years, in better moods, I would have found quite charming. Still, I'd found a delightful gift for my sister, thus completing the Christmas shopping for another year.

Yeah, maybe it was good to get out, invigorating to be back in tune with the rural life of Lincolnshire. What had I been expecting from my romance with that New Yorker? It hadn't been part of the deal. Fate had thrown us together only because I needed some work. That's all I'd been in it for as I'd stepped into his razzmatazz world. I merely had to look on it as a bonus from the hand I was dealt, a rogue ace that shouldn't have even been there.

"Did you read the papers?"

He looked at me as though I'd just asked if he watched *Love Island*. 'As if I bother with that rubbish, Hazel!'

"Nope. Well, not the nationals. You'll be glad to know you didn't make it in either the *Sleaford Standard* or the *Target*, so nobody in these parts will have a clue about your affair to remember. I expect they all see you as just another muppet."

As though this were a goofy comedy, a couple of passing teenagers paused in front of us, one of them nudging the other and saying, "Here, ain't that Eddy Partridge's bit of fluff?"

"Except that one," Martin added. "He's most probably from out of town."

While he shooed them away, I pulled my woolly hat down, wishing it would cover my entire head.

"Want a drink?" Martin asked me after dealing with the loud-mouthed rapscallions.

"Yeah. Anything with alcohol."

He peered up and down the line of market stalls. "Hot chocolate with Irish Whisky?"

"Perfect."

The guy with the guitar finished his opener, then announced over the PA system that he would have some help with his next number. Accompanied by a tall chap who was likely the headteacher, a choir of young children gathered round an additional microphone. As I glanced across the crowds, I sensed that many of these people were the parents of these kids. The song appeared to have been custom written about their school.

The moment took me back, transporting me too many years into the past when I was a young schoolgirl.

The nativity. I wasn't part of the crowd that time, not one of the *supporting artists* shoved into the background. No, they gave me a leading role in this. I was Mary. My entertainment career had started off right at the very top and it seemed I'd worked my way down to the very bottom with my uncredited role of unnamed party-goer in Eddy's

257

film. What range my star had spanned, from mother of the saviour of mankind to complete nobody, from one end of the universe to the other.

Gazing into the audience in my school hall as we'd sung about following the star, wearing my white and blue cloak, baby Jesus in the form of a plastic doll cradled in my arms, Joseph and a donkey either side of me, I spotted my mother. Her eyes glistening, she couldn't have looked any more proud of me.

It was the same expression I saw in the faces of these people watching their children sing about Christmas trees and lights and Yule logs burning bright. My eyes panned from one to the other, and then they froze.

Standing by a big red postbox, she was facing the other direction from everyone else. She was looking my way, gazing directly at me.

Mum?

She appeared exactly as I remembered her, wearing her black denim jacket with all those pin badges. Peace signs, rock bands, The Clash, Pink Floyd, Carter. The Boss, of course. A big smiley yellow face, one with a single word, 'Relax'. Time had not ravaged her. She was still just as beautiful. I could picture every single detail of her, just as I still knew every line of that nativity carol.

What child is this who, laid to rest, on Mary's lap is sleeping?

Why had she come here dressed like that today? Nothing but a thin vest on beneath her jacket, flip-flops on her naked feet. She'd catch a cold in this weather. It was more the sort of attire she would wear on our summer holiday trips when Phillipa and I would travel down south with her in her old VW camper van, our excursions usually coinciding with a music festival.

Whom angels greet with anthems sweet, while shepherds watch are keeping?

258

She smiled at me, raised her hand, and waved.

"Here you are. This should defrost you," Martin said as he held up a cardboard cup. "Hazel?"

"Do you see her?"

He followed my gaze. "Who? Nan? She's over there with Kitty."

My eyes instinctively tracked his pointing finger as it blocked my view.

"No, I meant... Doesn't matter."

As he lowered his arm, I returned my focus to the postbox. She was gone. Well, she hadn't been there at all, of course, because Mum had been dead for over twenty years.

"You okay, maggot?"

"Yeah. Fine," I replied, taking the hot chocolate from him. "Losing my mind."

"Not you as well."

"Thanks for the drink." I swallowed a mouthful and nearly choked as it burnt my tongue.

"It's hot by the way."

"I'll just wait till the next ice age for this to cool down."

I could feel Martin's eyes on me. When I looked up at him, he said, "It's going to be okay, Hazel."

"How did you manage to do it so well, looking after Nan? You made it look so easy."

"I'm a master of deception."

"You never found it a struggle, what with handling everything in your own life too?"

His lungs inflated. "Explaining the same things over and over to her? Getting a call from Kitty because she'd been seen wandering down the fens again? Trying to fix her television because she'd somehow pressed a sequence of buttons on the remote that had unlocked a level in the settings hitherto unknown to man? I should have given her my old Sega, see if she could unlock the hidden levels on *Mortal Kombat* I could never find."

"You were so rubbish at that game."

"And I would be the first to admit it. I know; You frequently kicked my head in." Our conversation ran dry as we both focussed our attention on the singing schoolkids. "It's all a losing game, Hazel." He didn't need to tell me he was no longer talking about his childhood video games. "There's only one way it ends, no matter what we do."

"Listen at you, Martin. Now who's the one being morose?"

It was natural to assume this was all about us being there for Nan, serving her now she was what society labelled 'vulnerable'. But what if we'd got that wrong? What if we saw beyond the immediate trivialities of making her porridge and filling her pill planner and ferrying her to the warfarin clinic? Perhaps, within the bigger picture, she was there for us.

"Anyway," he said, taking another sip of his drink. "I suppose we'd better fetch her before she wanders off and ends up in the Slea."

As Kitty and Nan stood there yards away from us, I could read their body language; Nan looking increasingly confused, Kitty resting a reassuring hand on her shoulder.

"Yeah. Time to get her home, I think. With any luck, by the time I get back, this drink will be at a consumable temperature."

"Good to see you again, fuzzball."

"You too, nerf-herder."

Chapter 30

"NOW THEN, IN A COUPLE of days, you'll all be getting a visit from the big, fat fella," Robin said as he stepped back up to the microphone, his throat freshly oiled with whisky between sets. "If you've been good girls and boys, that is. But were you aware that Santa actually came from round here? That's right, Santa Claus is one of us, a true yellowbelly. And we know a song about it, don't we, guys?"

The lead guitarist, Glen, kicked off the number with his opening riff before Robin sang about how Father Christmas indeed lived in a village not too far away from New York, the glamorously named Anton's Gowt (a place that sounded like a *Strictly* dancer with painful joints). Putting a fresh Lincolnshire stamp on the whole Saint Nicholas mythology, it also turned out that a visit to Sincil Bank inspired the colour scheme of his outfit, the Mighty Imps playing in their red and white.

The Mall was as packed as it could be to see the Black Grass Bandits' Christmas gig, festive jumpers and hats on display, mulled wine flowing, mince pies piled high on trays. Even Nan had turned out tonight and she hadn't refused a dance from Melissa's twin brother, Randal. There was a lot of 'the Morris' in her moves.

We had so much to be grateful for, all those scientists that had come up with the vaccines. I wondered how long it would be for them to invent a vaccine for heartbreak, although I had to admit an evening of live music and drinks in the local was effective therapy.

"So, did you two, like... you know?"

I leant closer to Melissa, cocking my ear as if waiting for her to finish her question, even though I knew what she was on about. Thanks to that newspaper article, a certain

261

transatlantic love affair was common knowledge, in the public domain. Although there were plenty of details known only to me and Eddy, those gaps provoked speculation.

"Yes?" I prompted her.

"Did you two make it a *special relationship*?"

"You mean did I sleep with him?"

"Uh-huh."

"A lady never tells, Melissa! But I am from the fens, and I've had one or three shandies, so I guess I can tell you. Yes, we took it to the next level. He shot a home strike, scored a touchdown at every base, or however their euphemism goes. I'm not really into sport."

She hung on my every word in our girlie chat, in awe of my affair with the Hollywood superstar, that vicarious look on her face saying, *Why can't something cool like this happen to me?* Nan was sitting down again, catching her breath. Although she was right next to me, it was most likely she couldn't hear my words over the music. Not that I would have filtered anything for her. She and I could have had the exact conversation, most probably in greater detail, too.

"So... what now?" Melissa asked.

"What do you mean?"

"Where do you two go from here? I take it he's gone back to America, yeah?"

"He has, and that's the end of the story."

"Is that what he said?"

"Not exactly. He's so reticent. Really smashes the perception that Americans are outspoken."

"Maybe he's working things out."

"Melissa, look; The reality is, you don't see him on my arm, do you? In fact, I've not heard a thing from him since he left. Guys like him don't have time for girls like me."

"That's so sad."

"It's nothing I didn't expect, if I'm honest. You just have to make the most of these things while you have them.

Nothing lasts forever. Listen to your Auntie Hazel here."

I looked towards my Nan and she caught my gaze and smiled back. Perhaps one day I might create a coping mechanism as she had done, find a way to carry on after losing someone. As far as she was concerned, Grandad was genuinely visiting her every evening and sitting with her in the living room watching repeats of game shows.

"So, aside from the *Notting Hill* aspect, what did you make of being a film extra?" Melissa asked. "Would you do it again?"

I hadn't thought about this at all, and I needed a moment to reflect on my feelings. Might it remind me of him? Lightning would not strike twice, I would not feel this thrill again. My next gig would not involve another romance with another film star, not that I wanted that. But even more unlikely was the possibility I would be cast in another film starring Eddy. This kind of thing was a once in a lifetime deal, like winning the lottery, and I had already spent all my riches. I didn't see any other way the universe would put us together once more.

"In the absence of any other work coming my way, then no, I wouldn't turn anything down."

Her eyes lit up. "Great. I had an enquiry for a job in January for a Ryan Reynolds film. If you get it too, you have to go for it. Bring some of your luck with you to rub off on me. But hands off Ryan. This time it's my turn."

"I promise he's all yours. But I'm not sure Blake Lively will be too happy about it."

"Oh yeah, forgot about her. Well, she doesn't need to know. What happens in Vegas and all that."

My head was feeling rather light, much like some of those moments I'd shared with Eddy, drunk on the endorphins. Nan had insisted we both had some drinks tonight, so we'd left Clarence at the bungalow and taken a taxi here.

"What are you doing Christmas Day?" Melissa asked.

"We're both off to Martin's house in Sleaford. He has plenty of space for us all. Phillipa's coming over too from Norton."

"That'll be nice."

"How about yourself?"

She frowned again. "Working."

"Bummer. Still, I'm sure you guys are just glad to be back up and running."

"Definitely makes a change from Christmas last year."

The song about Santa being a yellowbelly concluded, and the room clapped and cheered.

"Thank you," Robin spoke into his microphone. "Now, you may have noticed that Hollywood has been in town recently, shooting a war film. Eddy Partridge was here, Janice Daniels. My own daughter worked on it so you'll have to look out for her lurking in the background somewhere, much like she is at the moment."

Heads craned round, and I held up both my arms to point out a blushing Melissa.

"One of her co-stars is with her tonight..."

Oh, don't do me as well.

"Film critic turned film extra, Hazel Nightingale, who's come all the way from a certain village down the fens. I don't think that's the place Shane MacGowan had in mind when he wrote this next one, but this one's for you, duck."

There were cheers as the band began their rendition of everyone's favourite Christmas song.

Melissa turned to me and said, "You've got his number, right?"

"Shane MacGowan's? Afraid not."

"No, dummy. Eddy. Message him. Let him know you're thinking of him."

"I'm only thinking about him because you keep thinking about him."

"Rubbish. You miss him like crazy. I can tell, Hazel. You need to tell him how you feel."

He already knows...

"Do it," she went on. "It's Christmas. You know what Andrew Lincoln wrote on his cards to Keira Knightley. At Christmas you speak the truth."

"So why hasn't he messaged me once? He's been gone days."

"Because he's busy making films. What's your excuse?"

"If his hands are full, then what good is it me causing a distraction?"

"Just do it, Hazel."

I humoured her and typed out a text. It was simple, merely a few words. Nothing much. My finger hovered over the send button.

"You done it?" she asked.

I couldn't bring myself to punch it. "Yeah. It's gone." If I'd glugged a couple more drinks, perhaps I would have. I'd seen it with Maddox, the way he'd chased after me, trying to rekindle something that had already sailed. I would not be like that. It didn't look good, coming across as desperate. What Eddy and I had going on was like everything else in this world, transient. That's how it was for Gerrick and Polly.

"I think what happened with his on-screen romance was a bit of a sign for me," I said.

"How so?"

"His character got shot down over France and the Nazis captured him. What you call a death knell."

"Huh?"

"Come on, what are the Nazis going to do with a black guy?"

"Shove him in a prisoner of war camp with everyone else."

"A concentration camp, more like."

Melissa shook her head. "Nah, that's not what they did."

"They shot him on the spot then?"

"No. Gerrick James survived the war. He returned to England when it finished, when the allies freed him."

"Huh. And he got back with Polly?"

"Of course. They got married, had children. In fact, she was already carrying when he got captured. One of his descendants still lives round here. Didn't Eddy tell you this?"

"Perhaps I should have done a little Googling on the matter."

He came back...

"Oh well. Nice to know there's a chance he could return for the sequel."

"When he comes back, it'll be for *you*, Hazel."

The song reached that rousing section. The Bandits didn't have an accordion or a fiddle, but they used a keyboard to emphasise the melody.

Nan leant over the table and asked, "Who's coming up for another dance?"

"Come on, Dora Nightingale," I said. "Show me your moves."

I was expecting Nan to ask me when we were going home so she wouldn't miss Grandad's nightly visit, but we made it to last orders at *The Mall*. Perhaps she was too caught up in the revelry, or perhaps she didn't mind missing him tonight as he was planning to stay longer over Christmas?

Our taxi was on its way and our coats were on as we waited for it to arrive. My glass was still half full, and I really didn't need to finish this last one off, but I necked it anyway, a decision I would surely regret come the morning.

"Now then, Dora, thank you so much for coming this evening," Robin said once he'd finished packing up his gear. He still wore his festive Santa hat. "Did you enjoy the music?"

"Oh yes," she replied. "You just need to turn it up a bit more."

Robin chuckled as I rolled my eyes.

"And how about you, Hazel Nightingale? It's been quite the whirlwind since you've been back in the Shire."

"You can say that again."

He sat down beside me, his voice taking on a different tone. "So what about that prat of an ex of yours? Has he been any more bother?"

"Dad, just leave it," Melissa butted in as she milled around us collecting empties.

"It's fine," I said to reassure her. "I haven't heard anything since the tabloid sensation. I doubt I will now." For some reason I checked my phone to see if he'd sent me any ill-timed messages in the ten minutes since I last checked my phone.

Talk of the devil and he shall appear.

To my relief, there was nothing from him. Nothing from anyone, in fact. Perhaps my subconscious was using Maddox as an excuse to check if I'd received any communication from a certain someone else. Not that I'd sent him anything to reply to.

"That's one good thing, I suppose," he said. "Still can't believe he would do that."

"I should have seen it coming."

"He deserves something in return," Robin muttered, so only I would hear. "What about giving him a taste of his own medicine? Try to dupe him with a scam like what he does."

"We could text him," I said, humouring him. "We'll say there's a parcel waiting for him for a large fee."

"Yeah. Or I'll ring him, pose as a banker, telling him he needs to empty his account."

"You have to speak like George from Uganda, though. That'll get him."

He didn't laugh at this. Either he'd never seen *Phonejacker* or he was deadly serious.

"Honestly, Hazel. I really don't like what he did to you. Never liked the guy, you know."

"You can't con a conner, Robin."

"So you're saying we should take a different tack? I've got some friends that owe me a favour."

With a wry smile on my face to diffuse the dark direction this conversation was taking, I placed my hand on Robin's. "Don't worry about it. He's not worth the bother."

He nodded, his sneer slowly dissolving. How had he gone from singing jolly Christmas songs to vengeance-seeking gangster so quickly?

"It's like what Fred says in *A Christmas Carol*," I said. "His offences carry their own punishment."

"Let's drink to that then." He clashed his glass with my empty. "Do you two want another? On the house."

"I should get her to bed." Right on cue, my phone pinged with a notification. "That's our ride now."

"Righto, you have a great Christmas," Robin said as I got to my feet. On seeing me do this, Nan did the same.

"Are we off back now?" she asked.

"Yes. Taxi's waiting."

We said our goodbyes, before stepping out into the cold air.

The taxi had parked right outside. Once we'd got in and I'd done up Nan's seatbelt, she turned to me and asked, "What was he on about Christmas for? It's not that time of year, is it?"

"Yep. That's what all those fairy lights are about," I replied as I pointed to the windows of *The Mall*.

"Ooh. I'll have to get presents for everyone."

I was too tired to explain to her we'd already done all the shopping. We had that conversation, we'd only be having it again the next time someone mentioned Christmas.

"Back to New York?" the taxi driver asked me. He was the same chap from earlier.

"Yeah. Sounds like a nice place to go."

Chapter 31

IT WAS CHRISTMAS EVE, AND although I awoke with a fuzzy head from the shandies I'd consumed last night, I did not find myself in a drunk tank, nor hear anyone singing *The Rare Old Mountain Dew*. However, it might have been preferable to the sound of Nan snoring.

This New York was no place for fairytales, Shane. It was no place to hold on to your dreams, Kirsty. If you can make it there, Frank, it didn't mean anything. Nothing you can't do, Alicia? There's nothing *to* do. You're no alien here, Sting; you're just *frim*. And it most certainly has not been waiting for you, Taylor, nor you, Alice.

But despite no singer ever writing a song about the village, and no filmmaker using it as a setting, I still dearly loved the place.

The frost had been so hard last night that it looked like fresh snow had fallen. The pink blush across the sky made all the ice crystals sparkle. That North Sea wind of which Cliff spoke was absent, all the trees standing completely still in a calm, as if hypnotised by the beautiful scenery and sunrise around them.

I didn't need any early morning television as I sat there in the living room, taking in the festive scene around me, the stockings we'd hung over the fireplace yesterday, the sacks of presents ready to take to Martin's tomorrow. Nan had even made some of her eggnog, using up the rest of 'Grandad's' bottle of whisky. I wouldn't be drinking any of it just yet, not while I was in this delicate state. Perhaps by the evening I would feel better.

Memories of Christmases past drifted through my mind, the ones we'd spent here. Nan and Grandad had always made it a magical time. I'd taken it for granted back then, but now, more than ever, I really appreciated what they had done for us.

Tragic circumstances had brought us here in the first place, and my grandparents had stepped up. Without them, we would have been completely lost.

By the time I'd finished my coffee, the dramatic colours had almost faded, the sky restoring itself to its normal blue, so I swiftly got dressed, leggings underneath my jeans, a vest underneath my jumper, a scarf around my neck. With all the buttons done up on my coat, I stepped outside to breathe in that crisp winter air, charged by the invigorating solar rays.

These were the kind of days I enjoyed most of all living in these environs. I headed down Sandy Bank Road, a serene feeling within. Much like the trees that lined the road, I too felt calm, no longer being pushed and pulled by the winds of fate. In that stillness, the sweet chatter of a red-breasted robin carried along the air to fill my ears. I looked for him but could not see him anywhere.

Farther on I discovered that someone else was up early too, evidently much earlier than me, judging by the glorious sunrise landscape on his canvas.

"Hazel. Good morning."

"Morning, Montgomery. Merry Christmas!"

"And to you."

I thought that was the end of the conversation, that he would need to rest for the remainder of the day to catch his breath after the two lines he'd delivered, but I could not have been more wrong.

"Can you spare a couple of minutes?" he asked.

"Got all the time in the world, my friend."

He placed his paintbrush down on his easel, slowly rose to his feet, then took a deep breath before he walked towards me. The tip of his nose was red from the cold, a thick woolly hat on his head with one or two holes in it. It

271

wasn't obvious at first, but it seemed to be a Christmassy hat, one he'd probably had since he was a boy. Sticking out of it was another paintbrush cradled by the top of his ear.

"Hazel, we've known each other for a long time now," he said once he'd walked up to me, his face directed down the road towards the village, as though reflecting on the sporadic interactions we'd had over the years.

"Ever since I moved here, yes. Twenty-one years ago."

"Twenty-one years and eight months," he replied, nodding. He still wasn't making eye contact with me. "I was well into my twenties at that point in my life."

I imagined that 'point' in his life was barely any different to the one he was at now, but no doubt to him they were vastly different.

"So I realise there is a significant age difference between us, seventeen years, four months and seventeen days, and I'm not sure how many hours as I'm unaware of what time of day you were born."

"I believe it was four in the morning but my memory of that period isn't so good."

"Right," he said, his eyes twitching as his brain processed the new information to update his mental data banks.

Why the heck was he talking about age differences? Only people who were involved with each other talked about that.

"And I hope it isn't a strange prospect given that I've known you since you were nine when I was a grown adult."

"What um... what prospect do you mean?" *You want to draw me like one of your fen girls?*

"I hope now you are a grown adult too you can see past that."

"Sssure?"

"You see, Hazel Nightingale, you may have noticed over the years that I've created many paintings of these surroundings."

"I had an inkling there was a little pattern there, yes."

"Even yourself and your siblings, the portrait your grandparents commissioned."

"Nan still has it up in the bungalow."

"So you'll appreciate that I'm rather qualified to appraise the aesthetics of New York and its populace."

"I'd say you know the area rather well."

"In intimate detail. I suspect many of our fellow villagers don't even see it themselves, the unheralded beauty of these fields, its sky, its mellow, straight-arrow character."

"You do seem a fan."

"I have painted this village from every angle you can imagine. I have seen all the people that have come and gone and come again, and I can honestly say, Hazel Nightingale, that you are the most beautiful feature that my eyes have had the privilege to behold. A beauty that transcends what anyone or anything else could ever strive to match."

I must have blushed at that moment. I could practically feel the heat humming from my cheeks.

"Wow. Thank you, Montgomery. I think... No, I know; That is most certainly the sweetest thing anyone has ever said to me."

And where exactly are you heading with this proclamation, my friend?

"And so I just wanted to ask you something," he said, now turning to face me, a deep reverence in his eyes as they took in my form. "Whether you might like to consider going out for dinner with me some time, once the festivities have concluded. I'm sure you have lots planned over the following days, so perhaps next week, before New Year's, in that Chrimbo limbo period. Not that I had anywhere in particular in mind for us to go, as I know very little about your tastes, although I have spotted you walking out of the Chinese in Tattershall on more than one occasion."

The poor guy looked so nervous now, trying to disguise it with this ramble.

Had I got this so wrong for so long? Had I not realised that, all along, the love of my life was under my nose the whole time? Of course, I would never be destined to find my happily-ever-after with Eddy, my polar opposite. No. It would be with one of my own. It *should* be with someone from this New York. Someone who would bravely enunciate his feelings to me. In two minutes, Montgomery had disclosed more than Eddy had done over an entire week.

"Wow, Montgomery," I said, a smile on my face. "I did not see this coming this morning one bit."

"Sorry, yes," he muttered, his eyes returning to the inferior beauty of the plain fields he'd been painting earlier. "I realise that this is something you may want to give some thought to. I've had years to think about it. You've barely had a minute."

"The thing is, Montgomery..."

He nodded as though he knew what was coming, as though he had already imagined me delivering these very friend-zoning words.

"I've just been through a couple of intense relationships, so I think right now I need to focus on myself. Try to sort my life out."

"I understand."

"We possibly work best as friends."

What was I saying? All our friendship entailed was randomly shouting greetings to each other every now and again, but I had no doubt those fleeting interactions meant a lot to him.

"I hope you find happiness one day," he said. "Have a good Christmas."

"You too, Montgomery."

He returned to his easel, resuming the finishing touches of his painting as if nothing had happened.

Could my life get any more ridiculous? What kind of film would this pitiful story make?

Fiasco of New York (2021)
Directed by Unknown. Evidently some sadist, quite likely Satan himself? Film Review by Hazel Nightingale

A tragic tale of falling in love, failure and forgetfulness, *Fiasco of New York* stars Hazel Nightingale as the Girl, someone who must be worried by now that her career has descended into perennial typecasting as she forever seems to play the girl that never catches a break.

Fiasco starts as a classic story of Girl meets Boy, here played by heartthrob Eddy Partridge, a Hollywood star who is far, far above Nightingale's league. He's from New York. She's from New York too. Yet these two could not be more worlds apart.

Girl returns to her rural roots following the loss of her job as a film reviewer for a community magazine in London. Back in Lincolnshire, Girl takes on the care of her nan, not that she can even do that right. Nan is played by Dora Nightingale whose dementia provides some comic relief. Not that it is required. Girl's love life is laughable enough.

Pursued by her obnoxious Ex, a tour de force performance here by Maddox Morales, Girl resists his attempts to rekindle their relationship. No, Girl is taking a million to one shot at that Hollywood superstar, and against all odds, he even seems to like her.

But in a deft stroke of subversion, the director of this tale sees that Girl's fortunes go from bad to worse and there they remain. Throwing away the usual trope where everything culminates in a Hollywood kiss, the rain pouring down as the orchestra swells, the frame freezing on that epic smooch, Girl is instead heartbroken when Boy suddenly has to return to his homeland, with no talk of their future, no attempts to give it a go with an ocean between them, not even a letter or a phone call or a text message to ask how she's doing. Boy doesn't even send her a Christmas card, not unless one arrives in this morning's post, which, let's face it, it won't because even if he had sent one, it wouldn't have got to England that quickly. Although, perhaps he could have sent it by some sort of special delivery? Does such a service exist between America and England? Girl will have to check this when she gets back home.

Talk about ghosting. Had their romance really meant so little to him?

Girl is bereft. The sun can't even set in her world when her horizons are filled with clouds.

Perhaps she should wish that madness would take over her as it has with her nan. Dance away with the fairies. Hallucinations are probably preferable to this constant stream of misfortune.

Verdict: 0 / 10

Chapter 32

WITH MONTGOMERY BACK IN HIS usual place, I turned around and headed for the bungalow before anyone else wanted to declare their feelings for me. The village looked far away, the road stretching before me in a long, straight line.

My eyes fell to my boots as they trampled over the frozen blades of grass held rigidly by the frost. I heard the crunch of the ice crystals as I stomped along.

Raising my head, I saw the figure in the distance. He stood in the middle of the road, facing me. Close enough that I could presume it was a man, but far enough that I could not identify him.

Maddox, perhaps? Cliff coming to nag me again about my wheelie bin? The ghost of my grandfather finally appearing to me? Because I had slipped down Nan's rabbit hole too? It was Christmas Eve, after all, the day the ghosts manifested to point out all the mistakes you've made.

Rub my nose in it, why don't you?

So much hope I could have mustered for it to be the one person in the world I wanted it to be. But that kind of thing didn't happen to people like me, did it?

It can't be him, Hazel. He left. What would he want to come back here for?

As my footsteps took me ever closer, I had a strange sensation that I could manifest whatever person I desired in this anonymous figure before me, mould him into the form that my heart pined for.

He waved. I paused, the mist billowing from my open mouth.

"Eddy?" I whispered, as though in prayer.

I ran. It must have been the first time I'd run in years,

probably since I was in school, my body wondering what the heck was going on. The sprint was all I could do to hold on to this manifestation, a morbid fear that, in one blink, he might disappear.

About ten yards from him, I paused to catch my breath. My lungs felt bruised.

"Are you really here?"

He smiled and nodded.

"Say something. Please say something."

He took a breath then said, "Got some bad news." It wasn't the proper reaction to such a statement, but I sighed in relief.

He spoke. That was a good sign, right?

Collecting myself, I asked, "What bad news?"

"I didn't get the part."

"You didn't?"

"Nah. Looks like they're going with Regé."

"Oh. I am sorry. But... silver linings and all that? I mean, you're here. I can't believe you're here."

He stepped up to me, a look in his eye that I had only just seen in someone else back down the road. He reached out his hand and trailed his finger down the side of my face, pushing a lock of hair behind my ear. I felt his fingertip.

"I missed you, Hazel Nightingale."

"I may have missed you a little, too, Eddy Partridge."

"Seems I've fallen for you," he said as he wrapped me in a warm embrace and kissed me.

We were a long way from the end of the day, but I would have gladly remained in that moment until the sun in that big sky began to set.

Afterword

The Second World War Through the Eyes of My Grandparents

Everybody Has A Story

I once worked on an educational scheme called *Making History*, whereby young children were given the necessary resources to research their family histories. Lincoln-based actor Colin McFarlane (who helped me on my research for *Fairytale*) ran the project as a *Who Do You Think You Are?* for kids, with celebrity mentors such as Jim Broadbent and Miriam Margolyes lending their support. Back when we were doing *Making History*, Colin would speak passionately about the importance of investigating what our ancestors did, particularly for children, so they might understand where they came from and who they are. With time on their side, it's important for children to begin this research at an early age, before the memories of their grandparents would fade, or, inevitably, they would no longer be around to recount their stories. My role in the project saw me filming interviews and compiling the videos the children made, but that thought was always there; Should I be taking a leaf out of this book?

Writing this novel, it was inevitable that I finally dipped into researching my own family history. This began with talking to my parents, aunts, uncles and cousins as I investigated what my grandparents did during the Second World War, the things I already knew, the things I'd forgotten, and the things I never knew because I never thought to ask my grandparents when I had the chance.

Both of my grandfathers served in the RAF in the war. Some of their tales passed down the generations into family lore, but I soon realised how much of it has eroded, at least in my own mind. With all of my grandparents now deceased, my father's generation has become the custodians of these wartime tales... And one day it will come to mine.

Many of the things I wrote about in *Fairytale* had a kernel of truth to them, but don't worry; I'm not about to go on a step-by-step explanation of everything. This is just my own little stab at a *Making History* report as I research my own family history.

Paternal

My grandmother, Ethel, was an intelligent lady, and very family-oriented, so had the foresight to document her and Grandad's life as she created an album of important photographs and keepsakes, complete with annotations; Undoubtedly she would have understood the importance of describing the context of these images, so future generations would understand what was going on in them. I found so many old photographs that had no explanation to them, as you'll see here, and so they'll probably remain a mystery forever more. But who knows? Perhaps someone reading this may be able to throw some light on these photos, might recognise a face, or have some expertise on some of the specifics I write about, and so might be able to help me fill in the gaps. If that's *you*, then please don't hesitate to get in touch with me.

The eve of war... What a year to get married. My grandparents tied the knot in April 1939 at St Elphin's Church, Warrington. The following year, Grandad joined the RAF.

Great-grandparents I never met, great-uncles and aunts I did meet when I was young. It may be a strange mirroring of history that both my brother and I were married (not to each other) 80 years later in 2019, right before the world got crazy with covid.

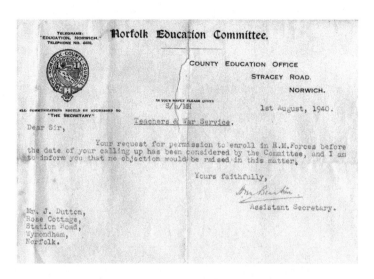

Norfolk Education Committee.

TELEGRAMS:
"EDUCATION, NORWICH."
TELEPHONE NO. 4400.

COUNTY EDUCATION OFFICE
STRACEY ROAD.
NORWICH.

ALL COMMUNICATIONS SHOULD BE ADDRESSED TO
"THE SECRETARY"

IN YOUR REPLY PLEASE QUOTE
S/E/MH

1st August, 1940.

Teachers & War Service.

Dear Sir,

Your request for permission to enroll in H.M. Forces before the date of your calling up has been considered by the Committee, and I am to inform you that no objection would be raised in this matter.

Yours faithfully,

Assistant Secretary.

Mr. J. Dutton,
Rose Cottage,
Station Road,
Wymondham,
Norfolk.

Grandad puts himself forward as history beckons...

"Teachers & War Service.
Dear Sir,
Your request for permission to enroll in H.M. Forces before the date of your calling up has been considered by the Committee, and I am to inform you that no objection would be raised in this matter.
Yours faithfully,
Assistant Secretary."

Grandad Joseph Dutton (whom I was named after) was a Corporal in 353 Squadron (pictured above), which was active mostly during World War 2 as it carried out "maritime patrol and transport tasks," (as described in Wikipedia). The Squadron was based in India. I think there may have been some Indians in its ranks, but in researching this book, I happened to read the account of a serviceman from Trinidad who was posted to the Squadron in 1945. Whether he knew my grandfather, I have no idea... I presume Joseph is somewhere in this photo, but I've not been able to place him categorically. He *might* be sitting on the plane's left wing (right of image, 5th from end).

One story we were told as kids was how Grandad played in a series of football matches during the war, representing his country. *'My Grandad played for England!'* I would tell my mates at school. One of the heirlooms passed on to my dad was the shirt Grandad wore in these games. We're sure he did wash it at some point, but you can still see the sweat marks on it. In this photo of the 353 Squadron football team, he's on the back row, second from right.

I'll stick my neck out and say Grandad was the best sportsman our family has produced. I believe he was good enough to have had trials with some of the big clubs. My cousin John told me that Bury FC offered him a contract but Joseph's father pushed him towards a more steady career, and so he became a teacher.

But during the war, Grandad had his moment of glory, representing England in a series of charity football matches.

They played weird formations back then, but it appears his position in this particular match from 1943 (see overleaf) was something akin to right-back. My cousin told me he normally played as a centre back, a position that requires plenty use of the head...

In Grandad's later years, he suffered terribly from Alzheimer's. I don't have too many memories of him where the shadow of his dementia was only faint; the curve could probably be plotted back to the early eighties. Heading towards the turn of the millennium, it was very pronounced.

Recently there has been a lot of talk about the link between dementia and former professional footballers, a study from August this year indicating that the most at risk position is defence. Whilst I was researching my grandparents, this link did occur to me with Grandad, and on discussing it with my cousin, he suggested the very same thing. The balls back then were indeed rather heavy objects. I also remember my dad telling me how Grandad would suffer from crippling migraines.

Even though I may have inherited *some* of his footballing genes, my game is limited to 5-aside where the ball is played more to feet. On the rare occasions the ball does demand a header from me, I am always reluctant, even with the softer modern balls. I wince at the thought of what damage those older footballs may have done.

A newspaper clipping my grandmother saved may also be telling... The *Eastern Daily Press* reported on a game Grandad played for Wymondham Town, highlighting him as "the star turn". In this particular match, he played with "his usual coolness and skill," as he "repelled all the onslaughts hurled against him". It all sounds so brutal, doesn't it?

★   ★   *Programme*   ★   ★

CHARITY SOCCER MATCH
IN AID OF
THE BENGAL RELIEF FUND.

INTERNATIONAL

ENGLAND
versus

SCOTLAND

AT

IRWIN STADIUM, NEW DELHI

ON

9th OCTOBER, 1943

*The price of this programme is whatever
you care to give. (Minimum—One Anna)*

★   ★   ★   ★   ★   ★

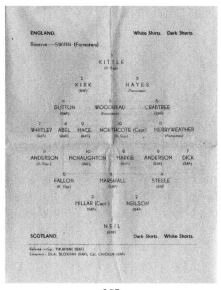

ON THE FIELD TODAY.

Any Englishman will tell you that Scotland have hardly any chance against England today, and any Scotsman will tell you that England have hardly any chance against Scotland. We hope that they are both right because that would mean that our efforts to field two sides of equal standing had succeeded. The money which gained you your admittance goes to the Bengal Relief Fund, but in taking that money from you we have tried to give you, in exchange an evening's entertainment of good class soccer. None of the names in either team is 'news', but almost without exception they are well known in their respective counties in U. K. Furthermore they have played themselves into the teams over a series of trials held during the past six weeks. Everyone of them is dead keen today and when they hear you roar for their country they will play better football than they ever dreamed of.

After the match a small cup will be presented to each player. The teams will then dine at Davico's to celebrate the union of England and Scotland.

Sgt. Thurman who has charge of the game is a professional referee of the English Football Association. Similarly S/Ldr. Bloxham and Cpl. Chicken who have kindly offered their services as linesmen.

The ball which is an 'Improved T' made by Tomlinson of Glasgow was purchased for Rs. 40 and is being raffled at two annas per ticket.

Music has been provided by the Band of the Rajputana Rifles by kind permission of the Commanding Officer.

My father told me Grandad was a fine cricketer too, an outstanding golfer, and a strong swimmer. There probably weren't too many sports that he *didn't* have a go at. When we were young grandchildren, we often played games with him, darts and bowls, and football, of course (my cousin also reminded me of a game he played called Colours where the players would be grouped into strangely named colours like heliotrope... I forget the rules but it involved throwing a ball high into the air and trying to catch it).

Sometimes Grandad would jokingly size me up like a boxer, spitting on his palms before holding up his fists; don't worry, we never got a beating, just a tickling. Although, he did exploit our ticklishness occasionally...

"Now repeat after me. Grandad..."

"*Grandad...*"

"I will give you..."

"*I will give you...*"

"All my pocket money."

If you hesitated to say these last words, more tickling would quickly follow.

Dad told me Grandad recounted that in these wartime matches he lined up alongside players that, before the war, were professionals playing for big clubs, some of them even playing at international level. My grandad was good enough to line up alongside them.

I do not know who took these photos, but it appears this is a Scotland vs England football match, and if so, that could be my grandfather in the white shirt on the left of shot.

The single lion on the blue(?) shirt tells me these are the
Scottish players.

The crowd look like they're enjoying the match.

The trophies on the table look like the ones Grandad was awarded. I don't know what the score was here, but 'champion' is written on one of his trophies, a match played in 1944.

As my character in *Fairytale* postulated, a number of these football matches took place during the war to help with morale and strengthen bonds, and also to provide the other servicemen with some entertainment. As far as rivalries go, there aren't too many greater than England against Scotland. I hadn't realised these games had a charitable aspect to them. In fact, I thought there was only one match, but actually there were several. It appeared that each of the players was given their own little trophy, my dad now in possession of the ones Grandad received.

Two of the trophies, the one on the right inscribed with "Winners 1944 RAF Palam B."

In recent years, I've read articles regarding the famine in Bengal where three million people died, and the criticisms aimed at Churchill and the British government. I hadn't realised that these football matches were an attempt to raise money for the Bengal Relief Fund, the British servicepeople in India at least doing their bit.

Back at home, his wife Ethel looked after two evacuees called Margaret and Anna. In this photo above (possibly taken by my grandmother) are these two girls, along with two other evacuees, Iris and Billy. At this point in their lives, my grandparents were living in Norfolk, which was strange as that is where my maternal grandmother was from. Both of my grandmothers were called Ethel. Both my grandfathers had a first name beginning with J.

"November 1940, Joe now in the RAF." Here he was on leave to see Grandma and their son (my uncle Peter) who was born in June that year, mere days after the Dunkirk evacuation. Peter sadly passed away this year while I was writing this book.

Never too early to teach them how to play football. Peter grew up to be a Liverpool fan. I don't know what Grandad made of that, he being an Everton fan.

Peter's son (my cousin John) told me Peter and Joseph had a strained relationship. Whatever interactions between the two that I saw all seemed pretty normal, but Dad also talked about witnessing certain frictions between the two of them.

During the war, young Peter caught diphtheria, and was doted on by his mother and his grandparents. When Grandad returned home after the war, the dynamics must have changed quite drastically. Peter was scared of this 'new' man.

Grandad would repeat history by doing as his father had done to him... Peter had a passion for cars, and when he entered adulthood, he wanted to become an F1 mechanic, but Grandad didn't approve of this career plan, and encouraged him towards something more stable, and so Peter became a draftsman for a building firm.

In his first couple of years in the RAF, it appears Joseph was stationed at various bases in England. By June 1942 he was in India. He had sailed from Gourock in Scotland (west of Glasgow) to Singapore. By then, Grandma and Peter had moved back to Warrington.

Grandad caught malaria while he was serving abroad. This photo was taken in the Himalayas as he was recovering. Without Grandma's notes, I probably would have wondered why he looked so gaunt.

My cousin recalled Grandad telling him about some large birds in India that he had a colourful term for (Grandma would castigate him whenever he repeated it; Let's just say it rhymes with 'kite-hawk'). These plucky birds would swoop down and pinch their food. Wikipedia tells me the term was indeed military slang that originated from British servicemen in India during the war.

According to the notes, this was taken in Cuttack in India. The plane is a Hudson. I always had it in my head he worked on the Lancasters, but they're not mentioned on the 353 Squadron Wiki page. I'm probably remembering when we once got him a decorative plate with a painting of a Lancaster on it.

"Close to the jungle north of Calcutta. Sorties over Burma." That's one way to have a shower; get your buddy to pour the water over you. The man under the fountain of water looks like Ernie, my grandfather's best friend, but he couldn't have been there in India with him... I don't think?

But this is definitely Ernie Greenwood (right) with Joe, presumably taken in Norfolk in either 1939 or 1940 (most likely the former), before they went their separate ways to serve. The two friends had plans to become farmers after the war, but Ernie would not return. His is one of the names on the memorial at the International Bomber Command Centre in Lincoln. My aunt Kathy remains in touch with his daughter, Diane, to this day. She was born 6 weeks after he was killed.

A member of 83 Squadron, Ernie flew in the Lancasters and was shot down over Germany on 25th April 1944, possibly by flak. At that point in the war, the squadron was based at Coningsby, Lincolnshire. If Ernie had survived the war, my grandfather's life would have worked out a lot differently.

A trip to the Taj Mahal. Grandma had written "dome in repair" by this photo, and it's easy to assume that, but it wasn't the case... In the war, the British thought that, naturally, the building was vulnerable to being bombed by the Japanese and Germans, and so they built bamboo scaffolding around it to provide protection and camouflage. This is from information I pulled from a quick Google search.

It had been reported that the entire building was covered in bamboo. Not so the day Grandad visited, it seems, just the dome. I'm sure that's him in the centre of the huddle. I also read that images of the Taj Mahal in protection are scarce... How many more are stored away in family photo albums up in the attic?

Army trucks. No notes with this one, so I don't know what's going on here or why he took this photo.

Again, no notes. An important-looking building somewhere in India.

He took various photos of elephants, including this one below where they are ridden just like they were in *Temple of Doom*. I seem to remember Grandad telling me when I was a very young boy that he'd once been bitten by a tiger on his arm. I'm not sure I was taken in by it, even at that age, but I wonder if the story was inspired by his stay in India.

A damaged bridge?

Are these guys knitting?

In a mysterious newspaper cutting Kathy showed me, Grandad was that day's lucky one as Grandma sent some sort of call to him at "RAF India Command". She tells him she is still missing him as much as ever and longing for the day they shall meet again. Sandy then plays a tune for him (like this is a radio station, not a newspaper). The song, *My Hero* from *The Chocolate Soldier*, brings with it all her love. "God bless and keep you safe always."

On the subject of the importance of recording family history, my cousin had the foresight to film an interview with Grandma and Grandad where they talked all about their experiences of the war, including Grandad's time in India. John shot this in 1993 when he'd come over to England for his sister's wedding (John emigrated to Canada in the late eighties). Sadly, it is most likely that the tape is now lost. John was burgled, his camera stolen. He thinks the tape was still in the camera.

History taken away from us.

Maternal

My other grandfather, called John (yes, there are lots of Johns in my family: my grandfather, my dad and my cousin), put together an album full of photographs he had taken during the war, or at least I *presume* he (or his mates) took them. My mother knew nothing about this book, although my aunt did. I discovered it only recently, whilst I was writing this novel. Stored away with the family heirlooms, among photos and documents stretching back to the First World War, was this tatty leather-clad book that looks like something out of *Indiana Jones*. Sadly, some of the photos have dislodged, and where Grandad had written some comments about the photos, the images are missing or loose. According to his notes, he served in Palestine, Egypt and also India during the war, along with time spent at various bases in the UK. His character was consistently graded as "V.G." which was "the highest character which can be awarded in the Royal Air Force."

He didn't write a great deal of detail in this photo book. One photograph sees a group of worshippers kneeling on their prayer mats, Grandad's note beneath it simply stating, "Religion".

Grandad John joined the RAF in 1933 at the age of 16 years and 95 days, ditching his school exams to pursue a career in the military. At the start of the war he was a Corporal in 6 Squadron and rose to the rank of Sergeant in October 1942. Among the heirlooms, I also discovered his RAF papers (a certificate of his service and discharge, along with his RAF service and release book). The certificate document details his entire RAF career, giving the dates of where he was posted, his promotions, his qualifications, etc. I was interested to discover that in 1936 he'd volunteered for training as an 'Airman Pilot', but during the war he was a Fitter Grade II.

Coincidentally, in recent years, 6 Squadron was based at RAF Coningsby, which, as you know, is right next to New York. It was disbanded in 2007 but reformed a few years later and is now based in north-east Scotland.

He must be young here. It's the only photo I've ever seen of him as an adult where he doesn't have a moustache.

His RAF papers demand a little translation, but it appears he transferred from 6 Squadron to various RAF units, many of which are written as abbreviations, and for a C student at GCSE History (hi there), it's difficult to interpret them. Google is not much help either, which almost makes me wonder if these abbreviations meant things only to him... I suspect not, though. In some correspondence sent to Grandad in India, someone has scribbled one of these abbreviations next to the address, so it all seems to be legit.

But from May 1941 to early 1943 I worked out he was with '56 Operational Training Unit' in Sutton Bridge, Lincolnshire, which is the area where my grandparents lived. 56 OTU was part of Fighter Command.

Was it this period where he met my nan and their first child was conceived? I did once ask Nan where she met Grandad and she told me the story. I never thought to ask *when* they met, but it all seems to fit that it was during this period. As a lot of young women did in that era, it appears she was fraternising with the influx of servicemen in her area. On that occasion she was supposed to be going out with someone else, on a double date I believe, but when she turned up, this particular chap had backed out for reasons unknown. However, the good old chaps had sent along a substitute in the form of my grandad.

My grandparents talked very little about this kind of stuff. One Christmas Eve, they'd come over to our house to celebrate Christmas with us, as they usually did. Nan made a very casual remark about it being their wedding anniversary. Until that moment, I had never wondered the where and when of their wedding. It was probably years later that I even saw a photograph from the day.

It's documented that in early 1943, Guy Gibson and the Dambusters used the Sutton Bridge base to train for their low-level flying needed for their operation, and it's possible my grandfather may have rubbed shoulders with him at this point.

Between 1943 and the end of the war, the only thing I can garner from Grandad's papers is that he served in India (which I already knew, as he mentioned it a number of times), just like my other grandfather. In later years, Grandad Joseph told me he met Grandad John in India, but Joseph was quite far into his dementia by that point in his life, and John, who remained sharp until the end, had no recollection of this meeting when I asked him about it.

I remember glibly asking my grandfather one time if he'd ever shot anyone. "Oh yes," he replied very seriously. It was during the war, he told me, and he was somewhere in the Middle East, in the area that is now called Iraq. Or maybe it was Iran. I'm sure he had said it was called Persia back then, which would make it Iran. I think I naturally asked him if he'd killed anyone, but he said he didn't know for sure, just fired off some shots in what sounded like a skirmish. Here he is with a rifle at hand (far left).

Hold the press! My other grandad played football too? That's him with the moustache standing next to the man in black. Where or when this was taken, it's difficult to say as there is little to go on. On the reverse of the photo, however, is a stamp saying "Sack Bros G506 Tel Aviv", so presumably this was taken while Grandad was in Palestine. It seems the chap bottom left is wearing military garb; Is he the manager? Initially I assumed the man in black was the goalkeeper, although maybe he's the referee and the man on the left in the white shirt is the goalie. Either way, with 13 chaps here, there are too many players.

I hadn't known of my maternal grandfather playing any sports, so this photo came as a surprise. Sure, we used to watch games together on television, but Dad told me he was a bit of a sportsman too when he was younger. The guy in black looks like he could be his brother, right? Grandad did have an older brother... although I don't think it's him.

"Natives in camp". In the photo album he's written descriptions for the Sphinx and the pyramids, but, alas, these particular photos are missing. I made a thorough search, but to no avail. I hope they'll show up one day.

"Arab brigand."

"Army truck burnt by brigands."

"Train wreck caused by landmines."

"Ancient walls."

"Nazareth."

"Jerusalem."

"Police search in Jerusalem."

"Street in Jerusalem."

"Wailing Wall."

The only photos, of which I'm aware, involving a grandparent during a wartime Christmas. On the reverse of this one is some writing: "Xmas morning, Officers mess. I think the fellow with the fez on his head is the driver or something." So presumably that's my grandfather in the fez hat leaning against the vehicle, although he looks a bit foreign here. The guy next to him looks like the actor John Cazale (Fredo in *The Godfather*... sorry to make this even more confusing by having yet another 'John' when there are three already. Let's call this guy Cazale).

He played darts, too. Looks like that's Cazale again next to him. In so many photographs, Grandad had a fag on. When he was younger, he was a heavy smoker but quit before I came along, so I never saw him smoke. The writing on the back of this photo explains that Cazale is his room-mate, and that this was Boxing Day 1943. Initially, I thought this was taken at RAF Sutton Bridge, but after doing some more digging, I discovered *another* photo album full of images from later in the war. Some of them corresponded to photos in the first album, so I'm not sure why he split them up. But from his notes, I know that Christmas 1943 was spent in India, at RAF Santacruz, which was in Bombay (now called Mumbai).

This photograph is so utterly bizarre. That's Grandad just creeping into frame far left. He appears to be wearing one of those garlands from the Christmas morning photograph, and with the celebratory mood these chaps are in, this could well be Christmas here, too. Why does that man with the missing tooth have a towel wrapped around his head? Possibly 'mimicking' the culture they were immersed within? Did he lose that tooth by making fun of the wrong person? For a long time, I wondered what was going on with that guy with the punk rocker hairdo. Surely no one in the RAF had hair *that* long. I think, however, it's just a trick of the eye, and maybe there's a plant on the other side of him.

This is definitely Boxing Day 1943. I'm not sure I recognise any of these guys. That might be Cazale just walking through the door. There appear to be decorations hanging from the ceiling. I love how, even when we're in a global conflict, we still get the Christmas decorations out.

"Jimmy gets a haircut." And my grandad is the barber. Was this the punk rocker chap?

Time for a cuppa and a fag... Finally, Grandad puts some names to faces. The man on the left is W/O Rogers (warrant officer, I presume). The other guy is Jock Burns. In every photo, Jock seems to have a twinkle in his eye. He looks like he was fun to be around.

If I were sent back in time to the war, I think I'd pick the RAF to serve in (not that I'm the best of flyers). But it seems these RAF chaps knew how to have a good time. Often a drink or a cigarette or pipe in hand. So many have that cliched look going on, a moustache, slicked back hair, dressed cool and dapper. Grandad kept his moustache for the rest of his life. I don't recognise any of these men, except possibly Cazale again. I presume Grandad took this one. What's with the dog?

In the other album, I found more photos from this occasion. For a while I struggled to make sense of what was going on, and even wondered if they were indeed Second World War era, but then I discovered another photo that appears to be from this same event. It was a photo I hadn't paid a lot of attention to...

There appears to be a stage set up, lecterns, possibly a drum kit, but behind those chaps is an emblem, also seen on something on the table. This, I believe, was the 27th birthday celebration of 6 Squadron (see the invite earlier) held in Palestine in 1941, a whole 80 years ago.

This photograph intrigues me. The older chap with the moustache seems like he might be top brass. The other guy raising his hat is in some of his other photos. Who any of them are, I don't know. What they're raising their hats to? Some beer bottles?? It's quite possible this, too, is from the 6 Squadron birthday party. Is the man 'Formby' as mentioned in the invite? I can't decipher the other words before the name.

Here he is again, more beer bottles on the table, and it appears they're writing, quite likely signing their names. The small pieces of paper that two of those men are holding are the same size as the 6 Squadron birthday party invite, and the markings seem to correlate. I can't read any of the signatures on Grandad's invite.

As he'd done in Egypt and Palestine, Grandad took many photographs of the places in India he visited. 'Breach Candy' is mentioned, as is Bombay. Various places that, I presume, would look a lot different today.

A young boy making mugs of tea? I wonder if he is still alive.

An old Indian man.

I can't think what caught my grandad's eye here.

I'm not totally sure, but I think that's my grandad petting a freakin' leopard. Just another day in India.

A fairly unremarkable photo, until I read the reverse...

"Crowd on beach to see Gandhi." I scanned this one in at a high resolution but I couldn't spot a bald-headed guy in a robe. A shame Grandad didn't join the crowd to get a closer view.

But then the twist... In the second photo album, I found this...

Grandad did exactly as I hoped. He got in closer.

Yep. That is Gandhi. I can't really get my head around the fact that my grandfather took a photograph of Mahatma Gandhi. This figure was the father of the nation, a man who famously advocated non-violence in his protests against British rule. And here he was photographed by a British man who was there because he was part of the deadliest conflict in history.

I'm not sure what's going on with the women in front of him. Gandhi's entourage? Are those perhaps microphones in front of them? Are they singing? Why do they all have 'Chicago' written on them?

My aunt told me that Nan used to joke with Grandad that Gandhi was his other lover. I can only imagine that he was so chuffed he'd taken a photo of such a famous figure and perhaps went on about it somewhat. I know I sure would!

Somewhere in my head, I can hear Grandad talking about Gandhi. I can hear him saying the name.

I wondered if there were any other photos from this occasion on the web... Unsurprisingly, there is, it seems. One photograph was taken from behind Gandhi, that barbed wire fence immediately in front of him, then the crowd on the beach, my grandfather somewhere within it. The internet tells me this was May or June 1944, and it took place on Juhu Beach in Bombay, Gandhi leading a prayer meeting.

He'd been under arrest in the two years leading up to this, held at a palace in Pune. The house on Juhu Beach belonged to a friend and Gandhi went there to recuperate as he'd fallen ill while in jail.

Four years later, he was assassinated.

"Bombing up." This photo was beside others taken in Ramle in Palestine. The plane just in shot may be a Hawker Hardy.

The RAF Ensign flying, and a heck of a lot of bagpipes playing.

Looks like a checkpoint.

Trench warfare?

So many photos of my grandad have a dog in them. As has been famously documented with Guy Gibson, it seemed it was the fashion for RAF personnel to have pet dogs, but on further research, it appears these animals performed an important role in the war, guarding camps, carrying messages, smelling out the enemy. My grandfather may have fitted the planes with bombs, but I don't think he dropped any in the naming of any dog. Incidentally, on further inspection of my *other* grandfather's squadron photo... Yep. There's a dog there too.

And again, a series of photographs that has me utterly perplexed. Seems they're in India here, but what's with all the fancy dress? RAF personnel dressed in drag? Dressed as Indians? Goodness knows what my grandad is supposed to be, but he's there on the far right. A complete head-scratcher. There is a football there, I noticed. Maybe it was someone's stag do, my wife suggested.

Next they're on a sports field it seems, a crowd forming in the background, and the guy in the yodelay-hee-hoo outfit looks like he's ready for a fight, not a football match. And there's another dog!

And it goes on. Strangest game of footie I ever saw.

I mean... maybe it's not such a crazy idea, the stag do theory. Here we appear to have an Indian wedding, men in uniform, western faces, an RAF hat, and there on the extreme left we have Grandad just about in frame.

Grandad in the centre of the photo, hanging out with some Indians, and I think the guy sitting down may have a dog on his lap. Or perhaps he's opening a present. I can't tell.

I wondered if this photograph may be linked with the wedding, westerners mixed with Indians. Grandad seems to be wearing a buttonhole.

More fun and games... and drink, Jock in the middle with a smile on his face, Grandad on the end. Judging by the decoration in the background, it looks like this was another Christmas snap. This photo almost looks like it was pulled from a booze advert in a gentleman's magazine.

"Busy at work." I'm glad he fitted some of that in.

"Note the new style in hats." Note a dog again. This looks like it was from the early years of the war, possibly even pre-war, as Grandad was at RAF Depot Aboukir (Egypt) in 1938.

Even more dogs.

I love this photograph, one of the last ones I discovered. Grandad has a pipe on. Jock is holding some mail. Are they all piled into the back of a truck?

Are they giving a V sign because we'd just won the war? Or had they just won a darts match?

"The big noises. Raising the cheers (beers). Wing Commander Smithies. W/O Turner."

P. M. Goodchild   *King's Lynn*

My maternal grandmother, who went by her middle name of Ethel, was eighteen when the war broke out. She would have worked on the land.

Just like my other grandmother, she had a child during the war. And similar to my paternal grandfather, she also suffered from dementia in her final years.

This looks like her. Looking rather patriotic here.

Nan far left in the flat farmland of South Lincolnshire / West Norfolk.

My aunt Jacque was born in 1942, early enough to have a very vague memory of bombs being dropped during the war, so she told me. She recalls running into the dark of the front room of her house near Walpole Cross Keys when enemy planes were nearby. It seems the Germans frequently bombed the area.

Given he was two years older, I wonder what my uncle Peter would have remembered of the war.

I don't know who this man is, but I feel as if I should know him, like maybe one day years ago it was explained to me, but I've now forgotten. The note on the back seems to address it to my grandfather: "Please desist from laughing. The negative dad can use if you want more." It looks like an anti-aircraft gun, maybe? I want to say it was taken in Kings Lynn, or maybe it was Sutton Bridge. Both are ports, so presumably required this sort of defence.

But I can identify one of the people in this photograph, a great uncle, my nan's younger brother Ron, who died before I was born. The note reads: "Taken Nov. 1944, Belgium. The Salvation Army Canteen. Casse and myself having our morning cup of tea. Me sitting on arm of Casse's chair. Ronald xx. Picture as was shown in British Newspapers." He must have sent this to his sister.

An invite to Hell's Tavern for soldiers of the United Nations. I'm guessing Ron picked this up, and I'm guessing he went.

Ron served in the army during the war and sustained injuries that he never completely recovered from. He was in a blast at Antwerp that created a hole in his lung. He died in the 1950s. My nan had a framed photograph of him on display for the rest of her life.

In a newspaper cutting announcing his engagement, he is described as a Sapper (Private) of the Royal Engineers, with the letters MC after his name, which presumably means he was awarded the Military Cross. Amongst Nan's keepsakes, I discovered a very puzzling newspaper cutting concerning Ronald. Apparently he'd written to the King of England to ask for help as he had fallen ill with tuberculosis and the Ministry of Pensions would not grant him a pension, even though he had fought for his country. The king intervened and Ron got sorted, meaning he could now buy himself a house.

So much of it rang true, but so much didn't. This Ronald was a resident of Blaengarw in Wales, his father was a retired miner, and Ron apparently served in the Royal Welch Fusiliers. It's true Ron had tuberculosis, and he was very young when war broke out, so might have lied about his age to join the army (as the article describes). Would the King of England really sort out someone's pension?!? The only theory the family can put forward is that this was all a strange coincidence, and this was another Ronald. Weird.

This looks like Ron in the sanatorium, following the war, perhaps late 1940s? The facility was in Holt, Norfolk.

Ron by the seaside. I'm guessing either Sheringham or Cromer.

He was a handsome chap. Over two decades separate our lives, and yet his ghost has been *there* throughout my life. My nan frequently spoke about her brother, often comparing him to my younger brother. One day, maybe 15 or 20 years ago, she randomly told me a story of how Ron obtained some binoculars during the war (the way she talked about anything from long ago was as though it had only happened a couple of weeks ago, so it was often difficult to judge the gravity of her words). I think she said he had pinched them off a German, his own spoils of war? Whether it was a dead or living German, a soldier or civilian, I either don't know or can't remember. For whatever reason, my nan passed these binoculars on to me. Sixty years she'd held on to them, and then out of the blue, with no ceremony whatsoever, she gave them to me. After venturing into the loft recently, I can confirm that I am still in possession of them. I guess one day I'll pass them on too. Or maybe I should track down the descendants of its original owner?

Well, there we go, Germany. Two world wars, one World Cup... and a pair of binoculars.

Amongst my nan's keepsakes, was this document about her father's demobilisation. My great-grandfather fought in the First World War. It's a morbid thought, but I can't help but wonder it; As a machine gun operator, how many of the enemy died by his hands?

And then Nan went on to a glittering film career... With the way this has been framed (along with other photos of people posing by this door), it seems the aim was to get the word 'Elstree' into frame. I'm sure this was taken at the famous Studios, but I don't know why she was there (she wasn't really an actress, by the way), or what year. I can tell you the date, March 26th, going by the note on the reverse. She looks young here, but would members of the public be granted access to these studios during the war? The other sign on the door, incidentally, reads "Mrs Moll, Nurse." I have a vague memory of her telling me about this visit. I can hear the word 'Elstree' stumbling off her tongue, and I can picture her speaking in wonderment about the place. On the reverse she has written: "This is the first day of parting. But never again. Love Et." My first instinct is here is a young, love-struck woman, pining for someone (is that why she's lurking outside the nurse's room, because she's lovesick?), Grandad has been posted away again... So that would make this wartime, maybe 1943. She looks around 20 years of age here, so the maths add up...

On a postcard sent to Grandad in India, my nan tells him of having a lovely day in Hunstanton. The picture on the front shows the bungalows by the beach at nearby Heacham, a walk I made myself with my parents and younger generations of the family, a mere two weeks before I found this postcard. The date of my nan's visit was July 28th 1945. VE Day was over two months ago; VJ Day would not arrive for another two weeks. My aunt was sunburnt, the bus filling with daytrippers ready to go home as Nan signed off the postcard; "All my love. Always yours, Et x x."

It's hard to imagine that, at some point way before I came along, my grandparents were young adults in love. What sticks out in my memories of them are all the arguments they had, my nan nagging my grandad, telling him to get up and help on the garden while he just wanted to sit and do the crossword. This photograph was badly creased, as though it had been kept in a purse. On its reverse was a poem written by the photograph's subject:

"I wonder what these eyes are trying to see. Someone who is far across the sea. God speed the day when I can be. So very, very close to thee. Johnny xxx."

Through looking at his RAF papers... and doing the maths... my grandparents *must* have first met in wartime when Grandad was sent to this 56 OTU in Sutton Bridge. He arrived there in May 1941. By the end of that same year, Nan must have fallen pregnant.

I had never known before how the war had brought them together... I don't think. How difficult must it have been to be separated? The longing, the worry. Maybe tragedy would befall him. Maybe she'd meet someone else? Maybe one of those 'oversexed' Yanks. Maybe she'd grow bored with waiting. In those days, your loved ones weren't immediately on hand with a quick WhatsApp message or a text.

Although they were the next generation, the legacy of the war would also bring together my aunt Jacque and her husband... She would meet a young American, Raymond, who was stationed at one of the many American bases that popped up during the war (Alconbury). They married in 1966.

I was close to being an American too, as my mum apparently dated an airman from the States... But that didn't work out. Obviously.

War is over? It would appear so. A lot more is conveyed in this one photo...

According to his papers, Grandad's second overseas service concluded in July 1946. Even when the enemy forces had been defeated, he would spend almost another year abroad with the RAF. And even when he'd returned home, he continued to wear his uniform in public, a cigarette on, looking badass. Why would he wear his uniform on a day trip to the seaside? After all those years in the forces, did he need some adjustment? Perhaps he missed it, the company of his fellow servicemen, the laughter and the drinks. Perhaps that accounts for the buddy he'd brought along with him this day. Or perhaps wearing the uniform proclaimed to the world that he had served, that he had done his part in winning the war. The sight of 'our boys' being home was obviously a most welcomed one.

Jacque is somewhere close to her fourth birthday in his photo, and clearly shares a closer bond with her mother. When Grandad returned from war, she would apparently say to him, "You're not my father." This echoed with the situation on the other side of the family, my uncle Peter needing a lot of adjustment from being the apple of his mother's eye to suddenly having a father figure in his life. I also remember Grandma telling me of going through the same thing as a girl. With the First World War over, a strange man appeared in the corner shop where she lived, her mother having to explain to her confused daughter that this man was her father.

Who is the other chap walking with Grandad? Jacque actually remembers him and told me he could be called Mickleborough or Mickleburgh, a friend from the Sutton Bridge base. He is/was an American, and apparently helped to supply Grandad with rationed items. Maybe that's why they took him out for the day at the seaside?

I discovered so many photographs like this, people walking along a high street. In this case, I can easily conclude this was taken in Skegness, even though the seaside town looks absolutely nothing like this today. On the reverse of the image is a stamp by the photographers, and it says they're based opposite the pier in the town of Skegness, and I think this is exactly that location: the entrance to the pier. Googling photographs from that era, it does seem to match the brickwork and lamppost positions.

It seemed it was something of a fashion back then for photographers to take candid snaps of random people in tourist spots and then sell you the photo (a bit like when you go on a roller coaster and it takes a photo mid-ride so you can take home a souvenir photograph).

It's difficult to gauge *exactly* when this photo was taken. Jacque and my nan are both wearing coats, but with Skegness's bracing reputation, you might want to take one even in the summer months. Perhaps they went out for the day to celebrate Jacque's August birthday. Perhaps we're getting into the cooler ~ember months. I don't think I'll ever work out the date, but something continues to draw me to this photo... Doing the maths, my mother would have been conceived mid-August 1946. So maybe... just maybe... Nan is carrying her here. So early into her pregnancy, maybe she doesn't even know it herself yet? I imagine it must have been so frustrating for my grandparents to have to be away from each other for years, and I have no doubt they would have soon made up for lost time... My mother's existence being testament to that.

Incidentally, the scene in *Fairytale* where Hazel and her nan visit the pier in Skegness was written long before I discovered this photograph.

In 2018, when my parents were sorting through my nan's estate, my mother asked if I would like Grandad's cameras. There were quite a few of them, so many in fact that I got rid of a load of them. The three that I kept were stuffed away under my wardrobe, and I hadn't thought anymore of them until I was writing this book. Were they still there? I couldn't even remember which particular ones I'd kept onto, but my wife immediately assured me they were still there. I know how my thinking would have gone three years ago: *get rid of the naff ones, keep whatever looks old*. One of the cameras is in fact a cine camera (I think from the 1970s). One was a camera similar to this model, with a lens that folds out from the body. I looked it up online and it appears to be a 1950s model. But then there is this one that was packed away in a brown leather case...

At first, I couldn't get into it, assuming the case was locked, and the key had most likely been missing for decades. I tried picking the lock, and then I got some wire cutters to see if I could snip the fastener open... I held off doing that, just in case I might miraculously find the key in my searches of the family archives. A couple of days later I had the brainwave of sliding that circular mechanism, and ta-dah! The thing was unlocked all along. Yah, not my finest moment.

I quickly conducted an internet search on this model, and it would indeed appear to be something manufactured in the 1930s, which is around when I would have guessed it was from; If it looks like something Indiana Jones might have, then you can guess it's from the war era. It appears it was produced in Germany, of all places.

I hadn't thought anymore about these cameras after stuffing them under my wardrobe three years ago, but the way this all unfolded (the events, I mean, not the camera), it was like this camera was patiently waiting there for me, waiting for me to come to this very point, where I'm piecing together my grandparents' history, understanding the truth. It's a fair bet this was the camera Grandad took with him on his overseas service. For what it's worth, my instincts tell me this is so. This camera once took a photograph of Gandhi.

I'm jumping around again, but here we have another intriguing photograph. Just what is going on here? We're clearly in a foreign land, quite likely Palestine. The man on the left seems to have a deformity. Is he handing the officer a bottle of wine? Why would he do that? Did it come from that shop beyond them? The man in uniform could be an army officer, or possibly a police officer as the British maintained a force there back then.

Maybe he's sourcing drinks for that 6 Squadron birthday party? But what also catches my eye is the other object the officer is holding... a camera. It looks *very* similar to my grandfather's model.

In the Mood for a *Moonlight Serenade*... Tea dancing (but no Morris Dancing).

At Lake George — Lake Steamers in background. Oct 1974 N.Y. state

My nan really did go to the US in 1974, visiting Jacque and Ray with her mother, the only great-grandparent whose life overlapped with mine (she died when I was about 3 months old). Dora's little road incident really happened too, except it was in Montreal, not NYC. Every time I visit my uncle, I get him to recount this story.

Something else from the colour years circa 1984... I discovered this in my digging. That's me, standing behind my nan, my little brother with us. Grandad would have taken the photo. I'm pretty sure that black case housed his Polaroid camera. They would often take us round the Norfolk coast, where we'd have picnics and collect cockles and mussels, or Grandad would go fishing. Such trips must have made an impression on my young mind, sowing the seeds for my love of the coast. The sights, sounds and flavours I experienced would form the setting for one of my book series.

This trip was most likely to Hunstanton or Heacham, maybe Snettisham, although it's near impossible to tell. And even though I was there, and I'm the only one aware our photo is being taken, I have no memory of this.

Like so much else, it all just gets lost in time.

Join My Mailing List

To get your hands on my exclusive eBook, please sign up to my Readers' Club here:

www.subscribepage.com/intothefires

On my mailing list, you can learn about my future releases, receive offers, and get information about my other books and projects. You'll also keep up with the negotiations on the option rights to *Fairytale of the Other New York* with some top Hollywood producers (we haven't started them yet but you'll be the first to know when we do).

If you enjoyed reading this novel, then please do leave a review (or just a rating) on Amazon, no matter how brief, to help spread the word. Reader reviews can make a big difference to authors and help increase visibility. They make a real difference.

Thank you for reading my book.

Books by Joseph Kiel

The Dark Harbour Tales is a supernatural thriller series steeped in 'seaside noir', involving soul-searching vigilantes, romance and enchantment, and the age-old folklore that still haunts us today.

The Broken Melody series involves vampires and other supernatural characters and is full of sex, drugs and rock 'n roll.

<u>The Dark Harbour Tales</u>

Into The Fires (prequel novella)

Halo of Fires (Book 1)

Night Shines (Book 2)

Untitled Dark Harbour 3 (Coming 2022)

<u>The Broken Melody Series</u>

Broken Melody

Moonlight Melody (Coming 2022)

www.josephkiel.com

Printed in Great Britain
by Amazon